TWO NICKELS

TWO NICKELS

A Novel

MICHAEL F. DECONZO

Full Court Press
Englewood Cliffs, New Jersey

Published in the United States of America
by Full Court Press, 601 Palisade Avenue,
Englewood Cliffs, NJ 07632
fullcourtpress.com

ISBN 978-1-946989-84-0
Library of Congress Control No. 2020925198

Editing and book design by Barry Sheinkopf

Cover art by Steve McCurry / Magnum Photos

FOR MY WIFE AND CHILDREN

Your unconditional love and support
have made this book possible,
along with everything else.

ACKNOWLEDGMENTS

Thanks to the wine industry for managing to produce some very decent reds for under fifteen dollars a bottle.

Thanks to all my favorite bands, who've made sitting on my back deck having a glass of the aforementioned red a near religious experience.

For the people on Staten Island, I meant what I wrote: sometimes crazy, never dull, but when push comes to shove, you always show up.

For Barry S., who was instrumental in making sure that *Two Nickels* put its best foot forward.

For my dearest friends and colleagues, you are all somewhere in this book.

For Dr. A., my friend and mentor, who has provided invaluable guidance and with whom I've had the absolute pleasure of discussing *The Great Gatsby* for twenty years.

For Dan, who had the good sense to move to California forty years ago and create a terrific life for himself just so I could get some writing done.

For Morreale, whom I met in kindergarten and whose talent is only surpassed by his heart and sense of humor.

For my sister, who doesn't really curse all that much, and whose family has always just been an extension of our own.

For Elsie and Frank, who saw all of my false starts but who somehow managed to support and never discourage.

For Bailey and Gatsby, for providing me with the opportunity to pick up their crap while we walked and waited for the muse to appear.

When the time machine is finally perfected, I want to go back to the Sullivan Street of my grandparents' courtship.

And speaking of Poppy and Mary the Blonde, too bad you're not here. You would've got a kick out of this thing.

For my beloved children, who have always made me smile and who have inspired their father to do his best.

For my wife, who has brightened every one of my days since September 29, 1984. (No coincidence that's the day Johnny and Laura meet.)

And for all of the above, along with a few thousand students I've had the pleasure to share a classroom with, I am very lucky to have stepped foot on this planet.

Salute!

For additional listening pleasure, check out the Two Nickels playlist on Spotify. The user name is *Juhasz300*.

"Midway upon the journey of life
I found myself within a forest dark,
For the straightfoward pathway had been lost."
　　　—Dante Alighieri,
　　　Canto I, "The Inferno," 1307
　　　Translation by Henry Wadsworth Longfellow,
　　　1867

"The sunshine bores the daylights out of me. . ."
　　　—Mick Jagger and Keith Richards,
　　　"Rocks Off"

DECEMBER 1997

"Tuesday Afternoon"

THE MANHATTAN SKYLINE IS PASTED against a cold blue sky that is just beginning to deepen into evening. The setting sun, reflecting off the steel and glass of the skyscrapers, shoots lines of orange-white sunshine back across the Hudson River. The rays of light skip over the scrappy towns of Hoboken and Jersey City and Newark and fall on a quiet street in the suburb of East Dorwood, New Jersey, where they announce the end of yet another sunny day.

Birch and chestnut trees, bare for the winter, line the wide sidewalks on both sides of the street, in contrast to the white-columned mansions set back forty feet from the curb. The rays spotlight the stone facades of the homes, the long driveways, and the manicured lawns, which now feature the white skeletons of snowmen and reindeer, red scarves wrapped around their metal necks, waiting patiently for their own moment to shine. There is not one car in sight, parked on the street or otherwise.

Out of the ball of reflected sunshine a velvet blue shadow emerges at the end of the street. Long, loopy strides make the shadow look like it's moving in slow motion. Then, as the sun drops a few stories lower on the office buildings, the two dimensions of the shadow become three dimensions of a very large man.

Not moving from the center of the street, the man stops and slides a pint of vodka from his coat pocket. He presses the bottle to his chest and unscrews the top with one hand. Then he throws his head back and polishes it off. It is evident from the look in his eyes that this is a deeply satisfying moment. When the vodka is gone, the man pulls the bottle from his lips and holds it out in front of him. The glass catches the sun and makes it look like his hand is on fire. Then he steps to the sidewalk and crosses one of the lawns. He gently nestles the empty pint in the basin of a birdbath.

And despite the booze, a buttonless pea coat that is at least one size too small, and a navy-blue GAP bag that he holds by its pull strings, Virgil Shepherd moves with the floaty grace of the divinely blessed or the criminally insane.

Two young boys, bundled in their winter coats, approach from the opposite direction. When they see Virgil, they stop in mid-conversation and run the numbers: seven feet tall. Shoulders and chest that take up four feet of sidewalk. Legs in brown sweatpants like two halves of a telephone pole. A trio of grey patches on his black face (cheek, chin, jaw) that pass for a beard. A pair of giant red sneakers that are closing fast.

The boys look at each other, then turn around and head back in the direction they came from. Quickly.

About halfway through his pilgrimage, Virgil pulls a scrap of paper out of his pea coat. He holds the paper at eye-level and squints until the squiggles settle into numbers. Then he checks the houses. When he matches the numbers on the paper to an address, Virgil pivots right and stops in the middle of the driveway.

He studies the paper again, then looks back at the numbers on the fancy copper plaque next to the front door. One story above, in a bed-room window, a curtain moves.

Standing as still as a statue, Virgil contemplates the garage door like it is Ghiberti's "Gates of Paradise" at the Baptistery of St. John.

The grey pavers in the driveway turn purple. The last rays of sun-light give way to dusk. Virgil slides the paper back into his coat pocket, then moves up to the garage and puts his elbow through a door panel. Reaching his long arm inside, he unlocks the handle and rolls the door up just high enough for him to slip underneath and disappear inside the garage. Then he rolls down the door behind him.

A soft silver light filters through the hole.

A minute later a car starts, the engine revs, and a brand-new met-allic maroon XJ6 Jaguar smashes through the garage door in reverse. It is met by two police cars that are angled like a flying V at the foot of the driveway. A very loud crash shatters the serenity of the neighbor-hood. A screaming woman and a barking dog, along with a staticky police radio, round out the mayhem.

Two of East Dorwood's finest stand on either side of the driveway. They stare at what's left of their cars, which have been twisted into the back end of the Jaguar and hiss steam into the cold air like a giant lawn sprinkler. Then the officers point their revolvers at the crash and spring into action.

One officer circles around the front of the Jaguar, his gun trained on the cracked windshield. The second officer, whose dark mustache makes him look like a popular 1970s porn star, slowly approaches the driver's side door. He taps the barrel of his gun on the shattered glass and yells, "Get out of the vehicle!" Then both policemen cock the triggers of their guns and take three steps back.

Slowly, the door of the Jaguar begins to open and then falls off at their feet. From the driver's seat, Virgil looks down at the severed door in the driveway.

"*Or discendiam qua giu nel cieco mondo*," he says quietly.

The first officer, his face as pink as the foam dice hanging from the rearview mirror, sticks his gun six inches from Virgil's head.

"In English, fuck face!"

Virgil opens his mouth to say something, then hiccups loudly instead. From behind a row of spruce trees, a timer clicks. Ten thousand Christmas bulbs light up the lawn like the Vegas strip.

CHAPTER ONE

"Good Vibrations"

THE IMPORTANT THING TO REMEMBER when you set foot on Staten Island was that it was its own little universe. Divorced from the rest of New York City and the shores of New Jersey by a handful of ominous-sounding waterways (the Narrows, Arthur Kill, etc.) the "forgotten borough" was a breeding ground for things that probably didn't happen in too many other places.

On Staten Island people behaved one way, then minutes later could become totally different. On a beautiful spring day, most neighbors would say "Good morning," but a "You don't know who you're fuckin' with" was not out of the question. When someone did something peculiar, it was waved off with a "Ahh, that's just him," or "Yeah, she's a little off," and forgotten immediately. The level of interconnectivity was a notch above "The Young and the Restless." Whoever you talked to (or dated) was someone you knew's cousin, best man, ex-wife, third grade teacher, law partner, allergist, bridesmaid, pet groomer. It was almost impossible to mention a name out loud and not have strangers chime in that they were somehow involved.

The borough had its own laws of logic, its own rules of human interaction, its own version of acceptable behaviors, its own definitions of truth and sanity and absurdity. Maybe it had something to do with the fact that tons and tons of the city's garbage had been dropped on the island daily since 1948, making it home to the world's largest landfill. (A mound you were supposedly able to see from outer space, along with a few active volcanoes and the Great Wall of China.) Affectionately known as "The Dump," it had become one of the defining features of Staten Island, along with the Verrazano Bridge and the ferry. And it made perfect sense. A half century of waste seeping into our bedrock and infiltrating our air had to wreak *some* havoc on our brains.

But while a big part of the craziness was the dump (despite what the politicians and the scientists claimed), it wasn't only the dump. There were other factors at work. For one thing, it didn't help that there were too many people on the rock to begin with. The population had doubled in the last thirty years, give or take a hundred thousand. Thanks to an army of backhoes, the areas of the island that were still clinging to nature were disappearing fast. Animals were everywhere. Pushed to the brink by their proximity to almost half a million crazy humans, they became crazy too. Wild turkeys stalked parking lots. Families of racoons took over back decks. Blue herons landed in kiddie pools. Ants carried off dessert.

Living on SI in 1997 was interesting some of the time and disorienting at other times. It was always exhausting. And for the most part it worked—the homicide rate was the lowest in the city.

THE ARCADE WAS A BLOCK FROM THE BEACH, across the street from the boardwalk. As I headed down the hill toward the water, I noticed that the houses on either side of Sand Lane, mostly two-family yellow brick or aluminum-sided homes, were shut tight. Probably a little too tight for eight-thirty on a Tuesday night, but unless you were a kid, there wasn't much to do in South Beach in the middle of December. Besides, it was freezing out.

I climbed up the ramp and stood in front of the boardwalk railing. Not a car, not a turkey, not one of the five hundred thousand souls that had crammed the island was in sight. Only the moon, which had set itself just above the horizon, surrounded by stars that for once weren't drowned out by the light from the Verrazano Bridge a half a mile away. It was close to full and threw its light over the water and across the wooden planks of the boardwalk. Even the sand was drenched in silver. But as much as I wanted to sit on the bench and enjoy the view, I turned around and headed back down the ramp. I had too much to do to let a moon, no matter how beautiful, fuck with my plans.

That was one of the first things my grandmother tried to drill into me when she brought me down to the beach. Stay focused. Pay attention. Be alert. To a four-year-old ankle-deep in sea foam, I had no idea what she was talking about. There wasn't too much happening in our little piece of the Atlantic that seemed to require my immediate attention: no monster waves, no riptides, no fins cruising the fishing piers. Even during the occasional big storm, the tide rarely crossed Father Capodanno Boulevard, the street that separated the beach from the arcade. There were only two things that caught my eye: the flashing lights on top of the parachute jump across the bay in Coney Island, and the two abandoned islands, Hoffman and Swinburne, that sat a few hundred miles off shore between Brooklyn and New Jersey.

But even back then, Mary the Blonde knew what we were up against.

While it spared us the drama, the ocean managed to sneak into our lives in more devious ways. Everything in the neighborhood was covered with a sticky, salty mist that burned off only on the hottest of summer days or popped like bubble wrap during the most arctic of cold spells. That was the thing about living so close to the water. It was hard to stay dry, and, like my grandmother said, even harder to get a clear picture of things.

When I crossed the street, I could make out the fuzzy outline of Dinino in the opening to the arcade, backlit by the neon colors of the video games.

"*Pucchiacha.*"

As soon as he realized it was me, Dinino mumbled his usual greeting, a term of endearment that sounded a lot nicer in Sicilian than it did in English. He'd been saying hello this way for as long as I could remember, and for probably most of his seventy-two years. I smiled and followed my frozen breath inside the building.

A boombox on the concrete floor was blasting a song from the Wu Tang Clan. Dinino shifted his form to yell at the only two kids in the place, who were parked in front of the car racing machine.

"*Madonne*, give me a break," Dinino complained hoarsely. "I got company."

Without taking his eyes off the screen, the taller kid tapped the machine with the side of his sneaker and the music stopped.

"I can't hear myself think around this fucking place anymore."

The only "doors" on the arcade was a pair of cranky metal gates, consumed with rust and touched up by graffiti, that faced the boardwalk on one side and the street on the other. Dinino pulled the gates up at ten in the morning and pulled them down at midnight. The two remaining walls were made of cinder blocks, painted black and lined with video games. Although the place was wide open to the elements fourteen hours a day, the air inside the arcade always smelled like overloaded outlets and fried electrical tape. A low tarpapered ceiling hung about six inches over my head, decorated with stick-on glow in the dark stars. The place was a perfect cross between a cave and a 1950s spaceship. Dinino's squeegee, his one magic wand against the mist, stood in a plastic bucket by his wooden stool.

I pulled a small white bag out of my coat pocket and handed it over.

"They might be a little *mushade*," I said. "The cab ride took forever."

"You never forget me," he said.

Dinino grinned and held a slightly compromised cannoli up to the fake starlight like it had just come off the dessert carte at the Last Supper.

"Where'd you get 'em?"

"Dante's. On MacDougal."

"Thank fucking God," he said. "These bakers on Staten Island, they should be shot for what they do to pastry." Dinino took a bite, closed his eyes and made the sign of the cross. "There used to be a place around the corner. *Years* ago. Every morning the owner made a hundred cannolis, sold 'em and went to the beach for the day. That was it, one hundred perfect cannolis. Fucking artistry. That was back when people gave a shit about how they made their money."

I pulled over a milk crate and Dinino squatted down on his wooden stool.

Dinino was the "*pecora nera*" of an old Staten Island family ("Real cut-throat ginzos," according to my grandmother. "Always crying with a loaf of bread under their arms," according to my grandfather) that had over time bought up most of the area around the beach and became very wealthy doing it. At one time they owned the corner bar, the deli, the gas station, the drug store, and a small amusement park directly across from the boardwalk, of which the arcade was an afterthought.

The story in the neighborhood was that Dinino had gotten into some bad trouble as a kid, and the family gave him the arcade to get him out of their hair and keep him away from the real money. But in one of those beautiful twists of fate, the baby boom hit the neighborhood. The arcade became an oasis for every kid within a mile of the beach who didn't feel like going home and who didn't mind having an older person around that wasn't asking a million questions.

When the family members grew old, they sold off their businesses one by one. But Dinino never sold. He kept the arcade open seven days a week three hundred and sixty-five days a year and made a fortune. Even when a builder knocked down what was left of the amusement park to put up condos, Dinino refused to go along with the family and sell off the last piece of the pie. And like a good Sicilian son who got the last laugh, Dinino took care of their hospital bills and eventually paid for their funerals and put several nieces and nephews through some top-notch colleges. A few years ago, he even funded a new roof for the rectory. All Dinino asked in return was for Father Ignatius to bless a string of rosary beads and hang them over the opening facing the ocean.

"Take one," he said, offering me one of the four remaining cannolis.

"I'm good. I can't stay too long," I said. "They're all up at the house."

He slid off his stool and moved over to the cash register, where he grabbed a fistful of paper napkins. Short and hunchbacked, Dinino had a center of gravity that tilted him slightly forward at all times. The white apron, which never left his waist, didn't help either. It was forever loaded with quarters and hung down to the buckles on his rubber snow boots. More than anything, my friend looked like a still from a silent movie—oversized black parka, white sunlight-deprived skin, the apron and a black felt hat that never left his head, even on the most brutal of summer days. His one concession to color were the gray callouses on his finger- tips, which were currently covered with powdered sugar. He was the rarest of human beings—content to be where he was, always himself, no regrets, no yearning, except the lust he

openly expressed for my grandmother. For years I had been trying to
talk him into a second career as a character actor, but he would only
curse me out whenever I brought it up and tell me I had a head full of
stars.

"*Che si dice?*"

"Good."

"Laura and the kid?"

"Terrific," I lied. Why get into it?

"*Il mio buon amico, che minchia fai?* While I'm still young."

"Soon," I said, trying to sound like I meant it, but Dinino noticed
when I looked down at the concrete floor.

"*Testa di cazzo.*"

Growing up in this neighborhood, I should've spoken a lot more
Italian than I did. But I could usually figure out what Dinino was say-
ing by the expression on his face. The look in his eyes was something
I hadn't seen before.

I changed the subject. "Why don't you come up for a drink and
say hello?" I knew exactly what his response would be.

"Next time," he said.

He tilted his chin at my new leather extravagance.

"You like the new coat?"

"*Non è male,*" Dinino shrugged.

"I gave myself a birthday present."

"What else is new," Dinino said, with a grunt that passed for a
laugh. "You look like Marcello Mastroianni in that movie I like."

I spread my arms wide and shook my hands. "*La Dolce Vita.*"

"*Dolce* my ass," he said, with another grunt.

I saw Dinino's eyes drift from the coat to my blue Brioni flat-fronts.

"How many times I gotta tell you, don't wear your good pants
down here. You're gonna ruin them."

"Nanny gets very upset when we don't dress up for special occasions."

At the mention of my grandmother, Dinino's face lit up like a pizza oven, a hundred times brighter than when he saw the cannolis.

How's Mary the Blonde?"

That was never an easy question to answer.

When my grandmother was twelve, she walked up to *capo di tutti capi* Vito Genovese, who was standing on Spring Street with a few members of his crew, and told him that he should be ashamed of himself for laughing at two young boys who were beating the shit out of each other on the corner. To make her point she wedged her skinny frame between the boys and broke up the brawl herself. Then she called Genovese an asshole. This brief encounter with one of the most powerful Mafiosi in Manhattan could've gone either way, but Genovese loved it. He immediately christened her "Mary the Blonde" and couldn't do enough for her and her family while she still lived in the neighborhood.

"Still married," I said.

"*Vaffanculo*," Dinino muttered, once again demonstrating his disappointment that Nanny hadn't been widowed yet. "I wanna make her an honest woman."

"Good luck," I said.

My eyes fell on two empty pizza boxes spread out on the alley of the ski ball machine.

"You still buying the neighborhood dinner?"

Dinino shrugged, then reached into one of the many pockets of his parka. "Happy birthday," he said. "I want you to have it."

"What are you doing?" I laughed. "I can't accept this."

"*Pucchiacha*, why not? All the quarters you put into these machines over the years, this is the grand prize."

What Dinino was thrusting at me was an 18K stainless steel and rose gold Bulgari watch, a perfect piece of jewelry that he had bought twelve years before for his sixtieth birthday. When he saw the way I was looking at it, he became defensive. "What? It still works perfect. Hasn't lost a second."

I took a step back. "You bought this watch for yourself. This is a special memento."

"*Speciale il mio culo*," he replied. "Anybody could live for sixty years."

He looked like he was ready to kill me, so I tried a different approach. "How are you going to tell time down here?"

"When I wake up, I come here. When the last kid leaves, I go home. I need a ten thousand-dollar-watch to tell me that?"

"I can't take it."

"*Fermati*," he snapped. "Why are you arguing with me? You gave me a present? I give you a present."

I had given him a bag of bent cannolis, but I already knew this was not my argument to win.

"Take it," he said, making the natural rasp of his voice softer. "Before I die down here and by the time they find me, some *pezzo di merda* from the Albanian pizza place up the block is wearing it on deliveries."

I reached out and took the watch from his hand.

"Put it on your wrist before you lose it."

He watched me, his dark olive eyes studying every move, as I slipped the watch slowly over my left hand and stared down at it.

"Fits nice. Was that so fucking hard?" he said.

I had to admit, it looked terrific, especially in combo with the new coat. "I'll hold it for you," I said.

"*Tieni questo*," he said, grunting again, this one accompanied by a grin and a gesture that you could probably figure out. "Let's play some pinball."

The two kids were still huddled in front of the racing machine. They were debating in very loud, very stoned voices what to do with their last quarter, play another game or split a bag of cheese doodles. Only when I waved them over could I see the faces of a boy and a girl framed in the ovals of their tightly pulled hoods. They were younger than I thought—eleven, maybe twelve. The girl had a very pretty face dotted with cold red freckles. The boy looked like the fifth Ramone, with thin cheeks and brown hair plastered down to his sleepy eyelids. Both of them had gone heavy with the cherry Chapstick and were wearing racing gloves with the fingertips cut off. They were a ragged couple, but not without some punky charm.

I handed the girl a twenty-dollar bill, which she immediately asked Dinino to change into eighty quarters. Then they both nodded appreciatively and went back to their game, completely forgetting about the cheese doodles.

"Thanks," Dinino said. "Mr. Bigshot. Now they'll be here 'til midnight."

"Who're you kidding?" Mr. Bigshot said. "You love it."

"Speak for yourself."

Dinino crumpled the empty pastry bag and dropped it on the concrete floor, where it was immediately carried into the middle of the still-deserted street. That was another thing about the arcade. Unlike the mist, which almost never went away, the breezes that swept through the open doors had a mind of their own. They came and went, with no connection to the weather and no regard for the ocean. They could kick up when the water was flat and vanish during a nor'easter. But put a five-dollar bill on the counter, and it disappeared faster than you could say, "Fuck, my allowance."

I reached into my pocket for four quarters and held them in my palm.

"You ready?" I asked. "My treat."

Dinino looked at the Bulgari and laughed. "You bet your ass."

There were a dozen machines in the arcade, from the skee-ball tables to the car racing game to the over-eaters of the Pac-Man family. Most of the games were swapped out every few months. But the one machine that never left the premises was Zenon, the most titillating pinball game ever created. I know that "titillating" is a weird thing to call an arcade game, but the truth was, whoever the genius was who thought that thing up knew *exactly* what "titillating" meant.

The gameboard was compelling enough. Drawings of beautiful nymphs in various stages of undress (picture the girl on the cover of "Candy-O," minus the Ferrari) posed for a crew of smirking devils in red tights. But the real charm of the game was the goddess herself. Once you put the quarter in, music that sounded like Black Sabbath backwards came pumping out of the speakers. Then a husky woman's voice claiming to be the one and only Zenon would taunt the player into screwing up: "Give it to me." "That's the best you got?" "What's wrong with you?" "Shoot again." And always: "Loser." Stinging words, especially to an army of eleven-year-olds, but right up our alley. From the day she arrived, kids lined up to play.

I checked the *First Player* score.

"Not bad for an old man," I said. I knew that would get him going.

Dinino took a long sip from a pint of blackberry brandy that had materialized out of his parka. Then he passed the bottle to me.

"You spend fourteen hours a day with a woman, you get to know her weak spots."

"*Salute*," I said, the liquor warm and sweet in my mouth. I put two quarters into the machine and waited for the music to kick in. "Wish me happy birthday, baby."

A surge of electricity sent me flying back on my ass. Sprawled on the floor ten feet away from the machine, I watched as lights flashed and then exploded inside Zenon's head, the glass over the board shattered, and finally sparks like a roman candle sent ribbons of color up to the stars on the ceiling, which smoldered briefly and then burst into flames.

The last thing I remembered was the girl with the freckles asking her boyfriend, "Is he dead?"

CHAPTER TWO

"Cut the Cake"

THE ROMANO COMPOUND WAS at the top of the hill, tucked into a ritzy neighborhood eight blocks from the beach and a two-minute ride from the second exit ramp after the tolls. The house would have been impressive even without the halo of the bridge looming behind it, a double-brick, four-thousand-square- foot fortress my father had acquaintances build with no money down and no questions asked. We moved two years after I was born, when a Hungarian quarterback (half my heritage, thanks to the lovely Elsie) from PA guaranteed a win in Super Bowl III and Jack Romano had the guts to believe him. The subsequent windfall provided all the bricks and lumber he needed.

God bless Broadway Joe.

As soon as I closed the front door, Laura tiptoed down the stairs, held her index finger to her beautiful lips, and nodded at the laundry room off the foyer. I figured she wanted to tell me something without twelve pairs of ears hanging on every word. Maybe cry a little about some misguided comment someone (Nanny? My sister?) had made while I was bringing the cannolis to Dinino. Instead she reached for my face with both hands and gave me thirty seconds of the most soulful kiss I'd ever had in my life. This was definitely not the reception I had expected, especially from someone who had just been fired.

"Whoa," I said. "Happy birthday to me."

Even in a moment of post-turmoil she was the loveliest person I had ever seen in my life. Strands of her blonde hair were bunched up around the collar of her red turtleneck and her blue eyes looked like the last thing Monet saw before he grabbed his paint brush. Her face was a little rosier, not as pale as it had been earlier in the afternoon when she first received the news. She had also been buffeted by the tender mercies of my mother Elsie and a few glasses of Corvo red. Laura's limit was always a half a bottle of wine or three mimosas, which had evidently been surpassed while Zenon was throwing a temper tantrum down the block. It was never hard to drink whenever my family convened for a special occasion.

Laura looked at me and smiled, then pulled open my coat, slipped her arms around my chest and kissed me again. For a second, I was positive that I had been electrocuted and this was my send-off to wherever the hell I was going.

"Your skin's hot," she whispered, working her lips over to my left earlobe and keeping her fingers pressed against my skin. I wasn't sure if it was the proximity of my family in the formal dining room one floor above or my near-death experience, but I was ready to explode. I leaned up against the Kenmore to brace myself.

"What smells burnt?" Laura pulled her head back and looked at me quizzically. I could still feel the surge of Zenon's voltage in my fingertips, among other extremities. I also noticed that I couldn't stop tapping my right foot.

It was time to resort to the truth. "We had a little fire in the arcade," I said.

"Oh, my God. Is Dinino all right?"

Laura loved Dinino. She told me right after our first trip to the arcade that she could tell how good a person he was by the way he talked to the kids (despite the curses and the "*pucchiacha.*") I did my best to assure her that he was fine (he was) and that the arcade had suffered only slightly more than minor damage (it had). But she was having a hard time wrapping her perfect head around an exploding pinball machine.

"I don't understand. . .*what happened?*"

"Basically," I said, "that bitch Zenon tried to kill me." I said it with a laugh, but when she didn't laugh, I explained, "The machine shorted out, and I got zapped. And then it caught on fire." In response to the budding tears and the 9-1-1 look in her eyes, I added, "See what happens when I do something nice?"

"Let's go to the emergency room."

"Nah, the firemen checked me out. They said I'm good."

"You're not good."

I could see by the way she was studying my face that she was going to be harder to sway than the two EMT guys in the ambulance, who were a little glass-eyed themselves and ready to pull away before I had the blood pressure cuff off my arm.

"Michael will take us."

My saintly brother, who could never resist doing a favor.

"No way," I said. "I'm not going."

Laura pulled her hands out of my coat and held my chin up to the moonlight, which was pushing through the window over the washing machine and had coated us in silver. With our faces so close, I felt like Heathcliff staring into Catherine's eyes on the moors.

"Your pupils are huge," she said. "How's your vision?"

"Perfect."

The thing that was between Laura and me was very powerful. Even four years down the line, and despite some of the recent moves I'd made, we were still pulled together like horizontal gravity. Always holding hands, arms around each other, head on shoulders, hands touching hair. My sister called us the "One-chair people."

"I'm serious," she said. Laura dropped my chin and took a step back. "How many of me do you see?" she asked, sounding very much like Iris D'Urberville, the brilliant no-nonsense nurse clinician she had played on her soap opera for five years. Funny, I had never thought of Laura in the medical sense, but I had to admit, the scene had some very sexy possibilities. I started to tingle again.

"The more the merrier."

A voice shattered the moment so completely that I could swear it was coming out of the washing machine. "Laur-rraaaa!"

"Jesus Christ," I muttered. I stuck my head out of the door and yelled up the stairs, "We're coming, Nanny."

"I was calling Laura," was Nanny's reply.

"Let me just throw this out there," I said to Laura, trying to delay the inevitable. "*Any* chance we barricade the door and make love down here?"

The most beautiful face in daytime television looked at me like I was nuts.

"Your grandmother's at the top of the stairs," she whispered. Then she took a step toward the stairway. "I'm getting your brother."

I put my hand on her arm.

"I'll make you a deal," I said. "Give me half an hour with Nanny. If I don't collapse, we skip the hospital."

"The clock's ticking," she said, but then added a smile to her Code Blue face.

I made an adjustment to my pants and pulled my coat closed to deflect Mary the Blonde's radar. Then I reached for Laura's hand.

THE FAMILY HAD MOVED UPSTAIRS for the dessert portion of the evening, after eating the platters of cold antipasto (always the highlight—everything after that was dessert, although no one would ever admit it) and the main course, Elsie's mind-blowing Sunday sauce over rigatoni, in the family room downstairs.

An array of sweets was already spread out on the formal dining room table, from the box of pastries we had brought to my sister-in-law Kristina's delicious homemade cheesecake to Nanny's delicious homemade cheesecake. (Whatever dessert anyone made, my grandmother had to make one, too.) There were also platters of colorful holiday cookies, including the seven-layer red and green jam-filled extravaganzas that fed my grandfather's diabetic sweet tooth like a morphine drip.

"I'll get everybody," Kim, my brother Jojo's wife, said.

"Let them finish the game," I said.

My twenty-seven-year-old twin brothers Michael and Jojo, their five combined kids, and Laura's son Chris had re-located to the family room, where they were screaming at the Knicks game. Despite the commotion, Poppy was sound asleep on the sofa, his eyelids fluttering, the baked potato-sized knot on his gold tie finally loosened a little at the collar. Ten years Nanny's senior, Poppy had recently started to spend more time in the past than in the apartment in the back of the house that he shared with his wife of fifty-five years. During our pre-antipasto grapefruit and vodkas (yet another ritual), he told me and Chris all about the Saint Bernards that he had taken care of in his uncle's butcher shop on Thompson Street seventy years before. I don't think I'd ever seen him happier.

The gravy meat that we had feasted on earlier in the evening was always courtesy of my grandfather. For every holiday/birthday, Poppy insisted that one of us drive him into the city to the butcher shop, even though it had changed hands twenty times since he worked there as a kid. He would pay for the meat in cash, "stake" the butcher a buck, and pocket two mozzarellas as a tribute to his continued patronage. Then he'd take a long nap and dream about the dogs.

I couldn't help looking at the empty chair at the end of the table, one piece of furniture that had stayed vacant most of my life. I felt the cool green of Elsie's eyes on me. She was standing in the doorway between the dining room and the kitchen. I knew she wanted me to be the one to get him for the birthday cake. Even though we'd been through this dance a thousand times, it never failed to piss me off that it was still such a contest of wills.

THE DOOR TO THE DOWNSTAIRS DEN WAS OPEN. The room was dark, lit with the flicker of two television sets, one on top of the other. Knocking twice, I walked in and sat down on the loveseat.

The bottom television was playing the fourth quarter of the Knicks-Celtics game on MSG cable, the same one everybody else was watching upstairs.

The top screen was much more pathetic. The Rangers were getting their asses kicked once again, this time by their rivals across the Hudson. Unfortunately for us Ranger fans, the New Jersey Devils had been playing terrific hockey all season. The Rangers, on the other hand, were skating like they had just left an open bar at Mustang Sally's.

"Jesus Christ," I said, watching one of the Rangers take another bad penalty. "How many years since the Cup? Five?"

"Four," my father said, without looking up.

Jack Romano sat in his brown leather recliner, a red-and-green Christmas throw across his legs. He was studying a small pile of bet slips in his lap. His black hair was cut short and pushed straight back, and his blue-tinted glasses hung on a cord on the front of his brown velour V-neck. Even though he'd never exercised a day in his fifty-four years, he enjoyed Nanny and Poppy's genes and didn't look a half an hour over forty. As a matter of fact, given the right dim light, somebody could've taken us for brothers instead of father and son. But either way, it wouldn't have made much of a difference. We were better off the way we were.

He glanced up at the television sets for a second, then reached for a pen on the snack table and made a mark on one of the slips. What was left of Elsie's dinner was sitting in a dish on the table next to the remote.

"How's business?" I asked, then immediately regretted it.

"Like that," he said, glancing in my general direction. "You?"

"Not bad," I lied. "Elsie wants you to come to the table."

"You mean your mother?" he said quietly.

"Yeah. My mother."

He slipped on his glasses and turned his attention to the end of the Knick game.

"Tell your mother that I'll be there in a couple of minutes."

And with that our conversation was over.

WHEN I GOT BACK TO THE TABLE, I could hear the girls talking in the kitchen: Elsie, Laura, my sister Pamela, Kim, and Kristina, Michael's wife. They always seemed to have a lot to say to each other. The strong aroma of freshly brewed espresso was suddenly very much in the air.

That left me and Mary the Blonde as the sole Romanos at the table.

"They eat and they run," Nanny said. "They finish, they get up, they disappear. Like a race. God forbid they should sit at the table and talk to their grandmother."

"I'll talk to you, Nanny."

"Big deal."

The gold Christmas tree on Nanny's lapel, dotted with five half-carat rubies, rose and then fell as she sighed and dropped her fork on the empty plate for effect.

My grandmother, the aforementioned Mary the Blonde and the object of Dinino's unrequited affection, was the matriarch of the Romano family. She was in her "work clothes," a nifty navy Liz Clairborne pants suit cut extra slim to accent her still petite shape. At 72, she worked full-time as a store detective for one of the high-end fashion stores on Fifth Avenue. Sauntering around the store like she was both Lord and Taylor, Nanny sifted through pricy merchandise, pretended to shop, flitted in and out of dressing rooms, and eagle-eyed the clientele. Then, when she saw something promising, she moved in for the kill, with instincts sharpened from a girlhood spent on the sidewalks of Sullivan and Spring.

Nanny had gone back to work at sixty, claiming she was bored with us. She quickly became the Babe Ruth of store detectives. Before she stepped up to the plate, the record at the store for shoplifting arrests had been 22 in one year. In Nanny's rookie season, she snagged 108 perps from all walks of life—waitresses, bank officers, socialites, secretaries, lawyers, Rockettes. She had an uncanny ability to sense, even in the most fleeting of encounters, the deceit, desperation, and sense of entitlement that lurked just beneath the shoplifter's often very fair exterior.

One of her favorites war stories was when she wrestled a second-grade teacher to the curb on Fifth Avenue. When the teacher started sobbing and told my grandmother what she did for a living, Nanny held the stolen Louis Vuitton bag in front of her face and snapped back, "Whatta ya teach 'em—how to steal?"

As soon as the reinforcements arrived, Nanny explained to her boss that it had been a terrible misunderstanding and sent the teacher on her way, minus the Louis.

At five feet one and maybe 110 pounds without the brooch, Mary the Blonde was fearless, a legitimate force of nature, mostly for good.

She reached for the carafe of white wine and filled her glass to the brim. Nanny drank cheap Chablis like it was lemonade, but never appeared to lose a speck of her composure. She also liked to top off everybody else's wine glass while we ate, another old trick to loosen tongues that my grandmother used to great effect.

"My family, when my mother-God-rest-her-soul made dinner, my brothers and sisters, my aunts and uncles, we used to sit at the table for hours. It was beautiful (pronounced *bee-uuu-tee-ful*). Sunday dinner would start at two, and nobody would move 'til eight, nine o' clock."

"That's why they all weighed four hundred pounds."

"Always so clever," Nanny said. "Everything's a big joke."

Mary the Blonde pushed back her chair and picked up her wine glass.

"Why're you getting upset?"

"Don't make fun of the dead," she said. She stood up and looked at me as if it was the first time she had ever seen me in her life. "You're getting very peculiar," she added, then went to sit next to her husband on the couch.

Pamela and Laura came out of the kitchen, carrying the coffee and demitasse cups.

"I still can't believe what they *fucking did*," Pamela said. By far the sharpest of Elsie and Jack's four children, and, as Nanny had claimed since my sister was two, "the most *alert*." Pamela had the filthiest mouth of the four of us. She was also the loudest accountant I had ever met in my life.

Although she worked for the venerable Bank of New York and buttoned up like Stalin for work, in her leisure time my twenty-four-year old baby sister still had the Staten Island Mall look down to an art movement. Her well-moussed hair was teased up to the chandelier, her silver-sequined blouse was well off the shoulder, and her hoop earrings just about touched her bare shoulder blades. I'd noticed that Chris was not above catching a glimpse of Pamela's clavicle between mouthfuls of stuffed artichoke a little earlier in the evening. I made a mental note to buy my sister a very expensive extra-baggy turtleneck with padded shoulders for Christmas Eve.

"You were the whole show," Pamela continued, setting each coffee cup down on the thick Holiday tablecloth with the delicacy of a Sumo wrestler hitting the mat. "Those cocksuckers."

I looked up to make sure the kids were still in the den.

"It's terrible," Kristina said, following them out of the kitchen with a stack of dessert plates and silverware.

Just like her husband, Kristina meant well, but I had to side with my sister on this one. "Terrible" was much too tame a word to describe how Laura had been treated. It was painful enough to be written out of a show, but to be blindsided by her producers at a story meeting nine days before Christmas (and on her boyfriend's thirtieth birthday) was a truly *disgraziato* thing to do. When I first saw Laura's face after she got the news, it'd been like a giant hole had opened up in front of her on Forty-ninth Street. She was crushed. I had hugged her until the sun set, then steered her through the blockade of tourists surrounding Rockefeller Plaza. We'd grabbed a very shaky drink at the first pub I saw on Sixth Avenue.

Although the place had already started to fill in with an early shopping bag crowd, I had been able to snag two stools at the bar. The bartender had quickly sized up the situation, put drinks in front of us and kept busy with some customers at the other end of the counter. A true professional. After my initial outburst of "Piece of shit this" and

"Motherfucker that," I'd just sat next to Laura with my arm wrapped tightly around her shoulder. She had kept her blue sunglasses on and was holding the script to her chest with two hands like it was a puppy she had just pulled out of an icy lake.

When I felt the rhythm of her breathing steady, I had very gently extricated the pages from her hands and replaced them with a glass of Jameson.

We stayed that way for an hour—not talking, not looking at one another, just sipping our drinks and listening to the jukebox, until Laura sighed, checked her watch, and announced that it was time to get a cab and pick up Chris.

"How much of a dick do you have to be to think this was a good idea?"

This was my sister again.

"They were very apologetic about it," Laura said. "The network told Gus they felt a tearjerker right after the holidays would give the show a big ratings spike."

I could tell by the way she was fielding Pamela's moral outrage that Laura was already more resigned than angry. This was typical of Laura. She never stayed angry for very long—but she did stay hurt. Slowly, over the next couple of weeks, after we had a chance to talk it out, that hurt would melt into disappointment and then empathy for her character. She wouldn't mourn the job—she would mourn Iris. This would take some time. After four years of Laura playing television's favorite soap opera nurse, there would be a lot to miss. Typical of me, I knew there had to be a lot more to this than Gus Haliatokis, her scheming oil slick of a producer, was telling her, but I figured we could save that for later.

When we first talked about how—when-*if*-we were going to break the news, Laura seriously considered not saying anything at all. This was after I, while we were still in the cab heading over to her apartment, suggested that we seriously consider calling the night off. This made perfect sense to me, in the afterglow of four whiskies. I gallantly insisted that we had much more immediate matters to deal with than my birthday. But Laura said that wasn't fair to anyone. (In all honesty, I had known she'd insist on going.) And any excuse we could make up (including what had actually happened) would have been *especially* unfair to Elsie, who had prepared the dinner and was the last person on earth who deserved an eleventh-hour cancellation.

Laura said there was no way we could deprive my mother of having the opportunity to celebrate her oldest son's thirtieth birthday. And Nanny, even though she always seemed mad at me about something, would have been on the phone to her friend Vito, or whoever else was standing on the corner of Spring and Sullivan these days, to track us down like dogs and deliver us personally to the celebration.

So not going was never really an option.

Chris suggested, in his seven-and-a-half-year-old wisdom, that we get it over with and say something as soon as we walked in, like, "Guess what just happened? My mom got fired—hi, everybody!" Always good to be proactive, but then Laura was nervous that it would be a little too much at once. Makes sense. Coming home was always a little too much at once. And, to be fair to my family, they were not only big fans of Laura—they all loved the show. (Or at least the fact that someone they were very close with was the star of the show.) So when Laura did say something during the antipasto, an immediate uproar ensued, which ran from genuine expressions of outrage and sympathy to a half-assed bomb threat (my brother Jojo's wacky friend Neal, who for some reason ate the first course with us, wished me happy birthday, and then somewhat ominously disappeared.)

Much to our relief, the conversation seemed to wane a little when we served the macaroni and Elsie's monumental platter of gravy meat. But it had obviously flared up again in the kitchen.

Once Laura finished setting the espresso cups and spoons, she took a seat next to me, the lone celebrant at the table. She reached for my hand, looked at her watch and very discreetly checked my pulse under the table. Ex-nurse clinician Iris didn't look happy.

"Are you okay?"

"Yeah," I said and smiled. "Why wouldn't I be?"

She whispered in my ear, "Your pulse feels like it's hit triple digits."

I lowered my voice. "Good. Maybe I'll run back to Manhattan."

"I'll be right behind you," Laura said, her voice low. "If your sister asks me one more question about getting fired my brain's going to explode."

I heard the door to the family room open, accompanied by some residual shouting and an army of footsteps.

I raised my wine glass.

"Cheers."

Chris was the first to emerge from the pack.

"How'd they do?" I asked.

Laura's son looked at me and tightened his jaw. Whenever he got upset his lips became thin and a little crooked, like two strips of over-cooked bacon.

"They *lost*? They were up by eleven." This was actually good news for me, or at least good for business. But the look on Chris's face broke my heart. "What happened?"

Chris shrugged. A die-hard fan, he was still young enough to believe in the essential invincibility of the teams he rooted for, especially the New York Knickerbockers. He took the seat next to me.

In the background, Nanny and Poppy were treading their way over, arm in arm. My brothers' children were also beginning to swarm the table, followed by their fathers.

My brother Jojo was talking about turtle wax. "So I get back from K-Mart, and the can's empty," he said to no one in particular. "Someone scooped the wax out in the store." He looked at Chris. "Who does that?" Then he sat down next to his wife. "You know, I thought the can felt a little light."

"Only on Staten Island," Michael responded, but, despite the turtle wax episode, my twin brothers loved living here. Michael had been planning on marrying Kristina and buying the five-bedroom Colonial across the street from our parents since he was twelve. They married as soon as Kristina graduated from St. John's University. The year before, they had signed the papers on the house.

Five years married, three kids and a house. And Jojo was right behind him.

"Can you sue the network?"

Pamela was relentless.

"The more I think about it," Laura said patiently, "the more it makes sense."

Honestly, considering how talented she was and how she had carried *The Daze of Night* on her back since the first day she stepped into Rose Hills Memorial Hospital, it would've made even more sense for Laura to pack up her stethoscope three years ago. But Laura was one of those people who took whatever she did very seriously.

Even me.

"They've been trying to kill me off for six months," Laura said, looking across the table at Pamela. "First the car bomb, then the brain cancer. At least with the tumor I could linger."

Chris looked upset.

"Mom, why do they want to kill you so bad?"

For some reason Nanny looked at me, so I spoke up.

"Because her producers know she's been getting offers to do movies."

"Wait—what? Movies?" Pamela asked, a complete 180, suddenly aglow, thrilled that she might share future holidays with a movie star. She gave Laura a big happy hug and sprinted into the kitchen to pick up the telephone.

"That's terrific," Michael added, beaming at Laura.

Laura smiled weakly. She looked tired. "We'll see. My agent mentioned a couple of scripts that he thought might be a good fit."

Kristina put her hand on Laura's arm. "Things always happen for the best."

I saw the slight quiver in Laura's lower lip and knew we had to cut our losses. Laura needed a nightcap and a really good night's sleep. Chris needed to get ready for school tomorrow. And I needed to make one more stop for the evening before I could put my thirtieth to bed. "Any idea where the cake is?" I asked.

When I heard my mother's voice singing the first "Happy," I could've cried.

Elsie stepped out of the kitchen carrying a large Pyrex of homemade tiramisu. Everyone joined in while my beautiful mother smiled at us and set the cake down in the center of the table. The "3" and "0" candles were already lit and standing tall in an ocean of mascarpone cheese and cocoa powder like the masts of the *Nina* and the *Pinta* at sunset.

Thanking everyone for being there, I made my wish, blew out my candles and poured another healthy shot of Sambuca into my cup. And at that moment, as beautifully wrapped presents began to appear in front of me, I actually convinced myself that those three little coffee beans (health, happiness, and prosperity) in my espresso were going to keep floating and not sink like tiny anchors to the bottom of my cup.

CHAPTER THREE

"Tighten Up"

J ACKIE AND I WERE PARTNERS. We ran a bookmaking operation out of the back room of a gay bar on Hudson Street in the Village. The beautiful thing about the relationship was that we understood each other perfectly. I was an actor who would supplement my income by taking the occasional friendly bet over the telephone. Jackie was Jay Gatsby with a hair weave, a man of large dreams, of expensive appetites, all five feet three inches of his chubby body bursting out of black nylon jogging suits and sockless Gucci loafers. Between our separate careers and our partnership, we both made almost enough money to support ourselves in the style to which we had grown accustomed.

From the night we met two years ago it was a very uncomplicated arrangement. We weren't new-found best friends. We weren't tied up in each other's lives. Most days, after we finished taking bets eyeball to eyeball in the back office, we didn't even like each other that much. It was all about cash flow. So when Pamela waved me into the kitchen to tell me that Jackie had just left a message, my gut reaction was, "Fuck." He knew it was my birthday. He knew I was on Staten Island to celebrate. He knew I was with Laura and Chris. Maybe he was just checking to make sure I had remembered to take the money? Or, even better, maybe Sally had cancelled our meeting? Maybe that was it— some Mob emergency had come up at the club, and Sally had to re-schedule. I could just head to Laura's apartment; we could say goodnight to Chris and then discuss the events of the day over a couple of glasses of Grand Marnier.

I stuck my head into the dining room and looked at Laura, who was carefully layering another piece of tiramisu onto Chris' plate. In twenty minutes, my beautiful birthday dessert had gone from a creamy ocean to a crater on the moon. The *Nina* and *Pinta* were nowhere in sight.

"Can I talk to you in the kitchen for a minute?"

Before she had a chance to tell me I looked a little shaky and maybe revisit a trip to the ER, I explained. "I just got off the phone with Jackie."

"Everything all right?" Laura asked.

"Not really," I said. "He needs a favor."

I could immediately see the tension slipping back into those beautiful features.

"What kind of a favor?"

I sat down at the kitchen table and gave her the few sketchy details that Jackie had relayed over the phone, with one or two slight edits. After I was done Laura sat down next to me.

"He wants you to do this *now*?" Her voice conveyed some concern over Jackie's predicament but was mostly tinged with a weariness that made it clear that this *particular* predicament (and my potential in-volvement in it) would have been much more compelling maybe a year ago. And definitely on a day when she hadn't been fired.

"Yeah," I said. "Definitely sooner than later." I made a face to indicate that it sounded crazy to me, too.

"Just tell him you don't feel well," she said.

"Absolutely."

She reached for my hand. Building on the goodwill of the birthday cake and my very thoughtful gifts, Laura was doing her best to snowball the love she had for me into a misguided faith in my ability to make a sound decision. She wanted to believe that, despite Jackie's latest emergency, there was no way her boyfriend, who had almost been fried by a pinball machine and who was as glassy-eyed as a branzino in an ice bath, could entertain such a ridiculous thought.

"Let's finish opening the presents," she said, standing up from the table.

"Definitely," I said, but I didn't get up. Instead I added, after a beat, "It's just that I hate to leave him stranded." When she didn't respond, I tacked on, "The guy doesn't ask for much."

Both Laura and I knew that this last statement was about as far from the truth as anything I had said since the cab delivered us to Staten Island four hours before. Jackie was a nuclear reactor of need, feeding off the low-grade plutonium of the people around him and splitting it into a billion favors.

"It's your birthday."

But when it came to Jackie, it was always a lot more complicated than that. I was very close to telling him myself that I couldn't make it until I stopped talking and listened to the sound of his voice in the receiver.

"Why don't we *start* to get our things together? I'll borrow my sister's car, we'll drive back into the city, I'll drop you and Chris off, and then I'll take care of this thing."

Laura offered me a closed-mouth smile that was never good. "Not after six shots of Sambuca."

"I'm good," I said.

She started to say something, then turned and walked back into the dining room.

THE STATIONHOUSE WAS ABOUT AN HOUR'S DRIVE, not too far from the Meadowlands and Giants' Stadium. Pamela, still elated about Laura's looming movie career, let me borrow her beautiful white Camaro, which had its little red gas needle buried a half inch below "E." Much to his delight, I asked the poor kid in the gas station to check the oil and the antifreeze too, just to be on the safe side. Then I took the Goethals Bridge into the lowlands of New Jersey.

Despite a few terrific beaches, Sinatra, the sublime voice of Frankie Valli (show me a vocal more stirring than "Rag Doll") and some really luscious tomatoes in August, the Garden State was never a place I held especially close to my heart. Not that I hated the place, but it was minor league, especially when compared to the Emerald City across the water. As far as I was concerned, the true brilliance of NJ was in what it did wrong. Greed and corruption were raised to an art form, the cities were mine fields that made some of the shittier neighborhoods in the Bronx look like Paris in May, and the cultural phenomenon of the moment was the guy who played goal for the red-hot New Jersey Devils.

I found the town of East Dorwood off 3 West in just over an hour. The precinct was just two traffic lights from the highway, a squat brick building with three police cars in the parking lot, two of which looked like they had been in a demolition derby with each other. When I opened the door and walked up to the front desk, the sergeant and two officers were watching the end of *Dateline* and eating Chinese food out of half a dozen containers. From the unhappy looks on their faces, it was obvious that they would rather have thrown themselves off the

George Washington Bridge than talk to me.

I pulled up the collar of my new coat and reminded myself that I was only a river and a tunnel from the city.

The way my partner had described the favor over the phone was both straightforward and ambiguous—just pick up a guy from Hudson Street (who?) being held (why?) by the cops and drive him back (when?) to the Onion. That was all I had to go on. But when I mentioned the name that Jackie had given me all three men leapt to their feet.

"Who are you?" the sergeant barked.

Good question. Who was I?

His eyes slid from my black Ferragamos to my leather jacket to Dinino's Bulgari, which I had slipped back on my wrist after hiding it through dinner. (We'd had enough to talk about.) I was pretty sure from the way he was sizing me up that the sergeant assumed I was a lawyer.

He pointed his chopsticks at my Adam's apple and replied with the utmost condescension, "I'm not sure how they do things across the Hudson, *pal*, but I think we're going to keep this one for a while. Why don't you try us again tomorrow morning? Around eleven."

For the splittest of seconds I thought about playing along (*Law and Order*, season three, college roommate of the campus rapist), but I knew I wasn't thinking clearly enough to pull off Atticus Finch.

I went with the solid but not too flashy "a friend of the family."

When that didn't make a dent, I added, "I understand it's very late, officer, and believe me, I appreciate your time."

Chopsticks paused, he nodded, then said, "Go home."

I took a deep breath. The thing was, I had never had a problem with the police in my life, not even close. But these guys were a masters' class in wasting taxpayer dollars. The sergeant running the show had that smug, small-town cop look, the kind of law enforcement official who'd made a career spending quiet nights on the payroll, eating dim sum and wrestling the occasional lawn jockey thief to the ground. His eyebrows had merged into one gray line, and one corner of his mouth was decorated with duck sauce.

"Would you be able to tell me what the charges are?"

"No."

"How about a date for a court appearance?"

Chopsticks looked back at his fellow officers as if they didn't know whether to laugh or lock me up, too. He glanced at the television set. "Maybe the end of next week," he said. "Outside chance middle of the week after. A lot depends on the holidays."

During my conversation with their sergeant, the two deputies had taken a few steps back from the desk and were studying me as if I was hanging on a wall in the Guggenheim. After a brief exchange that featured the words "It's gotta be," the shorter of the two deputies, with a mustache out of '70s porn, moved closer.

"You know," he said (as soon as I heard "You know," I felt the Sambuca and the Corvo red, with just a hint of Dinino's blackberry brandy, join forces and start to climb up my esophagus), "you look just like that guy who does that commercial on television."

To be fair, this was how I usually felt when anybody brought up the commercial. But now was definitely not the time to throw up.

I choked out a laugh. "Commercial?"

"Yeah," he said. "The sneeze?"

This was not a good development. Jackie lived less than fifteen minutes from this hellhole, in a huge Tudor on a half-acre of prime real estate with wife number four. For reasons still known only to my partner, Jackie needed to get this guy out of here tonight. And I, for reasons known only to me, had incurred Laura's disappointment in order to help him. How seriously were they going to take a guy who sneezed for a living? I gave them an annoyed, how-ridiculous look and tried to re-engage with Chopsticks, but he was much more interested in the sexy news girl on Channel 4 than anything else I had to say.

"He looks just like him," Ron Jeremy said, shaking his head. "Vicks 44?"

"I'm thinkin' Mucinex," his partner said, whose face, in keeping with the flow of the conversation, was as pink as a bottle of Pepto Bismol.

The '70s porn star turned back to me. "You have to be him."

"How could I be him?" I asked. "I'm here." This actually made no sense, but it seemed to shut them up. "*Officer,*" I said, in strict profile, trying to snag Chopstick's attention again, "what about bail?"

He turned back to me with a "Why are you still here?" look. "Tough to find a judge," he said, "at eleven o'clock on a Tuesday night."

The heat and the cheap plastic forks, the smell of the grease from the pork fried rice, and the pale green plaster of the walls, and especially the looks on their faces, were clouding my judgement and reminding me why I hated the commercial in the first place. Of all things to be known for in life—a fucking sneeze? I reached into my coat and *slowly* pulled the money we owed Sally out of the inside pocket. Then I slid one fat wad of twenties out of the envelope and started counting. True to form, the three officers lit up like bull sharks in a condo pool.

Within minutes phone calls had been made and we had come to an understanding.

THERE WERE TWO JAIL CELLS IN THE REAR of the precinct. Both appeared at first to be empty, but Chopsticks opened the cell that was nearest the security door and gestured with his chin for me to walk in first. "Your 'friend' is on the cot."

All three of the courtroom procedurals that I had acted in did not prepare me for the truly terrifying feeling of stepping inside a real jail cell. It was a lot more 'intimate' than the ones on a set. A lot darker, too. I lingered by the cell door.

"Go ahead," Chopsticks said, sensing some hesitation. "You paid for him."

I stepped into the center of the cell. A large mound that appeared to have a vaguely human contour was sacked out in the corner, under one end of a green canvas blanket. A pair of dirty red sneakers stuck out of the other end. "Excuse me?"

There was no movement, no sound.

Chopsticks looked at me and smirked. "No refunds."

"Hey," I said, louder. Still nothing. I moved closer to the cot and tapped the blanket with the tip of my index finger, then stepped back. Despite the sneakers, I half expected a rabid bear to roll out from under the lumps of blanket and tear the organs out of the both of us.

No response. The smell of dirt and sweat was so bad I had to turn my head and breathe into the collar of my coat.

I looked over at the sergeant. I was too tired to pretend. "What's his name again?"

"Virgil Shepherd," he said, not raising an eyebrow.

"Virgil! Hey, pal, come on, get up. We can leave."

Nothing.

The sneer on the sergeant's face made it clear that, despite the large amount of cash I had just handed over, we were not going to meet for a drink anytime soon. If I said the one thing that was on both of our minds, whatever was under that blanket would have a cellmate.

I considered my options. "Officer," I said, "you think you could help me out a little?"

Chopsticks stepped past me and kicked the leg of the bed hard with his jackboot, then calmly took a step back.

We both watched as one large arm slipped out from under the blanket and fell to the concrete floor.

CHAPTER FOUR

"Ride, Captain, Ride"

THE CIRCUMSTANCES THAT LED TO JACKIE OWNING a bar in his twenties were murky at best, much like Jackie himself, but here he was, thirty years later, legendary owner and operator of the Golden Onion. Once celebrated for being a safe haven back in the '60s when there were very few, it was now a quaint neighborhood footnote, the kind of place that kept its Christmas decorations up year-round. That was the history of most of the bars in New York City, if they managed to stay open at all, but Jackie insisted it was just our current economic downturn that had slowed the pace of the celebrations and kept the register quiet. Of course, it was other things too, terrible things, but Jackie didn't like to bring that up. Whenever someone came into the bar that he hadn't seen in a while, he showered them with drinks like they had just been resurrected by Jesus.

Brendan the bartender was putting the stools up on the counter when I walked in. It was already close to three in the morning and I felt like moving into my shower for a week. I waved to a couple of regulars who were finishing their drinks in the purple glow of the juke-

box, listening to Freddie's Scott heartbreaking fadeout to "Hey, Girl."
Brendan nodded toward the back room.

"He's a little crazed."

Brendan Halliday was the rarest of commodities, a nice guy in the
bar business. Anyone I ran into who knew him swore he was the greatest human being in the world, and in the two years I had been around
the Onion I had seen no evidence to the contrary. Black, late thirties,
slim, with a preference for pressed jeans and tartan sweater vests, Brendan had been a Wall Street guy until the great meltdown of '87, when
he was summarily canned like everybody else. With the economy in
the toilet, he asked Jackie if he could strap on an apron to make his
bills. A regular customer before the purge, he had been the steadiest
of employees since and Jackie's right-hand man in all matters pertaining
to the bar. Brendan had an MA in finance from U Penn, so he was a
bright guy and very good at stretching the diminished take from the
register. He would've been good with our other thing too, but Jackie
told me that Brendan had very politely made it clear from the start that
he'd had enough of the fluctuations of chance. He'd much rather slap
an olive in a martini.

The first time I met him, almost two years before, he'd stuck out
his hand, said, "Hi, I'm Brendan, Jackie's bitch," held my eyes for a
beat, then added with a straight face, "but only in matters of business."
I'd never had a gay guy quote *The Godfather* to me before. We'd been
close ever since.

"How was the night?"

"Not bad," he said, but he looked upset. "A few of the old faces
surfaced. How about you?"

"Not good," I said.

Brendan poured some Remy in a tumbler and nodded toward the
back room.

"Take this with you," he said.

"Thanks."

"I mean the bottle." Then, as if something had just dawned on him, he checked the clock behind the bar and smiled. "And happy belated birthday."

Jackie leapt up from behind the desk when I pushed open the door to the office. He was dressed as if he'd just come from a fundraiser—button-down light blue Alfani shirt, navy blazer, gray slacks.

"Where is this fucking meatball?"

I took a long sip of brandy and explained how his friend was dead to the world across the back seat of my sister's red leather interior.

"I should go out there and strangle this motherfucker," Jackie said, pacing past my chair and then back again behind his desk. "I couldn't've made it any easier. I told him ten times, show up after seven, we were going to her sister's house in Moonachie for dinner. All he had to do was open the garage door, start the car, and drive it back into the city. Could somebody tell me what's so difficult about that? Key, ignition, gas—goodbye. Simple, right?" When I didn't say anything, he added, "Am I right or am I wrong?"

That was never an easy question to answer.

"Meanwhile, he shows up at four o'clock, breaks down the garage door, and scares the shit out of my wife, who's watching the whole thing from the bedroom window."

"How do you know this guy?"

"He's been hanging around the bar the last few weeks."

"He's a customer?"

"Brendan found him sleeping in the doorway," Jackie said. I must have looked a little confused, so he added for clarity's sake, "You know Brendan, friend to the world, one brother to another, all that give-back-to-society crap. He gives him a cup of coffee and a bagel to sweep the sidewalk, throw out the garbage. Lets him warm up a little."

The headache I had developed on the drive back into Manhattan had just kicked into a full attack, and the tingling in my hands was making it hard to hold onto my Remy. Jackie stopped pacing the length of the office, which I realized was not much roomier than the jail cell. He flopped down in the chair behind the desk and mercifully refilled my cup.

"You made a homeless guy steal your wife's car?"

"I didn't *make* him, I *asked* him," he said, as if this explained everything. "And he wasn't stealing it. He was delivering it to me. I pay for that fucking car!"

When I didn't say anything, Jackie continued, in a much thinner voice that had lost its slings and arrows and sounded suspiciously close to the truth, "You ever drive an XJ6?"

"I don't think so."

"Do yourself a favor," he continued. "You ever get your hands on one? Drive it into a building. The car's killin' me. You have any idea what the insurance runs for a Jaguar? Half the time Courtney's driving she's fixing her make-up, she's playing with the radio. The next time she gets a ticket, they might as well walk in the bar on New Year's Eve and take the cash register. That's why I figured I'd pay him a few bucks, make the car disappear. Then, in a couple of weeks, I'd buy her a fucking Mazda and put it in Brendan's name."

A few words about Jackie's connubials: My partner had been married to Courtney Paiste Parker for three years, and while I can't say I was intimate with the situation, I was pretty convinced that Jackie's fourth wife was a *pucchiacha*. Very attractive, tall, curvy, early forties maybe. I could see her filing through a stack of cashmere sweaters in Lord and Taylor, Nanny watching her like a hawk. She was one of those people who was always going on about where she had just been and how terrific it was, like the immediate present could never measure up to the very recent past. When Jackie said, "Isn't the *crème brulée* delicious?" Courtney would act like she loved it, like it was going to cure cancer, then say, "Did you ever try it at (fill in with a four-star establishment)?" Laura wasn't particularly ecstatic about her either, which was telling, since Laura could find something nice to say about everyone. Not that Laura ever knocked Courtney to me, but she would get quiet during our very infrequent dinner foursomes, as though she was uncomfortable and couldn't wait to get the hell out of there.

"I mean, it's not like the guy couldn't use the money."

Jackie pressed the palm of his hand into his eye socket, took a sip out of a glass that was sitting on his desk, and wiped at his mouth with a cocktail napkin. He suddenly looked a lot older than whatever age he actually was. In the two years that I had known him, he'd claimed to be four different ages. But at that moment, under the dim circumference of the overhead bulb, fifty-five seemed like the over-under.

"Believe me, the last thing I wanted to do was bother you on the night of your birthday." He held up his glass for a toast. "Happy birthday, by the way." We clinked glasses. "But I had to get him out of there before he opened his mouth and told the cops that I gave him the car keys. I knew you were holding Sally's money. I figured if you spread a few hundred around, they'd let him go ROR."

Jackie shook his head in disgust. "I can't believe this *jomboni* got arrested."

It was my turn. "You have to understand one thing. He didn't just get arrested," I said. "The cops I dealt with tonight? You're very lucky they didn't shoot him."

I took the bail receipt from my coat pocket and read out the charges I had scribbled on the back: grand larceny, criminal possession of stolen property, attempted assault on a police office–here I paused to describe how he had tried to back the XJ6 through the two cop cars blocking the driveway–and my personal favorite, driving while intoxicated.

Jackie laughed for the first time since I entered the office. "He was drunk?"

"Bombed out. The cops pulled three pints of vodka out of his coat pocket."

"What the hell did you say to get him released?"

I detected the slightest note of admiration in his voice. "Sally's money did most of the talking."

For the first time since I sat down, I saw a glimmer of panic flash in Jackie's eyes before he was able to re-spin the wheels. "How much talking did Sally's money do?"

I explained that the actual bail bond was twenty, ten percent of the two hundred thousand the township had hammered him with. Three grand went to the judge (who had arraigned our friend over the telephone), one thousand to Chopsticks, and five hundred each for the other two crooks at the precinct.

It was Jackie's turn not to say anything. He sat there nodding, his top teeth perched on his lower lip, his eyes glued to the piece of paper in my hand.

When he was able to speak again, he asked, "When's the hearing?"

"Probably the beginning of next week."

Holding the glass with two hands, I finished off my Remy and watched as the last of the brandy reluctantly slid back down to the bottom.

The original game plan had been to meet up at the club at two a.m., triumphantly pay Sally back the money we owed, and maybe even bask a little in the glow of our re-established credibility. I checked the Bulgari—it was three-thirty. This sudden turn of events was not going to put us in the running for bookmakers of the year. "You think he'll give us another week?"

Jackie took a deep breath while he waited for his hyper-confident bullshit voice to return to form. He sat up straight, pushed his shoulders back, and expanded his chest, looking like he'd just finished taking a voice lesson from Stella Adler. "Of course he will," he said. "It's Christmas."

I stood up. "Help me get him out of the car."

I had parked the Camaro at a hydrant in front of the bagel shop, about ten feet from the bar. That was one thing about Hudson Street. The block got very quiet late at night, almost quaint, like a real neighborhood. Brendan came out to give us a hand, and the three of us walked over to the car. Everything was exactly as I had left it, with three exceptions. The car locks were up. The back seat was empty. And in place of the large, unconscious drunk who had been sprawled across the cushions less than a half hour before there was a crumpled piece of paper.

After a few seconds of staring at each other, Jackie reached in, uncrumpled the paper, looked it over, and without saying a word held it out to me.

It was one of Pamela's greasy oil change receipts from two years ago. When I turned it over, whatever was scrawled across the back was spaced like the inside of a Hallmark card and written in stop-and-start ink that could've only come from a frozen pen sitting in Pamela's glove compartment.

But the best part?

It was written in Italian.

CHAPTER FIVE

"Give Me Just a Little More Time"

MY PARTNER WAS AT MY APARTMENT DOOR Wednesday night coated in Hugo Boss and acting as if all the planets in our imploding universe were perfectly aligned. This was one of his best qualities. Jackie was the master of pretense. He was the anti-Dinino. Aside from occasional bouts of righteous indignation, usually directed at our bettors, or the semi-moment of truth, like the Courtney Jaguar story in the office the night before, the long-time owner and operator of the Golden Onion had perfected the art of appearing undaunted in public—"desperate casual," I liked to call it. He was so full of his own reality that it was often oddly comforting.

Except for now.

With my head spinning from the last twenty-four hours, I was in no mood for unbridled optimism, no matter how expertly it was manufactured. By the time the three of us had futilely cased the neighborhood and I had driven back to Staten Island with all the windows open to try to get the smell out of the car, it was after six o'clock in the morning. Pamela was already half-dressed for work when I handed her the car keys. She said that Laura and Chris were long gone, having taken a ride into the city with my brothers, who had very nobly dropped them home before heading off to work.

After I excused myself from my own birthday party, Laura had spent the rest of the evening at the kitchen table talking with Elsie. My sister also said there might have been some tears involved.

None of this was breaking news. Even before the latest favor, the fact that I was spending more and more time in the back room of the Onion had become a sore spot between us. And although I had managed to keep my mounting debts and credit card balances quiet, I could tell Laura thought I was swimming out too deep, especially with guys like Jackie and Sally hanging around the lifeguard stand. What Laura didn't know was that I was in way over my head already. My split from the sports operation was the only money I still had coming in, along with a few dollars from the cold syrup shoots. Without the vig, I would have been flat broke a lot sooner than now. And that didn't include the thirty grand we still owed Sally for the pleasure of doing business in his territory.

SALLY "SALLY TOAST" (BUT NEVER TO HIS FACE) Tosterelli ran his club out of a brownstone near Gramercy Park. The whole operation was very posh, with top-shelf liquor, hookers in Anne Klein eveningwear, and just enough upper-crust clientele (bankers and brokers, some sleazy diplomats, a few society types, a couple of corporate raiders, etc.) to make it one of the hotter night spots to hit. The place had been an after-hours club for years, but when Sally took over, he was sharp enough to put on a tux and turn it into one of the classier Atlantic City casinos minus the two-hour ride.

Jackie pushed the buzzer for the fourth time. The only light on the stairs came from the very dim glow of the doorbell.

"Maybe they had a fire," I said.

"We're not that lucky."

A black Range Rover rolled up over the curb at the foot of the stairs.

"Need help, fellas?"

Although I knew the voice, I let Jackie handle the greetings. "Butchie?"

"Yeah," the driver said, stepping around the front of the car and moving toward the dark stairs. "Who's that?"

"Jackie. Parker."

Butchie was not the first person we wanted to see on a night where we had to make excuses once again. As Mr. Tosterelli's right hand bone-breaker, he had a certain role to play, which he tackled with great relish and brutality. The fact that he dressed impeccably did nothing to diminish his reputation as a very large freak who scared the shit out of anybody he shook his cast-iron hands with.

"Jackie Parker?" he said. "Where you been hidin'?"

"Come on," Jackie said, smiling. "Who could hide in a city of eight million people?"

"You better believe that," Butchie said, then turned his attention to me. "Johnny Sneezes. How the hell are you?" He sized me up with a pair of glassy eyes that reminded me of the stuffed grizzly at the Museum of Natural History. He hated me for a variety of reasons, not the least of which was his unwavering suspicion that I was sleeping with Connie, his favorite bartender. I put my thumb on the buzzer and pushed again.

"Nobody home tonight?" I said.

He pushed past us and opened the door with his key. As soon as we entered the lobby, I saw the reason for the delay. An enormous young man, maybe twice the girth of Butchie and twenty years younger, sat slumped in a leather chair, sound asleep.

"Could you believe this?" Butchie said, trying to keep it light but definitely not amused. "Sleepin' Beauty. Get up."

He slapped the man across the shoulder with the back of his hand. The kid didn't budge on the second or third blow either.

"Get up, you fat fuck."

Not an eyeblink, not a muscle, not a roll of fat moved. Nothing.

Butchie nodded, then reached down under the leather chair for the baseball bat that was tucked inconspicuously behind it. When he cocked the bat over his shoulder, I had visions of *The Untouchables*, when De Niro uses a Louisville Slugger to leave a plate of brains on the buffet table. While I was pretty sure Butchie wouldn't murder anyone in front of us, an impromptu homage to the film was not too much of a stretch. But instead of bringing the bat down on the kid's skull, Butchie deftly shoved it under the leg and toppled the chair over. The young man hit the marble tile like an oil drum and scrambled to his feet.

"Butchie!" he said sheepishly.

Butchie grinned. "Good morning," he said. Then he smashed the chair into pieces. I looked over at Jackie, who had a smile frozen on his face.

"Now you stand," Butchie said. "And turn the outside light on."

He tossed the bat on top of the pile of busted up leather and chrome and escorted Jackie and me over to the old-fashioned wrought-iron elevator doors.

As was so often the case with such evenings, Jack Jones' inspired phrasing of "Wives and Lovers" greeted us as soon as we stepped into the casino, along with a wave of Paco Rabanne so strong I felt as if I was in a processing plant in Marseilles. The casino occupied the spacious third floor of the brownstone. (Whatever went on below us on the first two floors was nothing I wanted to know about.) Even though it was early, the five blackjack and four poker tables were full, and the paneled wall mirrors made the room look twice as crowded. The centerpiece of the room, what gave the club an extra glimmer of sophistication, was the antique art deco chandelier hanging directly over the craps table. Hundreds of clear and turquoise-beaded glass crystals were suspended from a pressed brass fixture, sending just enough shimmery light into the corners of the room to keep most people honest. The fixture was pre-1929 Robber Baron elegance at its best and looked very much like something Gatsby would have had stolen from a client's library in Manhattan and strung up in his castle in West Egg.

I recognized a few of the faces above the tuxedos and nodded politely as Butchie led us through the room up to the bar. If Butchie knew how much we owed his boss, he wasn't letting it get in the way of his wiseguy etiquette. He signaled for Connie to finish up her service at the other end of the bar.

"How's the gay bar business?" he asked Jackie.

"A little quiet," Jackie answered truthfully.

In addition to the money we paid for the privilege of taking bets, my partner paid protection money to Sally for the bar itself, so the boys had a hand in two of Jackie's pockets. That was the thing about extortion. It didn't matter if the registers were ringing, what your relationship was, or how much they liked you (and I believe a small part of Sally did actually like Jackie); Sally's enforcer was at the Onion every Tuesday before noon to pick up his envelope from Brendan, Butchie's favorite "tizzone," and have an amaretto on the arm, before he left to scare the shit out of other local businessmen.

"I don't get it," Butchie said. "When nobody wanted these people in their bars, they made a big deal about it. Couldn't shut up. Fucking riots. Now that their money is as green as anybody else's, they stay home, mix up their fag drinks in a blender, put on their disco records and fuck each other on the love seat. Who could figure these people?"

A much braver man would have asked Butchie how he knew any of this, but I kept my mouth shut and looked down the bar at Connie.

"Half the people in the bar are sober these days," Jackie said, repeating one of his favorite eulogies.

"At least when we went out, we went out. We stood at the bar. We showed our faces. We ran up tabs. We didn't pay our tabs, but fuck 'em. We *patronized*. These days joints that were goldmines are dying." Butchie said this with a snort of a laugh, as if he enjoyed the idea, which of course he did. "Then the asshole owners come to us for money. They don't realize, by the time they come to us, they should've put the key in the front door already."

Connie stood in front of us, her platinum hair under the soft blue of the chandelier shining like a sheet of ice at dusk.

"Hey, what're you drinking?"

Jackie asked for the standard Absolute and club (no fruit), which I also requested. Butchie had a Dewars and water and glared at Connie when she served me first. For her sake I hoped there was nothing going on between them. Connie set the drinks down in front of us, positioning them in such a way as to allow Jackie and Butchie to continue their conversation while dealing me out. Artistry.

"Watch the sleeve of your jacket."

Connie was wearing a black-and-orange body suit that would have suffocated any tiger I ever saw. As soon as I reached for my drink, she leaned a little closer, pretending to wipe down the area in front of me, enveloping me in a cloud of some very potent perfume. Connie's over-the-top sexuality reminded me of the late lamented Zenon, only her retribution came in one-hundred-dollar tips instead of quarters. She also didn't come with the option to unplug.

"You still do that sneeze on television?"

Why were people still talking about this?

"Yeah," I said. "Once in a while."

"Can I tell you a secret?"

"Maybe."

"I taped it on my VCR. I love the close-up of your dimples." She picked up a sip stick, dipped it in my vodka, then placed it between her lips. "You remind me of Montgomery Clift."

I was pretty sure Montgomery Clift didn't have dimples, but I was impressed by the reference. Also flattered—nice-looking guy, before he pilled his tortured soul to death.

"How do you know about Montgomery Clift?"

"My father was a big fan of *The Misfits*," she said.

I glanced over my right shoulder at Butchie, who was glaring at us, although still nominally talking with Jackie.

"How's Sally tonight?" I asked, lowering my voice.

"Wonderful," she said, then moved to the other end of the bar.

Butchie knocked, then ushered us into the room. Sally was seated behind his large antique wooden desk when we entered the office, a table lamp casting a soft light over what looked like the *New York Post* spread out in front of him. His eyes were on a closed-circuit television mounted on the wall to his right, and a facsimile of an old-fashioned radio on a shelf behind him was playing a tinny version of "Baby It's Cold Outside." From the cut of his tux jacket he was back to wearing Ermenegildo Zegna.

Sally had the compact, angular look of a man who had done very well for himself on his own terms. There was no wasted space on his body. His features were sharp and to the point, and his hard brown eyes gave you just enough: attention, patience, money, time, etc. The pinched look of aggravation around the corners of his mouth only added to the general impression of a Mob success story. With the right public relations firm, Sally Tosterelli could have been a poster boy for recreational gambling, but someone would have had to kill him to take the picture. That was also part of his old school charm.

Sally signaled that it was all right for Butchie to return to the casino, then waved Jackie and me over to the two chairs in front of his desk. His eyes moved from the television screen to Dinino's watch, but he didn't say anything. There was no "Hello," no "Sit down," no "How are you doing?" He just sat behind his desk and looked profoundly unhappy. Only when Jackie told him that, due to a "mishap," we were going to need another week, did Sally open his mouth.

"What the hell's going on down there?" he asked softly. "You used to have a good business."

"Everybody got lucky at once," Jackie said.

I looked over at Jackie to remind him to fork over the remaining four grand, but my partner sat perfectly still.

"What's that got to do with me?" Sally said, keeping his voice composed while looking exclusively at Jackie. He tugged his left shirt sleeve a quarter inch out of his jacket cuff. In a distinguished career dealing with connivers and brokesters, Toast almost seemed disappointed that human nature had let him down once again.

"You know, you haven't given me anything since June. Almost six months. Not a dime. Why does it always have to be bad news with the two of you? Just once I'd like to hear, 'Everything's fine, Sally, we just stopped in to say hello, drop some money at the tables, and pay you what we owe you.' I used to hear those words from you. Why don't I hear those words anymore when you walk into this office? After a while this bad news gets relentless."

Here Sally shifted his dark eyes and looked at me with the slightest suggestion of an understanding between us, as if to say, 'I thought you were better (smarter? sharper? hipper?) than this.' Then the look was gone.

"You seen *Othello*, right?

Fuck, the *Othello* bit again. (There was nothing worse than a literate gangster.) The guy *was* pissed.

Toast was referring not to the 1965 Olivier classic, or even the Royal Shakespeare production, but to the movie starring Lawrence Fishburne that had come out a couple of years before. Sally loved this movie. In more prosperous times he would ask me, "When am I gonna see you in a flick like that?"

"One of the best."

"You remember what happens in the end?"

Jackie looked over at me like the fate of the world depended on my response.

"Everybody dies," I said.

"That's right," Sally said, pausing for effect, his voice still on simmer, "*except* for Iago. Guess what? I'm Iago. Butchie's Iago. You're not." With that, he looked at Jackie. "Neither are you. Understood?"

It was not the best time to point out that Shakespeare had made it very clear that the Venetian noblemen were going to exact some major revenge on Iago after the play ended. I put on an act of contrition instead and told Sally how truly bad we felt about what had happened. "We just need another few days," I said. "Right after Christmas."

"Yeah, why? So you both go out and buy your girlfriends presents on me? Fuck Christmas."

Whether it was the close proximity of "Fuck" and "Christmas," or the thought of more aggravation bleeding into the holiday season,

Sally's face began to turn the reddish brown of a perfectly cooked to-mahawk steak. This was the one chink in his composure that he could-n't control. Much more than the suave formal wear or the carefully modulated voice, Sally Toast's hypertension let us know exactly how much we could get away with.

I could see by the way Jackie shifted ever so slightly in his chair that his mind was racing a million miles a minute.

"How about we see you next Tuesday?" Jackie said.

Immediately another one of my grandfather's favorite sayings popped into my head: "Beggars can't be chosen."

"Next Tuesday?" Sally said, then added for clarification, "The day *before* Christmas Eve?"

"Absolutely."

"With the full package?"

"Definitely."

"Without the shenanigans?"

"No shenanigans."

"And you're not going to make us look for you?"

"Sally," Jackie said, as sincere as a blind Eagle scout. "I know you for twenty-five years. Where am I going?"

Sally eyeballed us up and down, then stood up. "We'll see," he said.

CHAPTER SIX

"Pillow Talk"

DON'T FEEL SO SPECIAL. Butchie hates everybody," Connie said, a slight bob of her chin acknowledging the undeniable truth of her statement. "But he definitely hates you the most."

We were sitting in a booth in the back of the Empire Diner, a place on the West Side a few blocks from the Hudson River. With its art deco décor, from the black-and-white checked floor to the shiny outline of the Empire State Building on the roof, it was a place to go for people who weren't ready to go back to their lives. The food was decent, the Wurlitzer was stocked with records from the last six decades, and an upright piano in the front of the restaurant encouraged the occasional spontaneous drunken sing-along. My high school friend Ralphie used to bang out showtunes on our regular excursions into the city until I was able to convince him that he was a much better writer than he was a piano player.

When the waitress came around, I ordered two more Bloody Marys.

"I'm honored," I said, with great false bravado. "Let him hate me all he wants. What I really hate is to see you get dragged into this."

Connie took a bite out of her celery stalk and smiled. "I appreciate your concern," she said. It was obvious that Connie enjoyed her status as one of those very colorful angelfish in a tank full of hammerheads. But her flirtatiousness was so extreme that it was hard to figure out how seriously she took any of it.

Outside the club, and maybe outside Butchie, Connie looked a little different. She toned down the sexual magnetism and became more animated, more sassy than sultry. But she also had some serious light-refracting jewelry on her left hand that made me suddenly reconsider whether I should be sitting anywhere near her at six o'clock in the morning. When she said that she needed some advice and asked me to join her for breakfast I had hesitated just long enough to give her an opening. But I knew I needed to keep it very brotherly–sisterly.

"It doesn't help that you have that psycho watching every move you make."

She poured another dose of blueberry syrup over her pancakes and ate a piece, then put her fork down and polished off her cocktail. It was somehow comforting to watch Connie attack a plate of food piled six inches off the table, especially since I had no desire to order anything for myself except another pair of Bloody Marys, which were going down way too easy.

"You know Butchie thinks we're fucking."

So much for big brother. I was going to ask, How the hell is that his business? But I already knew the answer.

"Did you tell him we're not?"

"No."

"Why not?"

She looked straight into my eyes, laid her Atomic orange fingernails over my wrist and turned right back into Connie the sexy tiger. "Because I don't understand why we're *not* fucking."

The way she enunciated "fucking" sounded like we had already paid the check and were going at it on top of the checkerboard place-mats. I looked at my defenseless wrist under the five flaming scalpels of her fingernails and slowly slid my hand back to the relative safety of my sweaty glass.

"When are me and you going on a date?"

I didn't think Connie was intentionally trying to get me killed, but we were headed into tricky terrain. To quote the great Daryl Hall, "I need a drink and a quick decision," which was basically, I had to get the hell out of there.

"We're not."

"Then why are we here?"

"You said you needed to talk to me."

"I *do* want to talk to you," Connie said sincerely. "Among other things."

"No other things," I said, treading water. "You know Laura and I are together."

From the look on her face, I could have just announced that I was thinking of changing dry cleaners. It was obvious that this info held very little meaning for a woman of such sexual practicality.

"What about your *gumada*?"

"I don't have a *gumada*."

"You all have *gumadas*," she said, still keeping it coy. "All the boys in Sally's club. They all walk in Friday nights with their girlfriends be-tween their legs."

"And who do I walk in with on a Friday night?"

"The short, chubby guy who looks at me like he's already got his hand down my pants."

"That's my *gumada*."

Connie laughed and waved two fingers in the air for another round of cocktails. Up until that point, our waitress hadn't been particularly attentive to us, maybe even a little rude, actually more like openly hostile, but I didn't think too much of it at the time. I was pretty sure Connie didn't bring out the best in most of her female compatriots, especially those, ironically, who had the pleasure to serve her.

"I have to give you credit," she said. "You're a pretty good liar. I guess that's where the acting comes in."

"How long do we know each other?" I asked, trying out another tactic.

"Two years?"

"And I've been with Laura five years."

She looked at me with a new gleam in her eyes.

"She could join us."

Holy shit, talk about underestimating your opponent. This woman had all the answers, and not necessarily terrible answers, but definitely not the answers I could live with. I thought about Connecticut farmgirl Laura Winters, who was no prude by any stretch of my imagination, but who didn't exactly sit up and take notes anytime the occasional *ménage* scene came on *Showtime.* I laughed.

"I don't think that's going to work."

"Too bad," Connie said, with genuine disappointment.

"Everything on this planet is timing."

"Timing my ass," she said, shutting down sexy tiger again. She placed her fork on her plate which, dotted with blue pools of syrup, looked like a map of the Great Lakes, and opened up a second front. "Do you have any idea how many men would be very, very excited to have this conversation with me?"

Jesus, first Dinino tells me I should be happy to take the watch. Now Connie tells me I should be happy that she wants to fuck me. *And*

Laura. When did I become such an ungrateful bastard?

"Believe me, I know. I know. My partner would swim across the Hudson to be sitting here. But I can't do it."

"It's not that big a deal for people like us."

People like us?

"Are you going to tell Laura that we had breakfast?"

You mean if she ever talked to me again? Since last night I had left Laura six messages on her answering machine, all of them unreturned. So why was I still here? Laura needed me a lot more than this striped siren sitting across the table. Why wasn't I camped in front of Laura's building on Second Avenue, waiting to sidle up to her when she made her a.m. Starbucks run so we could talk? Two cinnamon dulce lattes (extra whipped cream), a hot chocolate for Chris, and a heartfelt apology by the window overlooking 28th Street and Third.

I guess I was a little lost in thought, so Connie reiterated, "Are you?"

Am I what? I thought. Connie took my lapse for a no.

"Why not?"

"Why would I?" I asked, picking up the thread from the look in Connie's eyes.

"Why shouldn't you? If there's no chance of us fucking, then we're just two 'friends' (she did the quote thing with her fingers) having breakfast, drinking Bloody Marys, maybe flirting a little, after spending another night together in a social club? Seriously, shouldn't you be able to tell your girlfriend something innocent like that?"

"You're absolutely right." I noticed I was chewing on my ice cubes. "But why does Laura need to think about that?"

Connie kept leaning closer to me and lowering her voice to a whisper. It was obvious that she was enjoying this. Her perfume, still powerful at six o'clock in the morning, was wafting over the lingering sweet of the pancakes and grabbing me by the collar of my suit jacket. But if I were one thing on the plus side of the T-chart, I was resolute in my commitment to my girlfriend, and I always had been.

"Think about what?" she asked. "Think about us having breakfast? Think about us flirting? Or think about how you gallantly decided not to fuck me?"

"First of all, flirting and fucking are two completely separate animals."

"Please," she said, rolling those dark mascaraed eyes. "You're telling me about the difference between fucking and flirting? I'm a *bartender.*"

"And second-*ly*," I said, pressing on, "she doesn't need to think about any of it. As far as Laura knows, I go to the club, I see Sally, I go home. Done."

"So you're gonna lie? I'm sorry—*act*?" she said with a grin.

"I'm not lying. I'm not acting. I'm just not saying anything."

"So omitting the truth is not the same as lying?"

"I have an idea. Forget bartending. Go to law school. You'd be a terrific prosecutor."

She shook her head. "I make too much money," she said matter-of-factly. "So if you can lie about this, why can't you lie about that?"

"Because 'that' is a lot more than lying." And then I added, "The defense rests."

She gave me a tired Connie smile. The darkness around her eyes, some but not all of which was last night's make-up, all of a sudden gave her the look of someone who needed to go to bed at ten p.m. once in a while instead of having breakfast with me at six a.m. on a cold Thursday morning. Or maybe that was just me in the reflection of her irises.

The conversation had ground to a mutually exclusive detente, and to fill the awkward pause, I took my napkin and made a small circle in the frost on the diner window. That's when I noticed a large man weaving himself through the few yellow cabs and trucks on Tenth Avenue. The man crossed from the diner side of the street to the water side, then back again. He stopped every few feet, looked back at the diner, then walked another few steps.

"What's so interesting?" Connie asked disinterestedly.

"I'm not sure."

When I looked again the man was *sitting down* in the middle of the street, the traffic moving slowly around him. He was staring directly at my window.

"I'll be right back," I said.

I bolted down the aisle and ran through the front door onto Tenth Avenue.

CHAPTER SEVEN

"Hooked on a Feeling"

LAURA AND I MET FOUR YEARS and three months ago, September 29 to be exact, on a cool, clear fall night, when the Golden Onion was just a bar I'd never heard of, and Jackie Parker and Sally Toast were still excuses waiting to happen. The first night I saw Laura was back in the old days. I was just another twenty-five-year-old actor piecing together a career (low budget theater, improv, a few ten-second spots in TV shows), heading off to workshops, and laboring in the market on Fulton Street whenever one of my brothers' employees called in sick, which mercifully wasn't that often.

After surviving a bit of a downward spiral in my early twenties, I had defaulted into the habit of taking care of myself, so anytime I had an audition I would try to get to bed early, even on a Friday.

Around eleven o'clock that night, my telephone rang. A distraught Ralphie, my piano-playing best friend from high school, was on the line, telling me his wife of two years had just decided to move to Boston with the UPS guy. Personally, having been a member of his wedding party and a witness to the massacre from the beginning, I had known the phone call was only a matter of time, but from the sound of Ralphie's voice I don't think he did. She was nuts, and he was gay—what was there to talk about? I listened for a few minutes, consoled, sympathized, listened some more, condoled, then tried to talk him out of driving into the city from Staten Island. "It's late, Ralphie," I said. "Go to bed. We'll have lunch tomorrow."

He told me he was thinking of blowing his brains out. To be honest, Ralphie was never that prone to happy moments to begin with, even before he met his lunatic wife, but the suicide thing was a new wrinkle. I told him I'd make some coffee. He arrived twenty-five minutes later with a quart of Southern Comfort, which turned out to be his second one of the night.

By the time we got to the club it was close to two a.m. The Warehouse was just what it sounded like, a giant concrete slab of a space off Broadway and 23rd Street, dark, cavern-like, musty and packed bare-shoulder to shoulder with models, clubbers, and coke dealers. At that time in the early '90s, details like occupancy laws and fire exits didn't matter as much as a bold sound system and a Puerto Rican deejay with an eyepatch and a Ziploc full of E. Ralphie wanted to numb his mind with music, etc., and this was the closest place I could think of to finish him off and get him back on my couch on Sullivan Street, so I wouldn't look like shit for my audition.

It was miraculous how Ralphie's spirits picked up as soon as we made it past the velvet rope and entered the club. Mesmerized by all the beautiful people on the packed dance floor, my friend announced how terrific it felt to be alive again. It was obvious, as Poppy liked to say, that the Southern Comfort was doing most of the talking. I told him to take a deep breath and find a wall to lean against while I grabbed two club sodas that I would insist had vodka in them.

The first thing I noticed was the way she tilted her head.

She was seated at the bar, a twenty-dollar bill in front of her on the counter. Her blonde hair, brushed back behind her ear, fell over the shoulder next to my shoulder. This gave me an unobstructed view of a profile that made my heart do one of those stutter-steps (freeze, shudder, resume) that you always hoped nobody saw. A tiny diamond stud in her earlobe caught the yellow glow from the bar lights above us. I heard the melody from "Come Touch the Sun" on side two of the *Butch Cassidy* soundtrack and knew I was done.

Her head remained very still, her chin at a forty-five degree angle toward the floor, no movement whatsoever, as if she had dropped something valuable, or was completely lost in thought, not an easy feat with Robin S.'s "Love for Love" pulsating through every cell in our bodies.

"Excuse me," I said, leaning closer. "You okay?"

Even in the sweaty confines of the club, Laura smelled like the most perfect early summer morning in my life. She didn't turn towards me, so I stooped over and studied the area around our feet. When she finally (and very slowly) moved her head to the right to look at me, I saw the neck brace tucked inside her long gray coat. I also saw a posse of some very protective girlfriends, huddled at the edge of the dance floor, barely restraining themselves from rushing over and dragging me to the other end of the bar.

"I thought you lost something," I said, straightening up.

She smiled and raised her eyebrows slightly, acknowledging my ploy. I figured I had thirty seconds to engage successfully and not make a complete jackass out of myself.

"I'm immobilized," she said with a smile.

"Yeah," I said, without taking my eyes off her face. "Me, too."

She reached for her drink, which turned out to be a glass of red wine, and propped her left elbow on the counter to steady herself. My eyes moved from her earlobe over to the fingers on her left hand—no jewelry. Then I asked her what had happened.

"I took my son skiing."

A sinking feeling.

"How old is he?"

"Almost three," she said, and smiled again, this time much brighter.

"A skiing three-year old," I said. "That's impressive."

"It's in his blood. His father's a—" I could see from the look in her eyes that she had a little trouble narrowing it down, before she finished the sentence with a tight-lipped smile— "ski instructor."

Moving the glass carefully to her lips, she took a very slow sip of wine. And then she asked, "Do you ski?"

A Ralph Kramden moment—do I lie and say that skiing was my life, that the judges would blindfold me on the giant slalom just to give everybody else a chance? Given the neck brace, she wouldn't be getting up on a lift anytime soon, which would give me time to take a couple of lessons and watch the Redford movie. Or did I tell her the truth, that the closest I ever got to a slope was tenth grade geometry, which I failed miserably?

"Not once."

"Good," she said.

WHEN THE DOWNSTAIRS BUZZER WENT OFF, I was lying naked in a bed surrounded by a dozen people. They all looked like versions of people I could've known, but they were just a little off—different height, weight, age, head shape, etc. The bed was in the middle of the stage in my old high school. Even though it was dark and quiet out in the black of the auditorium, I could hear some murmuring, throat clearing, seat shuffling. None of the people around the bed said a word—they just stared at me and my killer erection, courtesy of an overwhelming desire to pee. Finally, a man in a dark suit came charging out of the wings and pushed his way to the side of the bed. This man I didn't recognize at all, but he was very unhappy.

"Get up," he yelled. "You're ruining the play."

When I opened my eyes, there were wavy red lines radiating from the clock radio (a couple of 4s, maybe one 5), and the bedsheet was wrapped around my ankles. I threw on a robe and moved to the window, where I saw Laura standing by the open back door of a yellow cab double-parked on Sullivan Street. She looked up at the third-floor window and pointed to the doorway. Since it was dark out, my first reaction was, why is Laura standing in front of my apartment at 4:45 in the morning? The continued presence of the buzzer jarred my brain into the abrupt realization that it was almost five o'clock in the afternoon. I waved and gave her a hearty thumbs-up. She waited until I buzzed her son into the building, then got back in the cab and pulled away. Chris was standing at my front door thirty seconds later, a big, excited smile on his face, his New York Knicks jacket bulked up with seven layers of sweater underneath like he was doing research in Antarctica.

"Ready?"

I asked him to put some music on the stereo, keeping my voice in high spirits (one of the benefits of my thespian training) while I mercifully relieved myself and then stepped into the shower. Last night was coming back to me in sharp, jagged flashes, like frames from *The Cabinet of Doctor Caligari* (Intro to Cinema Studies): Sally's red face, Butchie's baseball bat, pieces of the fat kid's chair, chunks of Connie's pancakes, a celery stalk. And of course, the disembodied head of the black guy floating across Tenth Avenue.

I made the water stronger, even though the pressure in these prewar buildings was as unpredictable as the Mets' bullpen, and listened. "Mack the Knife" was playing out of my giant 1980 speaker towers in the living room. The *whomp* of the bass and the thud of the snare drum worked their way through the peeling paint on the back of the bathroom door and rattled the rings on the shower curtain. For my money, Bobby Darin (b. Walden Robert Cassotto) was the best pure singer to ever come out of rock and roll. If it hadn't been for the heart thing and Sandra Dee, he would've sold more records than any of them. The fact that Bobby spent his summers as a skinny kid on the board-walk a few blocks from Dinino's arcade, sorting out some fucked-up family situation, didn't hurt my opinion of him either.

"I'll be ready in ten minutes. Why don't you put on 'Splish Splash'?" I called out from the bathroom. Not to take anything away from Sinatra (the pinnacle), but I could never picture Frankie Boy sing-ing, "Ying yang, I saw the whole gang," with any kind of conviction. (Ever hear his version of "Mrs. Robinson"?) I was pretty sure Bobby Darin was the only white guy on Earth who could've sung "Splish Splash" and not sound like a white guy.

When I walked into the living room in my bathrobe, Chris had al-ready peeled off the majority of his sweaters and was sitting on the rug surrounded by stacks of my 45s, looking over the labels. I plugged in the lights to the Christmas tree, a twelve-footer we had picked out a few days before from a stand on Spring Street. It was a tradition Chris and I had started a couple of years before. While no threat to the mon-ster spruce in Rockefeller Center, the tree did give off a nice little holi-day glow, even though we ran out of room—the Santa hat at the top was bent horizontally against the plaster ceiling.

"Where'd you get all these records again?"

"From my father's business."

"I forget," he said. "These are the ones no one wanted anymore?"

I feigned a dirty look and put a short stack on the turntable. Chris watched me, a bit of a strange look on his face.

"Do you have 'Just a Little' in there?"

Ah, the Beau Brummels—something was up.

"Check the A-B stack in the corner."

The Knick game began at seven, so we still had about an hour to get into a cab and up to the Garden to catch the warm-ups. Much in the same vein as Laura's relationship with Nanny's *struffoli*, Chris had grown fond of some of the music I had forced on him since he was three. Actually, I think he got more of a kick out of my growing obsession with my collection of 45s, which had become one of my most prized possessions. I had to admit, this was somewhat peculiar, since the records were connected to my father. And like most things that came from Jack Romano, there was always a question about motive.

Back in the late '60s my father had maneuvered a piece of a vending machine business, which included servicing juke boxes. Every two weeks he would go to clubs, bars, diners, etc., empty the machines and swap out records, then leave half a dozen songs on the kitchen table before he went to bed for the day. To this moment, I have no idea whether they were even meant for me. We never talked about them, not one word, not "How'd you like those records?" or "You get those records?" or even "Where's my fucking records?" Nothing. When I mentioned them in a casual way, he'd look at me like he had no idea what I was talking about. But I took them anyway, and they were great—songs like "Tell Her No," "Kind of a Drag," "99 Tears," "Judy in Disguise," "Double Shot of My Baby's Love," "Midnight Confessions," "Time Won't Let Me," "Ball of Confusion," "Western Union Man," "Devil with a Blue Dress," "Spirit in the Sky," "Cry Like a Baby." All minor masterpieces.

We all have things that bring us back to the past. That was one of the reasons why I loved Professor Sklepowich's class my third (and final) semester at NYU. Every wanna-be actor in New York knew about The Studio and Kazan and Strasberg, but Sklepowich lived it. (He *swore* that he walked "my friend Marlon" on a dog leash down Broadway to the Ethel Barrymore Theater when Brando was doing *Streetcar*.) Sklepowich was a half-assed actor himself and showed up in a few Playbills from the '40s and '50s, but he told us he was just too odd-looking to go much further. (Freakishly tall, with crazy red hair and long skinny legs, he looked like a giant bicycle pump with the handle on fire.) His true talent was in the classroom anyway—aside from all the vintage stories that we couldn't get enough of, Professor Sklepowich taught us Stanislavski's sense memory theory and the Method like his life depended on it. And, to me, it all made perfect sense, at least the way he explained it. Honestly, unless you walked around in a coma, how could the sights, sounds, smells, and tastes that made up your life not hot-wire you to the past and tap into a few deep wells in your brain?

Whenever I was in class and I needed to tear up, I thought about the slightest of quavers in Elsie's voice just before she told us that our cat Clyde was hit by a car. (Immediate torrents.) And when I needed to act happy? All I had to think about was Laura—sharing some mozzarella fries with her and Chris on the boardwalk, drinking a bottle of wine with her at my kitchen table, walking down Prince Street with my arm around her waist. Even when I was nowhere near a stage, just taking in a spritz of Aliage, Laura's perfume, by the cosmetics' counter in Bloomingdale's would put my head in a very sexy cloud.

But the records were different. Each one of my 337 45s was more than a sense memory—it was a pocket in time. When I listened to "Brandy (You're a Fine Girl)," I was in the stupid tuxedo shirt that I insisted on wearing to first grade for the first week of the school year until Sister Margaret thought I was making fun of her and ordered me to start wearing my uniform. As soon as I heard the opening sax in

"Baker Street" I was crashing around on crutches after tearing the ligaments in my right leg playing touch football at PS 39. Whenever "Kiss on My List" played, I was at the kitchen table eating Oreos, watching Elsie cook, and trying to get over my first broken heart, that little *puttana* Denise and her hand-holding incident with some creepy middle-school kid. (As far as Clyde goes, Earth, Wind and Fire's "That's the Way of the World" was on the kitchen radio when Elsie very gently broke the news after she'd made us grilled cheeses.) Before the invention of the boom-box, Dinino always had a transistor playing in the arcade, so if I heard any song from 1972 to '85 I was eating fried calamari off a paper plate and waiting to be titillated by Zenon. Admittedly there were one or two back-of-the-boxers (no idea where I was when "Yummy, Yummy, Yummy" surfaced), but just about all of the other songs still gave me a memory check when I stacked them on the turntable, or a favorite came on the radio.

The beautiful thing about these records was that two sides (one really, except for those double-A side Beatles' singles, which were another beast entirely), with a max of three minutes per, were more than enough. No one threw themselves into an open grave and cried, "God, I really wish 'Woolly Bully' went on for another five minutes. What a loss!" It was perfection at 2:20. One blast of melody, some clever lyrics, a dose of heartbreak, a catchy chorus, the snap, crackle, and pop of the needle, pick up the tone arm, and put them to bed. What made them even better was the fact that the music was pressed onto a piece of wax the size of a dessert plate. Cleaning the songs up and putting them out on a shiny compact disc was like putting A1 on a veal chop from Ottomanelli's Meats.

I changed in my bedroom, slapped on JP Gaultier for a pick me up, and stepped back into the living room. Chris was lying on his back on the rug, headphones on, "Laugh, Laugh" playing out of the speakers.

When he saw I was ready, he slipped off the headphones and looked up at me. I could tell by his slim bacon lips that we were gearing up for a talk.

"I don't think Kunthea Triffiletti likes me anymore."

Jesus Christ, to be this young and already have to think about this, especially with a girl named Kunthea Triffiletti. While I usually tried to steer clear of the fatherly advice thing, we did have our occasional heart to hearts. And if it ever bothered Chris that his father wasn't around to share this with, I never heard about it, either from Chris or his mom. The closest Chris got was a postcard every four months from an icy mountain, when his father was off skiing the Matterhorn or doing whatever else a professional ski bum did with his leisure time.

"Kunthea's the little Chinese-Italian girl, right? The one I met at the ice-skating party?"

"She's Cambodian."

"Didn't you tell me you were annoyed that she kept grabbing your hand on the ice?"

"I wasn't that annoyed," Chris admitted.

"You guys are tight," I said reassuringly.

"She voted for Phillip Wong for best science project."

"What did Wong do?"

"He made a dialysis machine," Chris said matter-of-factly. "He had yellow water running in and out of a pink papier-mâché kidney with a dry cell inside."

Fucking Wong—what happened to the baked potato in a cup of seltzer? I tried not to look impressed. "Sounds bootleg," I said. "A Chinese kid should do better than that."

"Kunthea couldn't take her eyes off it."

"Maybe she has someone in her family with kidney failure," I said, my crass, intentionally stupid comment getting the hint of a smile out of Chris. "Or-r-r-r—" I paused for emphasis— "*maybe* she's trying to make you jealous."

"No," he said, too fast. "Why would she do that?"

"Girls do those things sometimes," I said.

"Why?"

Unfortunately, the next song to hit the turntable was "What Becomes of the Broken-hearted," so I knew I had to move this along before we both started sobbing. "Maybe you weren't giving her enough attention. Girls love attention."

I checked Dinino's watch, reached for my leather jacket, and took a step toward the stereo. Chris looked at me like, Where the fuck are you going? "She knows I look at her."

"But it's the *way* you look at her," I said, dropping my coat back on the couch. "Girls want to be treated like a princess."

"Why?"

He sounded annoyed again, but I definitely had his attention. I watched his little jaw clench and unclench as Jimmy Ruffin sang about walking in shadows and searching for light.

"Because it makes them feel special. Like they're the most special thing in the world. Like you notice everything about them. And everything about them makes you smile."

He looked over at the lights on the Christmas tree, rocking his body ever so slightly, just the way his mother did when something was really bothering her. That's when I knew where this conversation was headed.

"Do you treat my mom like a princess?"

So much for the tip-off, which was fine with me. The last thing my brain needed was nineteen thousand six hundred fanatical people screaming in my ear.

"I do," I said, sitting down on the floor next to him. "Most of the time I do. But not all the time. I always intend to. I just get caught up in things. My teachers used to say I had a hard time paying attention."

"Why don't you just focus?"

Because I'm an asshole, I wanted to say, *and I'm drinking too much,* but it came out, "Sometimes I'm not as thoughtful as I should be."

Chris's eyebrows ticked upward slightly, and I wondered if this was a word that had been bandied about in my absence Tuesday night. I could see him processing this info: thoughtful, hm, as in giving thought to things. As in thinking things through. As in thinking of others. Another hm. Then he said, not all that convincingly, "My mother thinks you're thoughtful."

"Because your mom tries to think the best of everybody." Then I added, "But disappearing on the night of my birthday? Not too thoughtful."

The short stack had come to an end, with the needle bobbing at the beautiful, wrenching conclusion of the Motown classic. We both listened to the *ssshhh*-scratch—*ssshhh*-scratch-*ssshhh*-scratch for a little while (oddly comforting); then Chris jumped to his feet and snatched up sweater number one.

"She'll get over it," he announced with surprising conviction.

"You think so?" I asked, still sitting on the floor looking up at him. He started pulling on his sweaters. "She always does."

CHAPTER EIGHT

"Walk, Don't Run"

WHENEVER YOU BET ON A TEAM in the NBA, the last thing you wanted to see was your investment ahead by ten or more at the half. In this respect, putting money on a professional basketball team was like picking a horse at the track. Unless you had legs like Secretariat, a fast start out of the gate usually didn't bode well for the finish line. The Knick game that night was no exception. After what we heard was a very solid first half (we listened to most of the second quarter in the cab), our hometown heroes had found themselves trailing by eight at the start of the fourth. And even though the Knicks were a legit team this season, this was a not-that-uncommon scenario, especially when the other team happened to be Kobe Bryant and the Lakers. But that didn't make the pre-Holiday crowd at Madison Square Garden, including the loyal young fan to my immediate right, any more resigned to the outcome.

"Kobe dribbled right into him," Chris said, upset. "How could he call that an illegal block on Ewing?"

"Say something."

Chris looked confused. "I just did?"

"Not to me. To the ref."

He looked at me, hesitant. I could see that the Triffiletti–Wong (Winters–Romano?) affair was still on his mind. What he really needed was a few sips of my Heineken, but even I knew where to draw the line sometimes. So I settled for the next best thing—let him scream a little.

"Go ahead," I said. "Yell at him. Pretend it's kidney-boy."

He scrunched up his face a little at the thought of his rival, but his "Poor call," came out in a voice that was a notch above a deathbed confession.

"That's it?"

Chris shrugged. "Weak?"

"Put a little heart into it," I coached. "Make it stick."

While our seats weren't in the Spike Lee/Woody Allen neighborhood, they were just about ten rows up in the first tier, two on the aisle courtesy of an old friend of Brendan's on the commodities exchange. Well within cursing out the ref and having him give us a dirty look range. Chris followed Kobe with his eyes as he moved to the foul line and cringed when the voice of the announcer came over the loudspeaker: *The foul is on Patrick Ewing. That's number four. The New York Knicks are over the limit. Two shots for Ko-be Bry-ant.*

"Very disappointing," he called out, a little louder but still not projecting past the tips of his white Air Jordans. He looked over at me expectantly.

"I'll make you a deal. You yell like you mean it, and I'll take you to see my brothers after the game."

Chris' eyes lit up as if Wong's papier-mâché kidney just exploded. "Really?"

"Absolutely."

He sank back in his chair.

"I don't know what to say."

I leaned over and whispered in his ear.

"I can say that?"

"This is Madison Square Garden. You can say anything." Then I added, "And stand up. Lean into it."

"Hey, ref," he yelled. I nodded my approval and motioned with my hand to keep going. "You wouldn't know a charge if a bull hit you in the ass."

I laughed and slapped him a high five.

"That was good," Chris said, impressed with himself.

"Time out, New York."

Ouch.

Every time an announcement was made, I felt like the Knicks' starting five were standing on my temples. It was an extension of the same headache I'd had since Zenon turned on me, only it was getting a little more intense. I fingered the next two-pack of Tylenol in my sweatshirt pocket.

"I'm going to get us two more drinks. Don't go anywhere."

I ducked down the corridor, stopped at the concession stand, which was just closing up, then slipped quickly into the men's room. I balanced the cardboard holder with a Coke and a Heineken on the edge of the faucet and leaned over the sink. I needed two minutes of quiet— no lights flashing, no screaming, and definitely no announcing. With one hand on each side of the basin, I pressed my forehead to the cool of the mirror and listened to the soft hum of the fluorescent lights echo off the tile.

I couldn't tell you how long I stood like that. With my eyes closed, the hum of the lights grew louder, as though there was a beehive on each side of my face. That's when I pulled my forehead off the glass and realized that the mirror had clouded over. There was no reflection.

I put my palm flat on the glass to wipe the mist away, but nothing happened. That's also when I heard the first toilet flush. But I was so focused on the gray mirror that I didn't turn my head right away—only when it flushed again did it register that someone else was in the bathroom with me. I took a couple of steps back from the sink and looked down the short stretch of tile floor. After the third and fourth toilets flushed, I expected to see a mob race from the stalls back to the game. When no one came out, I walked past the long row of urinals over to the stalls. The open doors all hung motionless. There was no suggestion of a quick exit. When I got back to the sink, there was also no suggestion of my beer.

I ran down the winding corridor. I was soaking wet, and my heart was beating like it wanted to push through my rib cage. There was nobody in sight—the concessions were all closed up, and the vendors had pulled down the metal gates. The beehive sound was still coming in loud and clear.

I was sure that Chris was gone.

I raced up the ramp and pushed past the two ushers standing in front of the exit. Nineteen-thousand six hundred fans were screaming *"dee-fense!"* at the top of their lungs. I looked over at our seats. Chris was on his feet next to my empty seat, cheering like a motherfucker.

"HEADS UP!"

Another loud thud, followed by a distant splash. I wasn't sure what was more of an assault on my already overloaded senses, the crack of wooden pallets hitting concrete, the sting of the breeze off the water, or the smell of five thousand pounds of calamari minus the tomato sauce. Buyers, sellers, vendors, customers, fishermen were in constant motion, unloading, hustling, flashing cash, making deals, the action at the market like the bathrooms at the Limelight at two in the morning.

I maneuvered my loafers around a thin paste of slushy fish parts on the floor while I kept one eye on my brother Jojo. Chris was already up on the hi-lo, riding shotgun. My brother spun the machine though narrow rows stacked with wooden crates of *baccala*, smelts, eels, *polpo*, *scungilli*, etc. Jojo liked to show off a little, an eight-year-old on his first ten-speed. Every time I heard another splash I looked at the East River and made the sign of the cross, admittedly an empty gesture but what the hell. I knew Laura wouldn't be thrilled with this turn of events, but my hands were tied. At least the sanctity of a promise would be preserved, if nothing else.

"He's not going to kill him, right?"

"Your brother is the Mario Andretti of the hi-low. Relax," Michael said with great admiration. That was one of the many beautiful things about Jojo—give him one thing to do and he did it with the concentration of a Tibetan monk, whether it was eating a sandwich or piloting heavy machinery through a packed warehouse on the coldest night of his life a few feet from the East River.

"I forgot how busy it was down here," I said. Once I hooked up with Jackie, aside from a few acting gigs, the concept of an honest day's work had gone out the window. My eyes drifted to a *Credit makes enemies. Let's stay friends.* sign placed prominently on top of a file cabinet.

"Thank God for the Feast of the Seven Fishes," Michael said. "During the holidays everybody remembers what good Christians they are."

Not everybody, I thought.

Philomena dropped four steaming hot chocolates on Michael's extraordinarily neat desk, a tiny island of organization in that churning sea of commerce, then charged off toward the river with a clipboard in her hand. My brother's secretary was a no-nonsense, iron-haired matron from the "other side" who had been with Michael for the four years he had owned the concession and with our Uncle Benny for forty years before that.

Michael handed me a cup. "What do you think about what I just said?"

I folded back the plastic lid and listened to the cars pass above us on the FDR Drive. The concern in Michael's eyes was genuine, but I hadn't come down there for medical advice. I was sorry that I had said anything.

"I don't have time to sit in the emergency room for three hours."

"I have a friend in triage. We'll get right in."

"Not for a headache."

"A two-day headache. After you almost passed out in a men's room at the Garden." I waved him off and took a sip of my hot chocolate. "And what about the tingling?"

"I like the tingling," I said, straight-faced, trying to lighten the tone a little. I thought it was funny, but he gave me a look that a big brother should give a younger brother, not the other way around. The truth was that, since Zenon exploded, I did feel different, a step outside the action, like when I first got my hands on a script and I was reading the lines but I didn't have a handle on the character yet. Maybe I should have gone to the hospital right from the arcade (the firemen begged me to get in the ambulance, the exact opposite of what I told Laura), but who wanted to ruin a birthday, aside from my partner?

"Michael, relax," I said. "I turned thirty, not eighty. I'm not having a stroke."

"When was the last time you ate something?"

Good question. Did I eat anything at the diner, or did I just drink Bloody Marys and watch Connie ravage her pancakes? I wondered. Did I have anything at the game? Aside from buying some drinks, I remembered Chris having a couple of hot dogs and a pretzel. Had I bought anything for myself? I couldn't remember.

Michael was staring at me while I ran this little soliloquy in my head.

"I ate like I was on death row Tuesday night."

"You know what Nanny would say?"

"What, that I'm peculiar?"

"She'd start with that," Michael laughed. "Come on. I'll drive us over to Beekman. Just get checked out. Jojo'll keep an eye on Chris."

"Speaking of," I said, seizing my opening and carefully returning my cup to his desk, "I have to get him back. It's a school night. Laura's not too thrilled right now as it is."

At the mention of Laura's name Michael's eyes moved from my face to Jojo, who zipped past and swung down to pick up two of the hot chocolates without spilling a drop. Although Chris's cheeks were as red as broiled lobster tails, his eyes were bright with concentration as Jojo provided a master class. Laura probably wasn't going to be too happy, but how do you deny a kid a ride on a hi-lo? Jojo had lent Chris his custom-made oversized work gloves, and he was actually holding Chris's hand down on the lever, taking him through the shifts. Only Jojo would have gloves specially made that were three sizes too big. The ends were doubled back to Chris' elbows, and tufts of what looked like matted rabbit fur stuck out over his coat sleeves. The smile on Chris' face said he was having an even better time down here, manhandling the fruits of the sea, than we'd had cursing out the refs at the Garden.

"I see Jojo's miserable as usual," I said to Michael, nodding my head with the admiration I reserved for anyone who put heart and soul into his gig. The look on Michael's face told me he had given up on trying to convince me to get checked out. He turned his attention to his other brother.

"He's got the clearest head of any human being I ever met," he said, and then added, "It's truly a beautiful thing."

Michael's last statement was accompanied by the return of Philomena, who slammed her clipboard onto her desk and was spewing curses in Italian like Mussolini. (She actually looked a little like Mussolini when she got mad.)

"What's the matter?" Michael asked, accustomed to her outbursts and trying very hard to keep a straight face.

"The matter?" Philomena repeated. She picked up her clipboard and slammed it down on Michael's desk, making what was left of my hot chocolate leap out of the opening in the lid and prompting another tirade when she saw where it landed.

"*Imbroglioni sporchi!*" she cursed. "*Che palle!*"

All three of us looked over at the two fishermen who were keeping a safe distance by the unloading dock.

"*Li mortacci tua!*"

"I'll talk to them," Michael said to Philomena. "You stay here."

"*Disgraziati,*" she muttered as we watched my brother calmly walk over to his vendors to discuss whatever had just happened.

I was struck with a bolt of inspiration.

"Philomena?"

"Cosa diavolo *vuoi*?"

Before she could lift the clipboard again, I slipped next to her and stooped down to eye level.

"I need your help," I said softly.

"*Now?*"

She looked at me like I was a complete pain in the ass, but she didn't move away. I pulled Pamela's oil change receipt out of the pocket of my leather coat.

"This is from a movie I'm doing," I lied. When she didn't seem all that impressed, I added, "I really want to do it justice, but I'm having a little trouble with the translation."

The note had burned a hole in my pocket for almost forty-eight hours now, and I still didn't have any idea what it meant. The problem was, whoever I knew who spoke Italian couldn't read Italian. And the people who could read and write Italian I wasn't showing it to. (Like Nanny.) The little I remembered from Ms. Arnone's tenth-grade Italian class helped me pick out a few words, but not nearly enough to make sense out of it. Laura had minored in Comparative Languages in college (whatever that was), but since she wasn't talking to me, I was still in the dark.

Philomena snatched the paper out of my hands and looked it over.

"You always get your scripts from a gas station?"

Still sharp as a sushi knife. No wonder Uncle Benny made so much money.

She flattened the receipt on Michael's desk and handed me a pencil.

"I'll tell you what it says," she said. "You write it down."

Philomena eyed the words on the paper and started dictating while I wrote what she said in the greasy space under the original message. When she finished, Philomena picked it up and looked it over. Then she folded it in two and held it out to me.

"Good luck with your movie," she said and walked off toward the water.

CHAPTER NINE

"Get Off My Cloud"

THE TEENAGE GIRL BEHIND THE COUNTER had her hair pulled back under a paper hat and was holding my freshly poured cup of coffee in the unwrinkled latex of a surgical glove. Nadia's only two concessions to personality were the one strand of blue-black hair that fell down the shoulder of her all-white outfit and the prog rock CD, in this case early Emerson, Lake, and Palmer, that she always had playing from her boombox next to the microwave. Despite the fact that she looked sterile enough to take out my liver, Nadia usually poured a very satisfying cup of coffee.

The bagel shop was, aside from the effervescent Nadia, nothing special, one of a thousand places in NYC that produced good bagels. It was two storefronts down from the bar. Its owner, the relentlessly grim Ivar, was one of our best customers—as unlucky as Siberia was cold.

"Very early," Nadia said, in her severe Eastern Bloc accent, puckering her pouty lips around every syllable. "You have audition?"

"I'm looking for somebody."

Nadia stretched a smirk across her lipstick, as black as licorice.

"Who do you know is awake at this time in morning?"

One of the perks of being non-commissioned in a nine-to-five gig was the luxury of not getting up with the rest of the world. There was something extremely gratifying about ignoring the racket of rush-hour traffic from under the cover of light sleep and a warm blanket, getting Chris up and off to school, then either shacking up with Laura or returning to my own bed for another four hours plus. I was an easy nine-hours-sleep-a-night practitioner, rising in the early afternoon to read the papers and plan the day's activities. (Not last night, of course. Laura gave me the slightest of acknowledgments as I ushered Chris into the elevator of her building at eleven-thirty, her son a little chilled but in obvious high spirits, a fact that I hoped would score some points with his mom before the elevator doors closed in my face.)

That sleep pattern was history. The fact that I was already semi-conscious enough to want a cup of Ivar's finest was a new sensation, one duly noted by my favorite counter girl. And I was definitely in need of a major sugar boost.

"Let me have some extra whipped cream on top," I said. "Maybe froth it up a little."

"You want latte?"

"Why not?"

She mumbled something Slavic under her breath.

"Nadia," I said, "How do you contain all that cheerfulness?"

"Is not easy," she said, but this time I got the hint of a half-smile.

Over by the rack ovens in the back, Ivar was shoving in another tray of onion rolls. The sweat from his thick head of hair had already turned his yellow bandana gold. I could tell from the erect hairs in his conch-sized ears that Uncle Vanya was hanging on every word.

I lowered my voice. "How's your boss this morning?"

"You want speak with him?"

"Not really."

"Ivar," Nadia said, turning to the ovens. "Johnny wants to know how are you?"

Ivar shrugged, then looked over his shoulder at Nadia, calling to her, "Ask him what's he got on Knickies tonight?"

After yesterday's stirring comeback victory, the "Knickies" were headed into Miami to play the Heat in a game that was destined to scare up a little action. With the Celtics struggling and the Nets on a ventilator, the Miami Heat, led by point guard Tim Hardaway and their half-a-nut shooting guard Archie DeAngelo, had risen to fill the void. The fact that ex-Knicks coach Pat Riley had his new team in first place in the Atlantic Division, three games ahead of the hometown favorites, only fueled the revenge fantasies of all the jilted fans who still felt that traitor Riley had reamed the team and split.

It was a terrific premise for a big game, especially on a Friday night, and if we played it right, it could turn into a nice windfall for us. A win and the Knicks moved a full game closer to first place, while kicking Riley's ass in front of the Miami worshipful. A loss and the two teams would have to slug it out in a rematch next Wednesday on Christmas Eve at the Garden, the Knicks saddled with the knowledge that they had lost six days ago. They'd be nursing a grudge as big as Riley's new contract. A lot of buzz, a lot of drama, a lot of ill will—perfect to get the once-a-month lightweights to pick up the phone and drop a couple hundred.

"He wants to know what you got on Knickies tonight."

"Tell him Miami's giving three," I said, and looked over at the clock. "As of—Jesus Christ—six-thirty in the morning."

Another half-smile as Nadia relayed the betting line to her boss. Ivar mumbled something out of the side of his mouth and turned back to his onion rolls. The heat from the oven came at us like a wave from hell.

"You must really like this job," I said to Nadia.

"Is all right," she said, not looking up. A couple of other customers had entered the store and were standing by the counter in front of the hand-written menu board. Nadia handed me my improv latte.

"You think he would mind if I. . . ?"

I raised my right wrist and played air pen, the universal signal for I have no cash on me.

"Ivar," Nadia shouted, "Johnny wants to know if he could put coffee on tab?"

Nothing like a loyal employee.

ARMED WITH MY "WE ARE HAPPY TO SERVE YOU" cardboard cup (to Ivar's credit, not the usual flimsy Styrofoam container that most stores were using those days), I walked over to the fire hydrant where our would-be car thief had disappeared over forty-eight hours before. A blue glaze of frost decorated the windshields of the parked cars lining the street. Even though we hadn't had any snow yet, any stray trace of water was frozen solid. The clouds had snapped a gray lid over the city since the sun set on Tuesday, keeping the sky the color of a wet sidewalk and the temperature in the mid-teens. From the early feel of the day, it didn't look like much would change.

I took a long look up and down Hudson Street and an even longer sip of coffee. I hadn't spoken to Jackie since we left Sally's club Wednesday night. But I figured if our fugitive had turned up, I would've heard something, if not from Jackie then definitely from Brendan, who took our welfare seriously. I slid the receipt out of my wallet: *Virgil Shepherd, booking #00213058607*. I had to call the court in a few hours to confirm the date of the hearing. My new best friend Sergeant Chopsticks had assured me that the case would be on the docket by next Tuesday the latest, just in time to collect the bail money and pay Sally off.

Of course, that was assuming we could find the lunatic. Without delivering a body to the court we weren't getting a dime back. And if I was capable of being honest with myself, Virgil Shepherd would have to be truly crazy to come back voluntarily. He'd fucked up and disappeared—a very old story. What did he give a shit about bail money? Once we got the bond back, he was going to jail. Maybe if he stumbled on a whiz of a public defender, he'd plea bargain it down to three-to-five. There had to be some point in the last two days when he was sober enough to realize that doing time in Rahway, New Jersey, was not a stunning reversal of fortune from being homeless in Manhattan.

But if that was his intention, why leave the note? It didn't make sense that he would leave a message for us, no matter how incomprehensible it seemed. I took the receipt with Philomena's translation out of my coat pocket:

Do not be afraid; no one can impede our journey.
It has been granted from above.
But stay here and wait for me.
Let your weary spirit rest, and feed on good hope.
For I will never abandon you in this low world.

I mean, what the fuck?

Number one, who knew Philomena had a poet in her? We always figured she was very smart (she had to be to keep Uncle Benny afloat), but we thought she was nickel-and-dime, bottom- line smart. The old bat was full of surprises—those words were art. I wish I could get my hands on a script half that well-written. Number two, what kind of disturbed individual leaves a note like that? What journey? Abandon who? Low world? It sounded like the type of message that winds up in the detective's hands right after they find the first mutilated body.

I should have just thrown the receipt out. Or maybe had it dusted for fingerprints. Either way, the thing made me nervous. The thought that the guy had taken the time to scribble this down at three o'clock in the morning and then disappear was a little too David Lynch for me. I have to tell you, even the handwriting was off. The letters were crowded together and slanted left, like they wanted to run off the page. But every time I went to dump it, I stopped, looked at it again and slid it back into the pocket of my coat.

Before I so abruptly left NYU, I had a professor for Scene Study class who would hand us pages from some of the greatest plays ever written and announce, in a British accent even though we all knew he was from Queens, "Let's strip this monster down to its hair and nails."

So here it was:

In addition to the now dozen messages I had left on Laura's phone, I had stopped by her apartment building before heading to Ivar's, where Val the doorman told me a couple of lame jokes and promised me, "Of course I'll tell her you were here," as he ushered me out of the lobby with a vigor that I wasn't expecting.

Despite two peculiar encounters and one extremely creepy note, Virgil Shepherd was nowhere to be found.

And while we had moved two and a half days closer to Toast's deadline, we were not a dollar closer to getting the money we owed back into his hands. That's where I was three days after my thirtieth birthday—no Laura, no Black guy, no money for Sally.

It had taken us the better part of four months to piece together the thirty grand we had neglected to pay Sally the past six months, and that was only because we had had a good run in the fall with college football. (Always a sucker's bet with the middle-aged business guys, rah-rah, alma mater, time of your life, take the over and squeeze into the old sweatshirt.) Jackie and I had accomplished this amazing feat the only way possible—whenever we had anything extra, we gave it to Brendan to hide.

How end of your rope did you have to be to ask a homeless man to steal your wife's car, even if she was breaking the bank? And then to use Sally's money to get him released? That was the thing with Jackie. Once the wheels started to come off, you never quite knew where you'd crash.

And honestly, while we all loved Brendan, how much could he vouch for a guy who slept in a doorway?

Then there was *my* part of the fuck-up. Should I have dragged him into the bar? Of course I should have. But the guy was a giant, smelled like the inside of an unplugged refrigerator, and was still sleeping the vodka off. I'd barely gotten him into the car, with the assistance of two of the cops (an extra twenty each.)

The pulse of the city was already starting to kick into double-time, pushing the tempo on the last Friday before Christmas, a lot more "You Can't Sit Down" than yesterday morning's "Crystal Blue Persuasion." People hustled themselves off to work. A few dogwalkers tugged on leashes, newspapers fat with holiday flyers stuffed under their arms, and glanced approvingly at the steam rising off their beloved's pile of crap. I stood there next to the hydrant, watching the street, checking the faces up and down the sidewalk. Unfortunately, there was no shortage of candidates—it wasn't too hard to find a homeless guy on the West side of Manhattan—just not the homeless guy I half-remembered from my sister's car and maybe the Empire Diner. And I was getting too cold to stand in one spot for much longer. I took a long sip of my hot and sweet coffee (thanks, Nadia) and licked the inside of the lid.

That's when I noticed an old woman staring blankly as her dog, the size of a well-stuffed veal chop tucked inside a red-and-green plaid sweater, left a huge mound of shit directly in front of the Onion.

"Excuse me," I said, before she could drag the dog away. "My partner owns this bar."

The old woman had her brown coat buttoned to her lower lip and her pink tam pulled down over her forehead. She peered through the front window.

"My condolences," she said.

"There's a pile of your dog's shit right in front of the door."

"Bingo," she said and started to walk away.

"You can't leave that there."

She looked over at the pile, then stared me up and down.

"Come on, Zelda."

"Wait," I said, maybe a little louder than I wanted to.

She and Zelda stopped in their tracks.

"Alright, alright," she said. "I'll make you a deal." She tugged Zelda a half-step back toward Mount Aetna. "If you pick it up, I'll drop it in the trash."

What choice did I have? "That works," I said, and looked dubiously at the overflowing metal trash can in front of the bus stop.

I took the bag from the bagel store out of my pocket, went down on one knee and started to shovel Zelda's shit onto the paper with the lid from my coffee cup. While the old woman studied this spectacle, her watery eyes suddenly became crystal clear.

"You're the boy who does the commercials."

When I didn't answer she winked at me.

"Such a beautiful face," she said. She stooped down and brought her own face so close to mine I thought she was going to kiss me. Then she asked conspiratorially, "Could you sneeze for us?"

Us? God help me. I stopped shoveling. "Absolutely not."

"Just one? So I could tell my girlfriends?"

The old woman pursed her lips and arched her eyebrows so high they disappeared under the pink of her hat. She was actually flirting with me. After thirty seconds she straightened up and tugged on the leash.

"By the way," she said, "you have whipped cream on your nose."

And with that they both took off toward Houston Street, leaving me standing in front of the bar with a bag of shit and a very strong desire to kill my agent.

CHAPTER TEN

"Take a Letter, Maria"

THE FELDER AGENCY WAS IN A VENERABLE BUILDING on Sixth Avenue and 23rd Street full of lawyers, world-class surgeons, and OB-GYNs for privileged pre-borns. I could see, through the glass door to Evan's office suite on the eighth floor, his secretary Loretta, who was already behind her immaculate desk, unpacking a Dean and Deluca shopping bag, a lavender scarf wrapped elegantly around her neck. A very stylish Black woman, maybe early fifties, with just the hint of a British Caribbean lilt to her voice, Loretta was a master of the even keel, keeping Evan's often frenetic office running smoothly through every variation of elation and disappointment. Her one concession to the insanity was an appreciation for expensive sweets, which she would pluck from a gold box whenever the needle bent a little too far toward either pole. I usually brought her a piece of Godiva or Vosges whenever I came to the office, and I suddenly felt terrible that I had showed up empty-handed, especially so early in the morning.

"Mister Romano," she said, looking up from her bag, a wry smile on her face. "You look like a popsicle." She nodded toward his office.

"Go on in. He's expecting you."

Her cup of tea was still steaming.

"Thank you, Loretta. Enjoy your tea."

"I plan to," she said. "Cheers."

My agent was sitting behind his desk in his own glass-enclosed office at the end of the hallway. Evan had "discovered" me at a bare-assed, one-man performance of *Waiting for Godot* (Estragon, Lucky, and Pozzo had the flu) right after I left college. Although I had been a part of his agency for almost ten years, lately the silence had been deafening. But one of the things I liked about Evan was that he still got on the phone when I called. He was an outwardly accommodating bastard, that much I had to give him.

"You're the last person I would expect to see at this time in the morning," he said with a smile. "Seven a.m. until ten is usually reserved for my below-the-line clients."

Good morning to you too, I thought, but at least he still seemed to consider me a client. When I told him why I was standing in front of his desk at eight in the morning, he seemed surprised.

"Didn't we already get the ball rolling on that?" he asked tentatively, as if he ever forgot one thing about his business.

"You know what Tuesday was?" I asked, not waiting for an answer. "My thirtieth birthday."

"Hey," he said, standing up and reaching out his hand to me. "Happ—"

"Why am I still doing cold syrup commercials?"

He sat back down.

"Do you know how many actors in New York would kill their mothers to do those commercials?" Evan answered defensively. "You could do a lot worse than be the face of a major cold remedy. Especially with what they pay us."

"I don't give a shit what they pay us," I said. "It's a joke. Every old woman in America—" (or at least one, I thought) "wants to stick a thermometer in my ass."

"You're famous," he answered, amused at the thought.

Famous for what? I thought. It was like the old if a tree falls. . .if you're famous for being an asshole, are you really famous? Or are you just a bigger asshole?

"I'm done."

"You're not done," he said with a grin. "You're cranky. Pick a bar. Let's have this conversation over drinks tonight at seven o'clock."

But I was done. I was done with people stopping me on the street for a stupid commercial. I was done feeling like shit every time I gave in and sneezed (snoze?) on demand. Unfortunately, I was also done with all the money I had made from the stupid commercial. And I still couldn't figure out why it had become such a big deal in the first place.

Whatever the reason, Evan and his agency had become a lot more successful in the last couple of years, partly as a result of my monumental sneeze. I didn't want to come off as the ingrate everybody seemed to think I was, but I was one of his first clients. Why wasn't I getting better gigs?

I resumed on a slightly more civil note. "I'm just asking you to get me a role that I could actually act in. Something a little more meaningful than spraying spit into a camera lens? That's not too much to ask, right? You used to do that. You used to get me some really good gigs." I paused, then added brightly, "You said I was great when I did *Zoo Story* at the Y a couple of years ago."

"You were outstanding."

"But?"

"What but?"

"I heard a hitch in your voice. You wanted to say 'but'."

"Remember what I told you when we first started—this is not a business for sensitive people. I paid you a compliment. You were great. No but."

I didn't believe a word he said, but I decided not to press him further. "Thank you for the compliment," I said, sounding sincere. "Please check into that play for me. I know I could kill that part."

The play I had my eyes on was an off-Broadway revival of Tennessee Williams' *Sweet Bird of Youth*. It was being directed by Scersa Wemblock, who'd created a buzz the year before with a stripped-down production of Inge's *Picnic* and who I'd heard was getting ready to open auditions.

"I'll reach out to them in a couple of hours."

"Thank you," I said, this time honestly sincere.

"That's quite a statement," Evan said. I wasn't sure what he meant until I noticed how his eyes were trained on Dinino's watch. "Coat, too." He looked impressed. "Business must be good."

I tried to wave him off using my non-Bulgari hand.

"Speaking of," he continued, "what time will someone be in the office?"

We concluded our conversation with a different business transaction.

"Give me Rutgers twenty times, a nickel on Villanova—" Evan got a kick out of throwing the bookie lingo around— "and put a dime on Gonzaga."

College hoops—the worst. How could anyone in their right mind put money on a nineteen-year-old point guard who might have just failed his statistics final?

"Nice picks," I said. "I'll put them in."

MY PARTNER WAS WORKING THE PHONES when I made it to the office around four that afternoon. He was dressed in his usual work ensemble, a purple jogging suit with a yellow onion on the jacket, and an

NYU baseball cap I had given him for Christmas the previous year.

"The Knicks're getting three and a half. That's right. The-ree and a h-a-a-alf-f-f-," Jackie said into the receiver, slow and obnoxious enough to avoid any confusion. Some bookies taped their betting sessions to avoid any unpleasant misunderstandings, but we found it was cheaper to enunciate clearly and repeat after the customer, like a nun teaching third graders grammar. "What do you mean, everybody else has three, can we do any better? What is this, a flea market? That's the line, take it or leave it." By the time Jackie hung up the phone, he had written three hundred dollars' worth of business. I pulled up a chair on the other side of the desk, took off my frozen Ferragamos, and rubbed my socks together.

"These people kill me. The guy's richer than a pharaoh, and he's got the nerve to complain about half a point. That's the problem with this business—people either got no balls or too much balls. There's no happy medium."

I wanted to be a lot more furious with him, sitting there in his warm purple outfit like a well-fed Prince, complaining about people and their balls. But I was more cold than angry, and more frustrated than anything else. One of my worst qualities, according to Nanny, was that I didn't stay mad at people. Typical of her worldview, Nanny was not a big fan of turning the other cheek. "Sounds nice in the Bible," she liked to say, "but it'll probably get you killed."

"Who was on the phone?" I asked.

"Jimmy the Jeweler," he answered, and then looked over at me like he had just really noticed I was there. "Where were you all day? You look a little glassy-eyed."

When I explained how I had spent a good chunk of the frigid day wandering in and out of the dive bars and homeless shelters east of Broadway, I could see Jackie's Adam's apple pulse slightly in his throat.

"To tell you the truth," I continued, "I wasn't sure I'd even recognize him. Most of the time I spent with him Tuesday night, it was dark and he was unconscious. We didn't get to spend a lot of quality time together. The main thing I remember is that he was Black and that the cops gave me his belongings in a plastic bag, which they said he had with him in Courtney's car."

"A Black homeless man with a plastic bag?" Jackie asked. "That narrows the field." He kicked back in his chair. "For a minute I thought we weren't going to find this guy."

I guess I looked like I was ready to choke him, so he added, "That's why I asked Brendan to take a walk with me. We actually closed the bar for a few hours."

"When was this?"

"Yesterday afternoon. We were all over the neighborhood." A funny look crossed his face, which was never a good sign. "They did fingerprint this guy, right?"

"Both hands," I said. I didn't think he was serious, but I made it clear from the look on *my* face that the idea of showing up with any guy off the street wasn't in our best interests. "Why would he leave us a note if he didn't want us to find him?"

"Maybe it was a suicide note."

"It didn't sound like a suicide note."

"I wonder—do we get the bail money back if the guy. . . ." He let the thought hang for a moment. "I think that's fair."

"How does your mind even work like that?"

"You're telling me you didn't think of that?"

"Absolutely not," I said, truthfully.

"Let me see the note," Jackie asked. I handed him Philomena's translation.

He reached into his top desk drawer and pulled out a pair of half lenses. Jackie could write numbers in his sleep, but any time he had to read anything he reached for his glasses. He studied the note. "Sounds like he's in love with you."

"Not me," I snapped. "You're the one who dragged him into this. That note was left for you."

"I don't think so," he said, as if he was teasing a nine-year-old. "You rescued him." Then he started humming the trumpet line to Herb Alpert's hit song. "Ba-bah, ba-bah, ba ba bah ba bah ba."

My eyes fell longingly on the half empty bottle of Remy sitting on the desk.

"Cheer up," Jackie said. "Have a shot."

Jackie put down his pencil, poured healthy shots into the two coffee mugs on his desk, and slid one towards me.

"Isn't there a people lost-and-found or something?" I took a long sip of the brandy. "This is New York City. There's an agency for everything. There has to be a place you can go to find a missing person."

"Yeah," Jackie said. "It's called the morgue."

"Let me ask you a question," I said. "You don't think Sally has anybody following us, right?"

"What's the matter?" Jackie asked, his antenna suddenly up.

"Nothing," I said, a little self-conscious, thinking about how Michael had tried to whisk me to the hospital when I mentioned the missing Heineken in the men's room. "Just a couple of times today, while I was looking for this guy, I felt like I was being watched."

"In this neighborhood, a guy that looks like you is always being watched."

"Not like that," I said. "I don't know. It was, like, wherever I went there was a pair of eyes on me." I should've added, not to mention the guy who was staring up at me through the frosted window in the diner Thursday morning, who may or may not have been our missing person, and who had disappeared by the time I ran across 10th Avenue, almost getting me clipped by a sanitation truck. But I didn't want to sound too paranoid.

"Sally knows where to find the both of us. Him *and* Butchie, that unrelenting prick." He added, almost amused, "You know Butchie hates your guts, right? He thinks you're fucking his bartender."

"Yeah, I've heard."

"You see her the other night in that tiger suit? My God, what a safari that would be."

Seeing the unbridled lust on Jackie's face, I couldn't help but ask, "How's your wife, by the way?"

"Comin' along," he said, not missing a beat. "Nothing that 500 milligrams of Prozac can't fix."

I picked up the stack of bet slips next to the bottle of Remy. I knew a little something about medication myself, prescribed or otherwise.

"How's it look so far?" I asked, changing the subject.

"We got about eight thousand in, mostly Knicks. I moved the line a half a point, to the-*ree* and a half." Jackie laughed, but when he saw my reaction, he added, "Relax. They're in Miami. Sucker's bet."

"Either that," I said, "or we're buried once and for all."

In a perfect world, half the bettors take one team and half the other team. The point spread is the great equalizer and keeps everything balanced. We'd happily collect the ten percent vig for providing a necessary service, and nobody gets killed money-wise, except the bettors who were on the wrong side of the spread. In the case of the game that night, moving the line encourages the woodwork guys to come out of hiding and bet with their hearts. As long as the Heat win by four or more points, all is beautiful. But if the Knicks win or the Heat don't cover the spread, we'd have an avalanche on our hands. Our humble office would be backed into a very ugly corner, one which at this point even Jackie Parker couldn't backpedal our way out of. In addition to Sally and Butchie, an army of righteous bettors would be looking for their payouts. That was one of the few roads left that we hadn't walked down yet.

I asked my partner about the possibility of edging off some of the surplus Knick money to our competitors.

"Fuck them," he said, with a look that would have passed for arrogance on a better day. "Why should we share our windfall with them? With that line we'll have every Willis Reed fan from '69 pledging his pension check." Then he added, with a little less testosterone, "Besides, I'm sure the other offices are in the same boat we're in."

Jackie got up from behind the desk and moved over to the coffee maker, which sat on top of the gray metal filing cabinet to his left. He splashed what was left in the pot into his mug with the Remy, then asked me if I wanted some. I waved him off, then slipped two aspirins into my mouth and washed them down with the pleasant sting of our winter drink of choice. "You seem like you feel pretty good about this."

"All we're doing is giving our loyal fans an opportunity to show how much they hate Patrick Riley. It's like a public service."

WHILE THE ONION WAS NEVER KNOWN as a sports bar, Jackie usually had a decent crowd for a Knick game, but the extra drama built into this one brought out some of the old faces, gay and straight. Both televisions mounted at each end of the bar were tuned to the game, which was usually not the case (Turner Movie Classics was a big hit), and the Christmas bulbs around the mirror behind the counter were blazing a little brighter than they had in a long time. The bar was two-deep for most of the game, and Jackie had to jump behind the stick a couple of times to help Brendan keep up with the flow of alcoholic beverages.

The night reminded me of the way it was when I first hooked up with Jackie in more prosperous times, the good old days of two years ago. Of course, it didn't hurt that the Knicks were down by twenty-three with three minutes to go in the fourth quarter.

"Could you believe this bum?" Jackie had lowered his voice, trying to contain his glee, and pointed to the television screen. Heat shooting guard Archie DeAngelo had just nailed his tenth three-pointer of the night, a beauty from the top of the circle. "Last week he couldn't shoot the ball off a bridge."

I thought of the stack of bet slips on the desk in the back office and asked Brendan to buy all the heartbroken Knick fans a drink. After being tapped for so long, I felt my spirits rise a little, knowing somebody owed us for a change, even though it'd probably take a week to collect. When Brendan picked up the telephone behind the bar, I never thought our luck could turn the corner with one lousy basketball game.

CHAPTER ELEVEN

"Black is Black"

THE "FIGHTING NINTH" PRECINCT WAS IN THE HEART of the East Village, two blocks from the Hell's Angels New York City headquarters and smack in the middle of the heroin capital of the East Coast. Despite these landmarks, the neighborhood surrounding the Ninth had a knock-around charm that was similar to what the West Village had had up until about twenty years before, only more drugs and a lot dirtier. A lot more dangerous, too. A couple of small theaters and a handful of seedy clubs and noodle bars had just enough hipness to offset the real menace that lurked on those streets. When we first started getting gigs there, Larry Rome, one of my actor friends, was robbed before a pass-the-hat show on Avenue A and then again right after. The guy actually waited for him. How sad is that, to make forty bucks acting and then hand it over to some creep in a dirty windbreaker? Needless to say, the "Fighting Ninth" had its hands full.

By the time we got a cab over to the stationhouse, it was after midnight. I knew a police precinct on East 5th Street wouldn't have too many lulls, but late on a Friday night the stationhouse was an epic of suffering, like *Les Miserables* without the orchestra. Everybody was either crying or bleeding, with at least half a dozen different languages echoing off the gray tile walls, coke-speed Spanish topping the hit parade. There were benches set up where whole families seemed to be wailing in unison, and the cops, to their great credit, moved calmly from one crisis to another, night and day from the little precinct that couldn't in New Jersey. It took Jackie twenty minutes to get anybody to speak to us.

"Excuse me," Jackie said to the desk sergeant when he finally returned. "We got a phone call about an hour ago to identify someone."

"Dead or alive?"

Jackie paused to consider. "Alive would be good."

"Name?"

"Virgil Shepherd," I said.

"Take a seat."

About half an hour later a very attractive officer, maybe mid-thirties, slim, with spiky black hair and heavy eyeliner, moved out from somewhere behind the desk and walked over to us. I saw Jackie's radar go up when he noticed the handcuffs swaying from her utility belt.

"Johnny?" she asked.

I looked into her coal eyes and smiled, not having the slightest idea who she was. She saw me checking her name plate, still racking my brain for a memory, then reached out to shake my hand.

"Galladin's my married name. I used to be Nicolette Goffredo." This woman was nothing but patient. "Nikki Gee?" After fifteen seconds of me staring stupidly at her face, she was kind enough to clarify. "Aniko's friend."

A white light seared through my brain. I felt like I'd been clocked with her nightstick. I asked softly, "You. . . .?"

She came to my rescue. "I've been a police officer for seven years," she said, with one of those ironic half-laughs that must come from being immersed in chaos for a living. "About a third of the way to retirement."

After I introduced Jackie and explained why we were there, she wrote Virgil's name down on a pad and said, "Let me see what's going on."

Jackie studied her as she disappeared behind the desk.

"What was that all about?" Jackie asked.

"Nothing."

"I have to say, I'm very disappointed." When I didn't respond, Jackie added, "How do you forget an ass like that?"

"Not easy," I answered truthfully.

"The way women look at you, they want to eat you like a Ritz cracker," he said, the expression on his face making it clear that the last thing he wanted to do was pay me a compliment. "I gotta work like an asshole to keep a woman, and all you do is show your dimples and they're kicking off their panties. Fuckin' genes, man."

He shook his head, lamenting the inequities of DNA, and I could almost hear him thinking, You must be one terrible actor not to be in Hollywood yet. What Jackie didn't know was that the way the officer looked at me wasn't about sex. It was about sympathy. And guilt.

Standing in the middle of a room full of misery and suffering was not the best place for me to think about it, after doing my best for a long time not to think about it at all. Mercifully, my mini-existential moment was interrupted by Officer Galladin's swift return, accompanied by a small man in a tired gray suit. Detective Harris had one of those panoramic vacuum stares that sucked everything in and instantaneously put people into one of two categories, victim or victimizer. His eyes were the color of a sharpened pencil point. Alert, as Nanny would say. He and Officer Galladin led us past the front desk down a corridor that opened into a windowless waiting room.

The man I had managed to squeeze in the back seat of my sister's car was slumped across the bench, his body bent on a forty-five-degree angle, once again dead to the world. Wrapped in a shabby pea coat and brown sweatpants, his legs were like a pair of sewer pipes—the same legs I remembered sticking off the end of the cot in New Jersey. But he seemed even bigger under the fluorescent light, with a scar that looked like a bas relief of an active volcano running from behind his left ear down the front of his neck that I hadn't noticed before in the darkness. His enormous arms were wrapped around a navy-blue pull-string GAP bag that he had pressed against his chest.

"That's our boy," Jackie said to Officer Galladin.

"I take it that one of you gentlemen is the owner of the bar," Detective Harris said, a mild distaste for us already evident on his face.

After Jackie produced his driver's license, Harris handed Officer Galladin the folder he was holding and told Jackie to follow him over to the front desk. When they were gone, she immediately reached for my hand.

"How've you been?"

I had to change the subject. "How'd you get Jackie's name?"

She very gently let go of my hand and started scanning the report.

"Evidently," Officer Galladin said, not looking up from the paper, "Mr. Shepherd requested that Mr. Parker I.D. him. He was unable to produce any identification of his own."

"Why's he here?"

"It says Mr. Shepherd was involved in a domestic dispute in a building on Avenue D."

Great, I thought, just what we need, a crime spree.

"If you don't mind me asking, Officer—"

"Johnny, please," she interrupted. "Call me Nikki."

"Nikki," I said, and smiled, acknowledging her kindness, "what was he arrested for?"

Officer Nikki closed the folder and looked over at the man on the bench.

"He wasn't."

LESS THAN A HALF AN HOUR LATER we were in a cab headed downtown with some minor paperwork on the seat between us and a twenty-five-thousand-dollar reprieve in the shape of our giant mystery man up front with the Chinese driver. As we left the stationhouse, Virgil was holding his stomach (knife wound? gun shot? dysentery?). He nodded when Jackie asked him if he was hungry. I could tell Jackie was running the options in his head, but I didn't care. I just needed to get out of the neighborhood.

The traffic on Second Avenue was tight, especially with all the taxi pickups and drop-offs at the bars still going strong at two in the morning. The more I tried not to look out the cab window, the more my eyes were lasered in on the old spots. Mercifully, a couple of them were out of business, but there was still enough going on to bring me back: the coffee shop on 4th, the Punjab deli, the laundromat on Second that played Tex-Mex music and passed out shots of mezcal in between loads.

I almost left the cab when we got stuck at the light on East Houston, but what difference would that had made? What was the better option, to sit in the cab and hyperventilate or walk past these memories with my eyes closed?

The one thing I did know was that there was no way I was letting this cabbie drive past our old apartment.

I started banging on the partition with the palm of my hand, much to the driver's delight, who, from the steady supply of murderous looks in the rearview mirror, hated us already.

"Make a right."

"What?"

"A right turn."

When he looked at me with blank eyes, I mimicked turning the wheel hard to the right like I was parallel parking a 737.

"When the light changes, make a right and then a left on Bowery."

"I go down Chrystie."

I hit the glass again when the car started moving.

"No Chrystie!" I yelled and banged out, "Take the Bowery."

The cabdriver half-turned in his seat. "You stop banging."

Jackie leaned forward. "Just a misunderstanding, pal," he said, sliding a twenty-dollar bill across the glass. "But do us all a favor—no Chrystie tonight."

Then Jackie turned to me and patted the sleeve of my coat.

"Let's get some soup."

CHAPTER TWELVE

"Lightnin' Strikes"

ANIKO AND I MET AT DUMPLING, a noodle bar on—that's right— Chrystie and Stanton Street, where she worked as a hostess. I had wandered in one night ten years before after doing the aforementioned *Godot*. Ironically, it was the same night that Evan showed up and almost pissed himself to get me to sign with his (then-fledgling) agency. My brain kicked high on adrenaline, I pulled open the velvet curtain and took a seat at a table for two in the corner, sliding past a crowd of people standing just inside the front door. I wanted to bang down a couple of cocktails and get something to eat before I figured out what shape my celebration was going to take for the rest of the evening.

When I looked over, a very beautiful girl in a flowery print dress and a geisha bun was waving me back to the front door. She was standing behind a music stand, the same music stand that doubled as the hostess station, the same hostess station that I had unwittingly ignored and moved right past five minutes earlier.

I had ten excuses ready, but all she did was ask me a question.

"Why do you look so happy?"

I told her I'd just been signed by an agent.

One of the group of people who was crowded around the music stand, a middle-aged guy with a goatee, wanted to know about his table.

The very beautiful girl smiled and held up one finger in her long black glove. Then she turned back to me, leaned over the music stand, and kissed me very softly on the lips.

I BECAME OBSESSED WITH EVERYTHING at Dumpling—the food, the loud dance music, the giant exotic drinks, and especially the very beautiful girl in the print dress, black gloves, silver crystal strappy evening sandals, and the geisha bun who ushered customers into the nightly whirlwind. It was the same routine every night after I wrapped the play. I'd walk past her, find a seat, she'd wave me back, kiss me over the music stand, send me to the bar. We'd catch up three hours later when the place finally emptied out, the owner locked the front door, and all the staff (and me) would stay at the bar until seven in the morning, drinking, eating, and dancing.

On my eighth consecutive night there, the very beautiful girl told me she lived above the noodle bar in a one-bedroom apartment.

I told her I was coming from Staten Island and falling asleep on the ferry.

She asked me who Stat Nylan was.

It was February. I was twenty. Aniko was very beautiful.

I moved in with her two days later.

SIX MONTHS BEFORE I MET HER, a pretty famous British rock star from the '80s, a regular customer at Dumpling, had asked Aniko to babysit his triplex on Ludlow Street while he went on tour. She'd agreed, moved in, and burned down the kitchen and half the first floor with a teapot that she put on the stove but forgot to fill with water. When the rock star returned, he couldn't thank Aniko enough for saving his cat, whom she had scooped up and brought to her new apartment, the one over the noodle bar. The rock star took the cat back and gave her a blank check, which of course she never cashed.

IF LAURA WINTERS WAS THE WAY MONK PLAYED the melody to "Sweet and Lovely," Aniko Forlini was Trane's solo.

I don't know if it was her half-Sicilian blood (the other half was Japanese), but her olive ice cream skin was always warm—Lily Pulitzer dresses in the dead of winter, almost nothing from March to November when she wasn't hosting. She had dark chocolate eyes and, when she didn't wear the geisha bun, the jettest of black hair with flame red tips that were layered and layered like waves at sunset. Wherever she went, her perfume would wrap you in white gardenias and let you think you were sitting in a garden at midnight.

Aniko was twenty-five. She had been working the front of Dumpling for a year and a half, but she did a lot of other things, too—modeling, graphic design, performance art. One night I came home after the play and found her practicing the oboe. She was one of those people who were talented and interesting in whatever they chose to do. But none of it was ever a big deal. Aniko very casually knew people— Yoko Ono came to one of her design shows and became a friend. One of the brothers from *The Brothers McMullen* was a regular at the noodle bar. She had a sax player from the Vanguard taking out her garbage every Monday and Friday. They were all very eager to play a role in the Aniko experience.

The apartment was packed with things she had picked up in her travels. She had a Warhol silkscreen of Mao leaned up against the bedroom wall that some poor soul in Times Square had insisted that she take in exchange for eighty dollars. She had an eight-foot dwarf citrus tree in the kitchen (southern exposure) that paid off in lemons, limes, and oranges like an organic slot machine.

She had the energy of a Columbian track team.

And she loved my 45s, especially the back-of-the-boxers.

Maybe it was a Buddhist thing, but she was kind to every living thing she encountered. She would catch water bugs in the bathroom and send them out the window in a parachute of toilet paper. She would find abandoned plants in cracked pots on the street and treat them as if they had just come from a halfway house. She was on a first-name basis with every mouse on Houston Street, and there were always a couple of them keeping us company in the apartment.

She was almost as tall as me, and I was six-one.

Naturally, throwing me into this mix was head-spinning, free-falling stuff. I did some of my best acting in the white Nova light of our courtship after *Godot* closed. I did an experimental play and received a terrific writeup in the *Village Voice*. I nailed a couple of guest spots in TV dramas, including an "edgy, riveting" (*Variety*) performance as a homeless bank robber in an episode of *Cagney and Lacey*.

I REMEMBER WALKING DOWN THE STREET, feeling different. There was the slightest hum around me, and the air felt like it was holding me up, even when Aniko wasn't at my side.

We lasted five months.

It was too much of everything—every day was like living forty hours in twenty-four. Neither one of us wanted to close our eyes. She worked a lot; I was busy with auditions and rehearsals. Exhaustion started to creep in, then some crashing, finally a few heated arguments.

In the end it was probably pretty typical of a relationship someone would have when they're twenty and they meet someone like Aniko.

And if it sounds too good to be true, it was, as least on my end.

One night, Aniko saw me kiss her friend, an actress we knew, in a club on Avenue A—one kiss, drunken kiss, stupid kiss, meaningless (I never saw the actress again—until tonight) kiss.

The next night, after not coming back to the apartment, she showed up at Dumpling with a new dress and a bloody nose, which she refused to either acknowledge or explain.

So in the end it was nobody's fault, except mine.

What came after was the terrible part.

CHAPTER THIRTEEN

"Too Much Talk"

WE ENDED UP AT UNCLE FENG'S ON DOYERS STREET, just a few blocks south of my meltdown on Houston. The food was decent and the clientele in the wee small hours ran to revelers and insomniacs. The odds of running into any stray wiseguys that late on a Friday night in Chinatown were pretty much in our favor.

The restaurant was no better or worse than a dozen other holes-in-the-wall that graced the landscape south of Canal and west of the Brooklyn Bridge. They all stayed open late and looked exactly the same. Outside, a mini-mountain range of black garbage bags blockaded the front of the restaurant, with a troop of skinny rats staking claim to each mound like it was the lunar landing. Inside there was one mirrored wall, one golden dragon nailed like a crucifix to one red wall, one row of wooden tables against the third wall, one row of booths against the back wall, two round tables in the middle, a small bar, and one skinny duck hanging over the cash register next to the front window. The outside of the place was papered over with flyers and yellowed permits and illuminated by one neon light that flickered on and off with the wind.

Uncle Feng's had become our Chinatown restaurant of the moment because of their *cha siu bao*, a steamed bun filled with barbecued pork that as a treat ranked right up there with Elsie's stuffed cabbage. None of the waiters spoke English, or at least they pretended not to, so we just pointed to the pictures on the menu and paid in cash, the language that everybody spoke.

Besides us, the restaurant had action at one other table, a crew of club kids, two boys and two girls, all very sleek and wasted and dressed like they had just stepped out of 54 in '77. They were huddled over a dozen dishes spread across the table. We took our usual booth in the back of the dining room, across from the restroom that doubled as a phone booth and diagonal to the swinging kitchen doors. In these places, no matter how tasty the dishes were, it was always good policy to keep one eye on what went down in the kitchen.

Virgil, sitting next to my partner, was at work on a big dish of cold sesame noodles that he was eating with great relish, using a fork to twirl the noodles in his spoon as though it was a plate of linguini. He appeared equally thrilled when our waiter dropped a steaming platter of *cha siu baos* in the middle of the table. When he leaned over to spear one, his chest seemed to push halfway across the table. For the first time it dawned on me how crazy I was to have allowed this man anywhere near me, not to mention putting him in the backseat of Pamela's car in the middle of the night. He could have beaten me to death in the time it took to buckle up. The fact that Virgil smelled like he hadn't changed his clothes in ten years didn't faze Jackie at all, who seemed preoccupied with his bowl of soup when he wasn't eyeing *me* suspiciously.

"Is it me, or is this soup a different color every time we eat here?" Jackie planted his spoon in the middle of the tureen, where it remained perfectly upright, buoyed by little tofu rafts and bamboo shoots and God knows what else floating around it. He studied the mix with some skepticism. "These Chinamen are like doctors. Everything's a mystery. God forbid they should tell you what the fuck you're eating."

The kids at the other table were just about finished with their smorgasbord and were contemplating in loud drunken whispers the old dine and dash. It would have been a very bad move that far from the front door, and I gave a quick shake of the head to the boy with the raccoon eyes. They lowered their voices.

Jackie glanced sideways at Virgil, whose eating utensils had been in constant motion since we sat down. "How's the soup?" Jackie asked.

"*Molto buono*," Virgil said.

You had to be kidding me. I was in no mood for this.

"What's up with the Italian?" I asked.

"*Sono italiano*," he said, and then added, "*Vengo da Mantova*."

Jackie registered the expression on my face. Unlike me, my partner actually looked amused.

"You speak English?" I asked.

"*Si.*"

"When you're ready," I said, "could you tell us *in inglese* why you went into that building and tackled that man?"

Virgil finally put his spoon down long enough to give me his full attention. "He was going to hurt them."

"You know these people?"

"*Si*," Virgil answered. "*Uomo molto cattivo.*"

A plate of spareribs, coated in a thick reddish-brown sauce, had materialized at my right elbow. I took a sip of water and turned back to Virgil.

"So let me get this straight. You see a 'very bad man' and a woman fighting on the street, you follow them into the shit-box projects on Avenue D, you walk into a strange apartment and then pin the man to the floor in his own kitchen."

"Only when he took out the—*come si dice*. . .How do you say?" Virgil picked up a spare rib and started beating it through the air.

"Hammer?" Jackie offered, like he was a contestant on a game show.

"*Grazie*," Virgil said, relieved. "The two little kids, they were crying."

"And what happens if the cops don't hear the woman screaming?"

Jackie, ever the diplomat, sensed that the conversation was taking a turn for the worse. "What our good friend Johnny is trying to say—"

"I'm not *trying* to say anything," I said. "Our twenty-five thousand dollars is lucky to be alive."

"What he's *saying* is that you can't walk around this city doing good deeds. They'll kill you for it. *Capisce?*"

A ring of waiters had very discreetly appeared around the perimeter of the restaurant, pretending to watch the latest/next edition of *Eyewitness News* on the small television set mounted on the wall to the left of the skinny duck. The kids in the booth were digging deep into their pockets, anteing up for the check. Racoon eyes looked over and gave me an equally discreet thumbs-up.

Jackie noticed me staring at the scar on Virgil's neck.

"*Scusa se ti ho disturbato*," Virgil said, then caught himself, "but the *polizia* said I needed somebody to pick me up."

"I'm very surprised you thought of *us*," I said, "after the way you disappeared the other night." I pulled Virgil's note out of the pocket of my leather coat and dropped it on the table. "What the hell is this?"

He dabbed at his greasy fingers with his napkin, then picked up the receipt.

"*Non male per una vecchia poesia,*" he said, looking pleased with himself. Then he added, "You like?"

Before either one of us could get a word out of our mouths Virgil slammed his hand down on the table when the score of the Knicks game was announced on the television. "*Fantastico!*"

"What's the matter?" Jackie asked.

"He knew he was gonna have a good game," Virgil said.

"Who knew he was going to have a good game?" I asked.

"Archie."

"Archie, as in Archie DeAngelo?" Jackie responded, finally expressing some mild disbelief. "You follow him, too?"

The headlines materialized in front of my face: *Psycho Stalker Kills Two in Bail Bond Massacre.*

"We play together," he said, then went about neatly rearranging his silverware, which had hopped around the table when he slammed his fist down.

My eyes moved from the television screen to Virgil's face, where a look of genuine something (concern? relief? insanity?) flashed across his eyes.

"Holy shit," Jackie said. I couldn't tell if he was playing along or if he was genuinely impressed. "Where do you know him from?"

"*Un vecchio amico,*" Virgil said, then turned his undivided attention to a dish of orange chicken. Jackie kept talking.

"DeAngelo was great tonight."

"Tonight" was the key word whenever it came to Archie DeAngelo. According to the papers, ex-coaches, and ex-teammates, the way DeAngelo played had very little to do with the talent he had and everything to do with whatever was going on in his head on any given night. He'd been in the NBA for over a dozen years with at least six different teams. He was the type of player who got traded to a new club, shot the hell out of the basket for a half a season, carried the team to the playoffs, then quickly wore out his welcome, usually sparked by some scandal involving another player's wife, a fistfight with an assistant coach, or some ugly incident in a night club. The guy was a menace, but to his credit, DeAngelo was on fire lately. His hot hand had a lot to do with why his new team the Miami Heat were in first place in the Atlantic Division, just past our New York Knicks, whom he had singlehandedly buried to our great relief much earlier in that never-ending evening.

Virgil picked up a bowl of pork fried rice, slid half of it onto his plate over the chicken, then turned to Jackie.

"*Per favore*," he said, and waved his fingers in the air. "A pen?"

Jackie reached into the breast pocket of his jacket and handed him a Bic. Virgil uncapped the pen, reached for a clean paper napkin, and wrote something down. As soon as his hand stopped moving, he looked over at the skinny duck, sighed, then scribbled something else down again on a different napkin. After about a minute, he put the pen down on the table, folded the napkins, and stuffed them into the side pocket of his pea coat. Then he picked up the pen and handed it back to Jackie.

"*Grazie.*"

"*Prego*," Jackie said magnanimously. "But keep it. I insist."

"How about we get the check?" I said, trying to put an end to the torture. "It's late."

The club kids had cleared out, a crumpled Christmas tree of damp fives and singles in the middle of the table. That was another good thing about Uncle Feng's—it was cheap. But now the waiters were eyeing *us* suspiciously.

Virgil started to slide out of the booth.

"Where you going?" Jackie asked.

Virgil lowered his voice, even though we were the only English-speaking people left in the dining room. "*Il bagno?*"

My partner looked at me.

I pointed to the wooden door with the *Phone* sign. As soon as Virgil closed the door behind him, I made a frantic scribble in the air for the check.

"Why are you squinting?"

My headache, which, in the hustle of our trip to the stationhouse, had been reduced to the low, steady ride cymbal sizzle of *Walk, Don't Run*, had exploded into the tom-tom attack of the Surfari's *Wipeout*.

"I got a headache."

"Didn't you have a headache Wednesday night?"

"Same headache," I said, washing two more Tylenols down with a glass of cold green tea. Then I let Jackie have it. "*Prego?* Are you fucking kidding me? I can't believe you're enjoying this."

"What's not to enjoy? We found him. We'll have the money back to Sally in a couple of days."

I took two twenties out of my pocket, put them on the table, and started buttoning my coat. My partner looked over at the closed bathroom/phonebooth door.

"You think he's all right in there?"

"You know what I think?" I said, trying to regain some equilibrium. "I think we're dealing with a very large human being who's clearly out of his fucking mind. *And* a stoned drunk. You smell this guy's breath? He's shit-raked. You know how drunk he must have been three hours ago when they picked him up?"

"The guy lives on the street. It's fifteen degrees out. What else is he going to do? Maybe we could get him into a shelter when this is over."

We're getting him into a jail when this is over, I thought, in no mood for Jackie's rationalizations, or his posture as a concerned citizen.

"You want to know what else I think? I don't believe one word he said, in English *or* Italian."

"You ever hear the expression 'Don't look a gift horse in the mouth'?"

"You ever hear the expression, 'Things aren't always what they seem'?"

"You ever hear the expression, 'When you're fucked you take anything you can get'?" He shook his head in disbelief. "We're out walking the streets like two jackasses looking for him, and when he's delivered into our laps you act like he's got leprosy."

"That's what I'm talking about. The guy disappears off the face of the earth, then calls *us* to pick him up? He knows how bad he fucked up. You don't find that a little suspicious?"

"Not at all."

It was classic Jackie. As much as he was trying to convince me (and himself) that the universe had finally given us a break, his eyes kept darting back and forth from my face to the closed bathroom door like a metronome.

"The cops, your sexy friend there, made him call us."

I must have winced when he mentioned Nikki.

"You all right?"

"Of course I'm not all right," I said. "The cops asked him to call somebody. A guy like this doesn't have a social worker he can call?"

"Maybe, if he calls his social worker, he gets in trouble."

"You really think he was in that building to help two kids?"

"The guy drinks a bottle, he wants to save the world. Who knows what goes through his head?"

"Exactly," I said. "For all we know, he could walk out of that bathroom swinging a machete."

The conversation, which had started as whispers, had steadily increased in volume, to the point where our stealthy ring of waiters was back in full force, especially at the mention of "machete." We lowered our voices.

"What? You think he's dangerous?"

"He's a survivor," I said. "Survivors are always dangerous." I looked over at the still-closed bathroom door. "This guy's going to outlive us."

"That's not saying much."

Finally, something I could agree with.

"And what about the stuff with DeAngelo?" I asked. "Please tell me you don't believe him."

"What do you want me to say? He's a liar? He's half a nut? Yeah— so what?" Jackie continued. "He's delusional? Good for him. I still dream about playing first base for the Yankees when I grow up. I don't get it. You act like this is not a good thing."

"*None* of this is a good thing,' I said, and then added, "And what the *fuck* is he writing on those napkins?"

The waiters closed ranks. Jackie looked from the bathroom to Virgil's coat.

"Take a look," he said, a conspiratorial glint in his eyes, as if we were two jerkoff freshmen peeking into the head cheerleader's gym locker.

"I'm not going in that pocket," I said and stood up. "I have to go."

The headache and missing Laura and the shock of seeing Nikki Gee were beating the crap out of my nervous system. Maybe I even had a premonition of how much worse things were going to get. All I knew was that I felt my skin was on fire and I was looking at the world through the inside of a sewer grate. I had to get the hell out of Uncle

Feng's, and I didn't want to see either one of them again for a long time, or at least four days.

When the waiter finally delivered the check to us, I dropped it in front of Jackie with my two twenties. Then I stood up, adjusted my coat, and walked over to the bathroom.

"You all right in there?" I asked, after banging twice on the door with my palm. As soon as I heard the toilet flush, I walked back over to Jackie.

"*Arrivederci*," I said, and hurried out of the restaurant.

CHAPTER FOURTEEN

"Sugar Sugar"

THE SET HAD BEEN ELEVATED ON A PLATFORM and designed to look like the interior of a cargo plane, all plexiglass windshield and fake instrument panels, with red crosses stenciled on boxes piled high on both sides of the open hatch just behind the cockpit. A backdrop of brilliant blue sky hung behind the plane, while three wind machines had been set up in front and on the sides of the platform to create the illusion of turbulence for the final heroic scene.

Nurse clinician Iris D'Urberville looked stunning in a clingy red flight suit and blue mirror aviator sunglasses. She sat in the cockpit, eyes closed, while make-up put the final touches on her soap-opera lover. Trey Callahan had been on the show for twenty-six years, working his way up from teen alcoholic to schizophrenic brain surgeon with hands of gold to dashing head of Rosehill Memorial Hospital. Jackie said that Trey was a regular at the Onion back in the day, where he wore an ascot and loved to serenade the regulars with poems from Shelley and Keats.

Laura had told us on the night of my birthday that they had already scheduled the final shoot for Saturday. None of this made any sense. Under what circumstances would the cheapskates who ran the network pay for a Saturday shoot? My cousin worked as a grip on *Good Morning New York*. He said the union guys wouldn't plug in a lamp on a weekend if they weren't getting quadruple time.

But here we were.

As soon as the make-up people were finished, the director, Brian Templeton, asked for quiet in a hushed voice that Laura said he used when he thought he was about to film something profound. He whispered some direction to the two actors, then climbed down off the platform and took his place next to Ernie the cameraman. Standing next to Laura's roommate Julie, along with most of the cast and crew who were crowded just behind the cameras, I noticed there wasn't a dry eye on the set.

DOWN ON THOMPSON STREET JUST ABOVE PRINCE, Fiorentino's didn't look like much from the outside, just a storefront with no awning, two black-barred windows, a pot of mixed begonias on the sidewalk in the spring and summer (the same pot filled with litter in the fall and winter), and a set of three patched concrete stairs leading down to the heavy wooden door. But once you walked in, the pink, blue, and gray mural of Positano that covered the entire back of the dining room, along with the exposed brick walls and the two inches of dust on the chandelier that permanently dimmed the lights, set the stage for a three-hour trip to the best food in Naples without the lunacy of Air Italia.

At Fiorentino's, the concept of free will was a tragic mistake. While there was a menu (in English) for the tourists who occasionally wandered in, the regulars trusted whatever the kitchen sent out to the tables. For starters, Enzo the maestro chef made the best rice balls in the city: tender saffron risotto surrounding a beef ragout, fried to golden perfection. And his grilled octopus? It slid down your throat like it'd just washed up out of the Tyrrhenian Sea. (They had been buying their fish from Michael for years.) It would have taken a real jackass to look at those two dishes and tell Misha, "I didn't order these." They also put out a hot antipasto (baked clams, mussels, eggplant rollatini, stuffed mushroom and zucchini) served over a base of tomato sauce, butter, olive oil, and garlic that could make your taste buds hallucinate. And his secondo courses were even better, from the seafood risotto to his masterful meat-sliding-off-the shank osso Bucco, to the cavatelli with mushrooms and lamb.

Mercifully, for a girl from Ledyard, Connecticut, Laura had an adventurous palate.

The restaurant was always crowded, but if you were fortunate enough to be seated in the alcove tucked into the far corner opposite the kitchen, it could be the perfect romantic setting for a first date, which it was a little more than four years ago, when one Johnny Romano, working actor and non-bookie, began his earnest attempts to woo and win the affection of Laura Winters, luminous shampoo model, rookie soap-opera actress, beautiful young (divorced) mother of one and a woman pure of heart and soul.

Misha, our linguini-thin, blue-eyed native of the Amalfi coast and nephew of Enzo, poured two more glasses of Moët & Chandon and nestled the half-full bottle into the ice bucket. He had always been starstruck by Laura, lingering a little too long at the table whenever he served us, this time being no exception. A newlywed, Misha had gone home to Sorrento for his cousin's wedding last summer and come back married to a pretty American tourist from Bay Ridge whom he met on the beach. Now he was working double shifts in his uncle's restaurant and, from the wistful looks he cast at Laura, already mourning his carefree youth of four months before.

"Thank you, Misha," Laura said, smiling as he stepped away from us.

"You think he'd be a little less captivated by you," I said, never that crazy about the extra attention he lavished on her, "now that he got married two weeks ago."

"Five months ago," she said, in response to my tone. "And he's just being nice."

Laura reached for her glass and watched the Moët bubbles race to the top. Looking across the table at her, I realized my heart was racing, too.

As soon as we got back to her apartment after the shoot, Laura had changed into her comfort clothes—a creamy beige sweater, her black J. Crew jeans, and a pair of brown Uggs. But she had the very slight head bob, accentuated by that oversized turtleneck, that happened when she was tense. Or maybe she was just tired. Either way, I was anxious for the champagne to kick in, for both our sakes.

There was definitely a level of awkwardness between us, but I'd been expecting worse. Maybe it was the hundred apologies I had left. Or maybe it was the three hundred dollars' worth of roses that I had managed to talk Stevie the florist into delivering to the foot of the set. The fact that she hadn't mentioned the night of my birthday was, I assumed, a good sign: I had fucked up, had apologized profusely, Chris and I'd had a terrific time together, a lot of flowers, and here we were, staring at our flutes.

So when she asked, "Everything go okay Tuesday night?" it was a bit of a heartstopper.

"Yeah," I answered, choosing my words carefully, "it turned out that it wasn't that big a deal. Something with Courtney's car."

I was praying she would leave it at that, but she brushed the blonde bangs away from her forehead and opened her eyes ever so slightly wider. I reached into the bucket and refilled our champagne glasses.

"You know," she said, "I was very mad at myself. There's no way you should've driven Pamela's car, after what happened in the arcade."

"You're right," I said.

Of course, she'd been right Tuesday night, too, but I left anyway.

Laura added, "I should've made a scene."

"You don't make scenes."

"I know," she sighed, obviously disappointed in herself.

Her incredible blue eyes, wider still and the color of the sky at dawn, were fixed so intently on me that if Misha hadn't come back to the table with a plate of bread to break the spell I was about to see how well the truth worked and confess everything that had happened over the last five days. Mercifully, in addition to the many things that Enzo did right, he put only the best imported olive oil on the table, the real stuff, not olive-colored at all but the green of sunlit grass on a summer lawn. Nanny always said, if you were going to splurge on one thing, make it a high-end extra virgin. Misha dropped the olive oil and a basket of bread on the table, and finished off our flutes, before heading back through the swinging doors. The expression of concern hadn't left Laura's face.

"Michael said you weren't feeling well."

"My brother Michael?" I asked, genuinely surprised. "When did you talk to him?"

"He called yesterday to apologize for keeping Chris out late. He told me that you've had some bad headaches, and that he was concerned."

What a pain in my ass. Good intentions were terrific, but why was my brother calling Laura and making her worry? "I don't understand why my brother is calling you to apologize. I took Chris down to the market. I kept Chris out late. I put him on the hi-lo with Jojo. If anybody has to apologize for anything, it's me."

As hard as she tried, Laura couldn't help but laugh at the absurdity of my last statement, which made me laugh, too.

"Did Chris tell you I was on death's door?"

"As a matter of fact," she said, with an actress's pause for effect, nodding her head grimly, "he said he had a great time."

"Yeah, well, it's impossible not to have a great time with him," I said, then added, "even though that little *Kunt*-thea is driving him crazy."

"Kun-*thea*," Laura corrected me, lowering her voice.

"You know he's got a killer crush on her."

"He tells you a lot more than he tells me."

"It's not me. It's the 45s," I said. "We slip on a few heartbreakers and everything comes right out."

"I'll have to remember that."

Interesting. I reached for my champagne flute and realized that my headache was gone. My brain no longer felt like it was pushing through the top of my skull.

"To Chris," I said, holding my glass up for a clink, "and first loves."

Laura reached for her glass and raised it to mine.

"I'll drink to that."

Although the episode wasn't going to air until the second week in January, someone (most likely her producer) had leaked a tease to the media, and the speculation about a beloved character's sudden exit from the show had already become a hot item in the entertainment world. In this restaurant, people tended to be a lot less impressed about a celebrity sighting—it was more about the two-second glance and the cupped-hand whisper than any actual intrusion. But tonight they were checking Laura out big-time.

"What's wrong?" she asked, when she noticed I was staring at her along with the other 160 eyes in the place.

"You are always the most beautiful woman in the room."

She gave me a dismissive bob of the head.

"In your eyes," she said. But I could tell by the look in *her* eyes that she knew I believed it.

"Trust me," I said, glancing around the restaurant. "My eyes know what they're talking about."

I raised my champagne for yet another toast.

"You were incredible today." We clinked glasses. "I've never been on a set where everyone was so moved by a performance."

"Thank you."

"When that episode goes on television, people will be crying for weeks," I said, then added, "Jojo will be crying for weeks."

For some reason my compliments did not have the intended cele-bratory effect. As a matter of fact, just the opposite—Laura was doing her best not to cry.

"I'm sorry. I didn't mean for you to get upset. . . ."

"It's not you," she said, then added quickly, "I mean it *is* you, but not the way you think. It's just starting to dawn on me that I don't have a job anymore."

Laura kept both hands on her flute as she contemplated the end.

"That won't last long."

She took another sip of Moët and put the glass down next to the cork, another addition to the collection she had started the night of our first date and which I had taken from the beginning to be a very good sign. I caught Misha's attention, pointed to the empty champagne bot-tle and gave him a very discreet thumbs-up.

"It feels weird," she said. "I've always worked. In high school, I tutored. In college, I was an RA. The only time I took off was when I had Chris. Then right after that, I started doing the shampoo commercials. I'm not sure I know how to not be busy. That's a little crazy, right?" She nodded to herself, not looking happy. "The few times in my life that I had a break and I wasn't that busy, I would get depressed and then upset with myself."

"I don't think I've ever seen you depressed."

"You have," she replied, the slightest note of resignation in her voice.

"Look, we can't let any of this happen," I said, trying to pick up the moment. "I'm pretty sure I can figure out some ways to keep you busy."

"That is *so* thoughtful of you," she said, choosing to play along.

I leaned closer to her.

"The work you've done on this show has been terrific. Everybody knows that. You were the star of a top-rated show for four years."

"If I was such a star," she said, her sweater starting to heave again, "why were they in such a hurry to kill me off?"

"Because your producers know it's time for you to move on," I said, a statement that suggested the show's producers actually had Laura's best interests at heart, which of course the slimy fucks didn't. Writing Iris out of the show had happened way too fast, especially in the chaotic world of daytime television, where a one-night stand takes a month. There was something else going on, some strings being pulled, but now was not the time to explore conspiracy theories. I did tell her, however, that I had seen Carlin Browne look at Gus and nod as soon as the scene wrapped.

Laura laughed. "You think Carlin Browne was there to see me?"

"Why do you *think* he was there?" I asked. "I mean, I like the guy, but Carlin Browne didn't fly three thousand miles to see Trey rub his crotch before every line."

Carlin Browne was the hotshot blockbuster director of the moment. His special-effects extravaganzas had grossed over a billion dollars over the last few years and he had nabbed a hot tub full of Oscars and Golden Globes, even though his characters were about as genuine as Taco Bell and his real claim to fame was nailing every major and minor actress in Hollywood, whom he had then cast in his director friends' movies and never seen again. (All this courtesy of *Access Hollywood*— not that I knew much about the guy.) He was the last person in the world you'd expect to show up on the set of a soap opera on 50th Street.

"Maybe he's a friend of Brian's."

"Maybe. All I know is that Carlin Browne was watching you like a hawk."

"Hawk" was the most polite metaphor I could use to describe the way Mr. Big Director was deconstructing the poignant swan song of Iris D'Urberville with a look not unlike the feverish glaze that came into Dinino's eyes when I mentioned Mary the Blonde.

Seizing an opening, I reached for Laura's hand. I could see she was thinking about what I had just said. And although I knew that she still had her heart in *The Daze of Night*, the look in her eyes told me she was preparing herself for the change that was about to come. But for that particular moment, despite the buzz of the restaurant, the stargazing of the other "patrons" and the inconsideration of my past actions, we were still in it together. I caught the slight lean forward and held Laura's beautiful, delicate chin in my hand for the first time in what seemed like an eternity.

When Misha returned to our table with a second basket of bread, I told him we'd take the bread, the entrees, and the next bottle of champagne to go.

CHAPTER FIFTEEN

"Sexual Healing"

L AURA LIVED WITH CHRIS AND HER COLLEGE ROOMMATE Julie in a three-bedroom apartment on Twenty-eighth Street between First and Second Avenues. Not that Laura couldn't swing her own place, but she and Julie were close, going back to their days at the University of Vermont. Julie had a very sweet personality, both emotionally and literally. She worked crazy hours as a pastry chef, so she wasn't around a lot. And when she *was* around, she smelled like chocolate ganache and buttercream. She was like a walking dessert cart, which wasn't a bad deal either.

The package must have arrived early the next morning. Julie had signed for it, then left it on the kitchen table when she went to work. I found it when I finally waltzed out of Laura's bedroom around twelve-thirty that afternoon. The rule had always been no sex in the house when Chris was home, even if he was sleeping, which, Oedipally-speaking, was a good system. Luckily for me, Laura's parents had picked up Chris after the shoot and driven back to Connecticut for a couple of days, giving them a little alone time with him before the holidays and giving Chris an early Christmas vacation. Laura wasn't crazy about Chris missing two days of school, but he was very excited to see his grandparents and it gave her some time to get herself together before her party that night.

The script inside the package was called *Family of Blood* and was based on a best-seller by a writer named Leon Littlefie. It was printed on paper as thick as a slice of provolone and bound in beautiful crimson leather with gold lettering. Tucked inside the front cover was a handwritten note:

> *Love for you to read for the part of Adrianna.*
> *Know you'd be fabulous.*
>   *Sincerely,*
>   *Carlin Browne*

I had to give Carlin credit—he didn't waste any time. Although Laura had yet to say a word, I'm sure she had taken a peek at it at some point in the morning while I was still comatose. The fact that she had climbed back into bed without mentioning a screenplay from the hottest movie director in the world was an interesting development. Luckily for me, I was able to sneak the script back into the bedroom and skim it while Laura was still in the shower.

I knocked on the door and carried the script into the bathroom with me.

She was leaning over the sink in her matching black satin panties and bra, layering strands of blonde hair into place with her blow dryer. Blessed with the flawless body of a girl who had grown up on a horse farm, the only time Laura ever wore make-up was when she was on the set. To be honest, I don't think I'd ever seen her put deodorant on.

I immediately started to get firm. Laura noticed and laughed. "Forget it. I have to get dressed."

"It's a compliment."

"Yeah, I know," she smirked, angling the blow dryer at me like a crucifix. "If you need to—you know—just go into the bedroom. I'll be in here for a while."

"I'm good," I said, smirking back. "I'm outta that business."

The Daze of Night had rented out a club downtown to throw Laura a farewell party, with cocktails starting at six. She must have been more touched by the gesture than I figured. I sat down on the edge of the bathtub and looked at the cover.

"Did you read this?" I asked, speaking loud enough to be heard over the turbo hum of the machine, which she had kicked up a speed.

"Some of it," she answered nonchalantly, looking at me in the mirror. "You were sleeping."

"Do you believe this crap?"

She turned slightly, holding the blow dryer behind her right ear. "You didn't like it?"

"Absolute garbage," I said. My response was accompanied by a loud snort of a laugh that suggested I couldn't possibly have taken it less seriously. "It's insulting, it's offensive. . . it's borderline racist. And they got everything wrong. On page two, they have an Italian family eating fish on Christmas Day, and a ham on Christmas Eve. My brothers would burn down the theater."

"They'd also see it the day it opens." Laura switched off the appliance, wrapped the cord slowly around the handle, and handed it to me. Then, to my great surprise, she turned to the cabinet over the sink and reached for a tube of eyeliner.

"I can't see you having anything to do with this."

She laughed and started in on her eyes. "Who said I'm going to have anything to do with it? I'm sure Brian told Carlin Browne how upset I was to leave the show, and they sent me a script just to cheer me up a little."

"Do you believe the values in this stupid business?" I asked rhetorically. "Just because a director ships someone a script, everybody's supposed to feel better about themselves."

She moved the liner brush over to her left eye. "It *was* a pretty nice thing for Carlin Browne to do."

Things were making a little more sense to me, and I wondered, from the meticulous way Laura was applying her make-up, if she was starting to put the pieces together, too.

"You say his name like he's Jesus Christ. He had a couple of hits. Big deal. The guy made a comet level Frisco. What the hell does he know about the Mafia?"

"He knows the book sold twelve million copies."

"If Don Corleone directed this script, he couldn't save it."

I stood up and held the cover in front of the mirror.

"Cut it out," she said, but I knew she wasn't mad at me yet.

"Look at this title," I said, pointing at the beautiful gold lettering three inches from her eyelashes. *"Family of Blood," by Leon Littlefie.* What insight could someone called Leon Littlefie possibly have about what it's like to be a wiseguy? This kills me. What kind of name is that? He sounds like an Indian."

"Native American," Laura said patiently.

"Anybody writes a book about anything today. And whatever they don't know, they just make up."

"That's why it's called *fiction*?" she responded, her voice rising on the last word. "You know you're not as sexy when you try to be obtuse."

"Obtuse? Isn't there supposed to be some truth in art? Isn't that the point? What truth could there be in this piece of shit?"

"I have an idea," she said sweetly as she capped the eyeliner, removed the script from my hands, and gently laid it on top of the toilet bowl. "Why don't you go on television tonight and make an announcement that the twelve million people who bought the book are assholes?" The frustration was just starting to blush into her cheeks. "All of a sudden," she added, "you have to be Italian to write about Italians?"

"As a matter of fact, yes, you do, without making them all look like idiots. You read this bullshit, you think every Italian is involved in organized crime."

Her middle finger slid into a jar of lip glaze, lingered for a second too long in the reflection, then moved over to her lower lip.

"Sally *Toast* is not an organized criminal?"

"That's one guy," I answered.

"And what about his scary bodyguard?"

"What about my brothers? They're the most honest, hardest working people I know."

"What about your father? He's not Mafioso?" she said, and then added playfully, "La Cosa Nostra?

"He's a bookmaker. There's a big difference."

"Can you hand me my blush?"

Moving directly behind her to get her makeup, I felt the soft satin of her panties brush up against my thigh. It was almost enough to make me lose the thread of my argument. "And as far as I know, my father's never drained anybody's spinal fluid in our basement."

"That's funny," Laura said, reaching for the blush. "I don't think I've ever heard you defend your father."

"I'm defending my ancestry."

"Half of your ancestry."

"That's not enough?"

"It sure is," she answered, with a knowing smile that stopped me cold.

"What does that mean?"

"What?"

"That look on your face?"

"What look? I'm just putting on my make-up," she said innocently.

"What're you saying, that I contribute to the stereotype?"

She shook her perfect head and tried to change the subject. "What're you going to wear tonight?"

"Cement shoes," I responded. "Do they go with a blue Perry Ellis pinstripe?"

Laura looked over her shoulder at me. "Exactly when did you become so sensitive on this issue?"

"I've always been sensitive," I lied. "I just never said anything before because I've never read anything this ludicrous." (Take *that*, obtuse.)

I picked the script off the toilet and started to flip through the pages. "This is like *Goodfellas* meets *Texas Chainsaw*. Every character in here is blood-crazed, sex-crazed. . . . He's got wiseguys sleeping with their sisters."

I actually shuddered when an image of Pamela's bare clavicle popped into my head.

"Are you all right?" Laura asked.

"Listen to this nonsense."

Putting her paraphernalia down, Laura leaned against the sink to look at me as I started to read.

"'Don't be a fool, it's not the money. It's the power we hold, the power to make men, the power to have men killed, that's what excites you. The smell of death, the thrill of death one phone call away, the fact that death is the currency of our way of life, that's what burns away in your loins, fires the desire to spend your nights in the bed of a man who had your husband—'"

When I glanced up from the page, Laura's mouth was open and there was a slight glistening of sweat around where her bra had just been.

"Lock the door."

Even though we both knew Julie was at her restaurant and Chris was seventy miles away in Connecticut, this was no time to argue. I dropped the script on the wet floor, then I reached behind me and pushed the button on the doorknob.

CHAPTER SIXTEEN

"The Elusive Butterfly of Love"

THERE WERE FIVE MESSAGES ON MY ANSWERING MACHINE when I finally made it back to my apartment about four that afternoon. Every one of them swore how wonderful Virgil had been at the Onion, what a good guy he was for a homeless person, how sorry he was that he had screwed us up, etc. And with each successive beep Jackie's voice sounded more and more like a high school kid trying to convince his prom date to swim naked in his parents' above-ground pool.

The thought did briefly cross my mind that I probably should've been around to answer the phones for a couple of hours over the weekend. It was the last full Sunday of the NFL regular season, the Giants were in first place in the NFC East, and the Jets weren't terrible for a change. The action always heated up that time of year—the bettors were either crazed with the upcoming playoffs or already nostalgic for another lost season. But the idea of sitting in the office listening to Jackie and looking at Virgil sacked out on the concrete floor, especially after a day and a half with Laura, caused my headache to come rampaging back into my brain and settle just above my eye sockets. Instead, I settled for a quick shower and a stack of Motown favorites.

My girlfriend was never the type of person to be fashionably late. I had an hour and a half to dress like I had just stepped out of *Family of Blood* and find a cab back to her apartment. But when I got back downstairs, the traffic on Spring Street was impossible and the cabs were packed. I pulled my collar up and started walking up Sullivan Street.

I had made it about ten blocks when giant chunks of sleet started to put a damper on my new leather coat. I checked the Bulgari—I still had forty-five minutes. I looked down Eighth Street for a cab, then decided that the pull of a single cocktail in One Fifth Avenue was too much for a wet actor to resist. I slipped gratefully through the revolving art deco door into the shiny warmth of the bar.

On the corner of Fifth Avenue and 8th Street, One Fifth was one of our go-to spots. It was the place where, on our third date, a songwriter who was drinking at the bar treated me and Laura to Dom Perignon because he said we reminded him of happier days when he first married his second ex-wife (who happened to be a much more famous songwriter.) When he finally told us his name halfway through the second bottle, I recognized it from one of my 45s: "The Elusive Butterfly of Love."

Laura and I had a lot of moments like that, times that seemed to take off into terrific memories while we were still experiencing them, heightened by this bubble that was ours and that other people wanted to enter. These were the things that lit up our relationship, the private moments in public, the asides for two that passed between us with a look or a half-smile. How perfect to sit on a dry barstool for ten minutes, order *one* drink, put the song on the jukebox, and toast to a perfect afternoon four years ago—and hopefully an even better evening tonight.

The legendary Joe D. was behind the stick, prepping the bar for the evening rush. (If you knew the spots to hit, Sunday was one of the best drinking nights in the city.) Sixty-five maybe, Hubble-thick lenses in black frames, and built like a bamboo shoot with silver-gray hair, Joe was a real professional, with a great baritone voice. He had perfected the art of never finishing a sentence.

"Johnny boy, how 'bout ahh. . . ?"

"I just have time for one. Surprise me."

My beautiful new coat looked like it had been worn by Kurt Russell in Carpenter's remake of *The Thing*. Some of the larger chunks of sleet slid to the floor as I draped it across the stool next to me. Joe D. eyed the ice but didn't comment.

There were just a handful of drinkers finishing up the afternoon shift. Joe D. had two rules set in marble: no profanity, and no television anywhere near the counter. But he did welcome the crooners: Louis and Ella's "The Nearness of You" was drifting from the old-school milk-crate-sized speakers on either side of the back shelf.

I reached for Joe D.'s *New York Post*, which was on the counter next to a bowl of mixed nuts.

On Page Six I saw the photo of Laura and me.

I squinted at the print from the gossip column: *We caught up with gorgeous Laura Winters and handsome Johnny Romano at Fiorentino's, that dirge of a restaurant downtown that plates some of the best pasta in the city. The champagne was flowing at their cozy table near the kitchen, and why not? A little bird told us that Laura's "daze" in the soap opera world may be numbered, as she is squarely in the viewfinder of one mega-director and his next mega-project. As for her long-term beau, he of the colossal sneeze, rumor has it he may have opted for something a little more 'organized.' Only in NYC.*

Joe D. set a sizable Manhattan down on a napkin in front of me.

"Your friend was ahh. . . ."

"Who?"

"Tall, ahh. . . . He was with a bunch of ahh. . . .Looked like he was very ahh. . . ."

If you drank in One Fifth often enough, you understood Joe D. perfectly. The only other actor I knew who stopped there on occasion and who didn't cry over the ten-dollar cocktails was Larry Rome, my old co-star and mugging victim from the East Village.

"Larry?"

Joe D. nodded.

"Good guy," I said and took a long sip of my perfect Manhattan.

"Got some ahh. . .good. . .ahhh. . .something about. . . ."

"About what?"

"A play. . .ahh—"

"What play?"

"Ahh. . .Tennessee. . . ."

"*Sweet Bird of Youth?*"

Joe D. nodded again. Then he poured what was left in his silver chalice of a cocktail shaker into my empty glass. I thanked him and knocked it back in one gulp.

I BANGED ON THE FRONT DOOR of the brownstone, which was around the corner from the bar a few blocks from the north end of Washington Square Park. When Evan finally opened the door, he was waving a palmful of twenty-dollar bills in my direction.

"I know what you're going to say and I apologize. I've had it in my pocket since yesterday."

He was wearing a rumpled Ohio State sweatshirt and a pair of black basketball shorts. It was obvious that neither Evan nor those clothes had left the apartment for a couple of days. His face was the color of a rind of parmesan Reggiano. Bluish-black lines of stubble came together just above his chin. And his jittery eyes reminded me of that painting of the guy standing on the deck of the boat with the wavy orange-red sky.

Jesus Christ, how could this be the same guy I'd seen behind his desk, raring to go, at eight o'clock Friday morning? I knew Evan dabbled, but this looked like eight-ball territory. I was slightly unnerved for a second, until I remembered why I was there.

"I didn't come about your bets."

Evan's disheveled state didn't jive with the inside of his home, which was right out of an Ethan Allen catalogue. Talk about spacious living. I realized I hadn't been to Evan's home in a while, but this was definitely an upgrade: royal blue sofa, floor-to-ceiling living room windows that looked out on the marble arch in the park, a wrought-iron spiral staircase (Who the fuck has a spiral staircase?) leading to a loft bedroom. The last place I remembered Evan living was on 18th Street near Gramercy Park, which was far from public housing but nothing compared to this palace.

"You want a drink?" he asked without meaning it.

I shook my head, and Evan dropped down on the loveseat. He was probably not in the best shape to have this conversation, but then again, neither was I.

"Sit," he said, nodding at the sofa.

The ice particles, which were sliding off my coat onto his beautiful oak floor, did not go unnoticed. I cut right to the ugly business at hand. "You sent Larry Rome for *Sweet Bird of Youth*?"

Evan looked up at me, half nervous, half restless, tapping his fingers on his knees.

"He fit the role."

"Sure, if Chance Wayne's a pussy, then Rome is perfect."

"That's not fair."

"You want to talk to me about fair? Just because I don't want to sneeze my brains out on television anymore means you're not going to find me any other work?" I looked around the apartment. "Obviously your agency has made a lot of money off those commercials. What'd you make off Larry Rome? How could you recommend him over me?"

Evan stopped drumming and fixed his eyes on a framed print just above my left shoulder.

"You're not going to like what I have to say."

"I haven't liked what you've had to say for two years."

"Larry Rome is a full-time actor."

"What the hell does that mean?"

"It means he's one hundred percent committed to acting," he said, launching into what sounded suspiciously like the opening line of a prepared monologue. "He's not distracted. He learns his lines. He shows up to rehearsals. He doesn't come to the theater late from God knows where." And then his gut punch. "He doesn't change the script."

"Are you serious? You think I would change Tennessee Williams?"

"You changed Banquo's lines in *Macbeth*."

"That's not true."

"You gave the middle finger to the witches."

"He didn't believe them. He thought they were a joke," I said. When I saw Evan wasn't buying it, I added, "How do we know that wasn't in the stage directions?"

"Because it wasn't in the stage directions."

"The audience loved it. They went crazy. And I only did it once."

"Because the producers threatened to fire you and sue the agency if you did it again."

"Fuck them."

"You know something? I can't fuck them."

With a boost from Columbia's finest, Evan was finally letting it all out. He got to his feet and took a step closer to the small pile of melting sleet that was pooling around me on the wood.

"It's *my* name on the agency. It's *my* reputation on the line." I could see that he was trying not to look down, but it was a losing battle. "You know why you never stick to the script? Because the only story you want to tell is your own. Anything I get for you is never good enough. You could've had that sitcom—you said you didn't want to work with a bird. I had the indie film for you—you said you heard the actress had herpes. I try to get you work, I try to talk your name up, I get you commercials, I give you bookmaking business. And then you charge into my home dripping water on my custom floor and make demands. You want to make art, and you want to make money. Good fucking luck. Only a handful of people get to do that and they're all named Keanu Reeves. Everyone else lives with it. They grind it out. They adjust their expectations. But that doesn't work for you, because of all the other bullshit you're involved with. Open your eyes. You're the one who's killing your career. So I don't know what you want from me. But whatever it is, I know I can't do it anymore."

And with that, he let out a deep breath, pulled a silver beaded throw off the back of the love seat and threw it triumphantly on the small flood at my feet.

CHAPTER SEVENTEEN

"Paint It Black"

FOR AN ACTOR, IT'S NEVER EASY to keep the confidence up. This was especially true after five more Joe D. Manhattans immediately following the blowout with my ex-agent. Once the doubt crept in, the questions didn't stop: How long was too long? How long was embarrassing? How long before you took a city job? A pension and a dental plan were not necessarily a death sentence. But in a way they were. As much as I loved him, did I want to turn into my grandfather and work for the Parks Department for 44 years, picking up dead leaves and re-painting monkey bars? A lot of merit in serving the masses, but not exactly a standing ovation followed by drinks at Palladium.

And the work itself—the rush of being on stage or in front of the camera, breathing life into words, connecting it back to the audience, and playing to that one person who may walk out of the shitty theater or their living room with a little extra juice in their step and a little more clarity in their brain? When things were going well (not all that long ago), when Laura, my family members, even Evan were the first ones in the theater to stand up and applaud, you always thought the bigger, brighter gig was one phone call away. But what if the next phone call was children's theater, or, God forbid, a fucking puppet show? Or no phone call at all? The valley quickly becomes the abyss— no work, credit cards maxed, bettors insanely lucky.

All right, enough with the self-pity—I had a relationship to kill. I checked the Bulgari, nodded a goodbye to Joe D., and stepped back into the killer sleet.

THE CATHODE CLUB WAS OFF VARICK near White Street. It was the type of place that no one would have ever suspected was there if it hadn't been for the small militia on the sidewalk, strategically positioned to keep anyone suspected of being unhip nowhere near the entrance. With its half-assed theme of technology run amok, the club had become a magnet for the end-of-the-millennium ravers and a hotspot for private parties. Gigantic pillars of colored lights were positioned across the dancefloor and sectioned off VIP lounge areas with couches that glowed were tucked into the corners. Lightning bolts would zap periodically across the high ceiling, and bouncers in hooded black jumpsuits circulated through the gloom, adding the requisite touch of menace. The place made you feel that you were in the lobby of a nuclear reactor just about to blow, with a burbling, synth-heavy soundtrack that would suddenly break into one of the peppier Joy Division songs. It was an interesting choice for a farewell bash, and I wondered who was paying the bill.

"Can I see your invitation?"

The doorman had positioned himself just inside the vestibule leading into the club. A leather biker cap was pulled down over his eyebrows, although the rest of his shadowy physique was under-dressed in a black T-shirt, black jeans, and steel-tipped work boots. A diamond stud in the form of an upside-down cross decorated his left nostril.

Just to be polite, I checked my pockets for the invitation that I knew was sitting on Laura's kitchen table.

"Sir, this is a private party."

"I know. It's for my girlfriend."

The doorman seemed to find my last statement very funny.

"Check the guest list," I added, again very drunkenly polite, and gave him my name. He reluctantly pulled a crumpled piece of paper out of his pocket, pretended to read, then shook his head.

"Maybe next time."

"Do me a favor," I said, as calmly as possible, "Could you move out of my way?"

The doorman glared at me and left just enough room to dare me to walk past him. I figured we were about two seconds from blast-off when I felt a sharp tug at the back of my coat.

"Just get here?"

It was Julie, Laura's roommate, slightly out of breath as usual and still smelling like whatever sweet dessert she had just whipped up on her last shift.

"Yeah," I said, nodding at the doorman. "Any minute now."

"Come on, we're late."

Julie waved her invitation in the general direction of my new friend, then reached for my arm and dragged me through the doorway and into the club. I felt the doorman's beady eyes on my back as we made our way past the first bar up to the edge of the dancefloor.

"Cool club," Julie said, pointing to the splashy colored tubes of light. "I'm going to get a drink."

The club was crowded with a hell of a lot of people I didn't recognize, but from the way they were spinning each other around, the evening appeared to have gotten off to an enthusiastic start. Out of the psychedelic light Trey Callahan stuck his bony hand out to me like the last survivor from an acid trip. I gave him a slap on the shoulder instead.

"Johnny," he screamed in my ear. "We're going to miss her."

"I know," I screamed back. "Where is she?"

"By the couches in the back," Trey yelled.

The first thing that stopped me dead was the dress Laura had on, a classic black cocktail affair highlighted by a necklace of pearls that I had given her for her birthday. She looked like she had just stepped off a yacht in Cannes.

She was leaning against a post, backlit by thick yellow light, her profile a cross between Grace Kelly and Betty Cooper from the Archie comic books. Brian her ex-director (decent guy), Gus her scheming prick of a producer, the genius Carlin Browne, and some other older guy with thin hair and a red beard had her surrounded in a semi-circle. Without knowing exactly why, I snuck up behind them, my back to the post, inches from her left shoulder blade.

The guy with the beard was gushing about the city of Vancouver as if they had just had intercourse. "It's just so beautiful," he said, repeating it five different ways. Then he added, "And cost-wise, which of course is one of my major sticking points, it would be less expensive to recreate Bensonhurst up there than it would be to film in Brooklyn."

"We'd have two weeks of rehearsal in LA and then move everyone up to Canada for an eight-week shooting schedule," Carlin Browne added, in a tight, clipped voice, almost the exact opposite of the other guy's post-coital rhapsody. The mega-director sounded as if each word cost him a precious second away from the soundstage—absolutely zero personality, which explained why the guy had to make blockbusters to get laid.

"When would all of this take place?"

"Second week in January," Browne said, without hesitation.

"Wow." Laura's exclamation of surprise was quickly followed by a delicate laugh, and then, "Fast."

Gus must've felt obliged to say something instead of just standing there with his hand around the shaft of a Michelob. "You'll see," he said to Laura. "When Carlin is excited about something he moves quickly."

As I continued to lean up against the post, taking it all in, it became obvious that this party wasn't just a celebration of Laura's work on *The Daze of Night*. It was a "Let's have some drinks and circle jerk each other because we all got what we wanted" going-away party. Laura's being written out of the show had been in the works for months. A lot of agendas had come together to make the move happen, and a lot of promises were already in motion. It wouldn't be the worst thing for a network, as well as a couple of soap-opera lifers, to be owed a personal favor by a director with a monster reputation. I figured this might be a good time to pretend that I had just arrived.

"Hey," I said, brushing up against her dress and kissing her lightly on the cheek.

"Hello," she said, barely looking at me.

I shook everybody's hands, mumbled a comment about what a great night this was, how deserved, etc., then suggested that Laura and I get a drink. Brian was very gracious, Gus nodded, Red Beard gaped at us, and Carlin stood there with a glacial look on his face, obviously unaccustomed to being interrupted. With the appropriate tight-lipped smiles, we backed away slowly towards the bar.

Obviously, now wasn't the time to tell Laura about Evan. I tried to keep my whereabouts vague, but under that cool black dress my girlfriend was seething.

"What 'things'? You told me you had to go home and change your clothes. You didn't say you had anything else to do."

With my hand lightly on her waist I had managed to guide her to a small alcove a few feet from the bathrooms without causing any great commotion. Although she maintained a smile, her fingers, clenched into a fist, had been pressed tightly against my thigh as we maneuvered through the party.

"Why can't I have something to do? Only everybody else has something to do?"

Laura gave me the "What's wrong with you?" look. "You were supposed to take me here. I was waiting for you," Laura said. "You didn't even call to tell me you were going to be late."

This was technically untrue. I had tried her cellphone when I realized it was later than I thought, but the call hadn't gone through. She didn't want to hear it anyway.

Laura waved to a friend passing by a few feet away, gave her a pleasant, "Thank you so much for coming" smile, then turned back to me. "I had to take a cab by myself to my own party."

"Maybe it was good that I wasn't here early."

"What does that mean?"

The lights from one of the big tubes had coated both of us in purple, and the dank smell from the alcove reminded me of Dinino's arcade before a thunderstorm. My face felt like it was on fire. I picked up somebody's empty drink off the ledge and pressed the cool glass against my cheek.

"When were you going to tell me about Vancouver?"

"I just found out about it now," she said. "How do you know about Vancouver?"

"Carlin Browne sounds like he has your bags packed already."

She poked at the corner of her purple eye with the tip of her purple fingernail.

"How long were you listening to our conversation?"

"Long enough to know what these guys are up to."

"And you make it sound like it's the worst thing in the world."

"*You're* not listening to what they're saying."

"What are they saying? That they want me to read for a part? That they think I'd be good?" she said, her voice rising with each word. "Maybe I should've waited for you and come two hours late. That would have been much better. Maybe they would've left by the time we got here. Or maybe they shouldn't have had a party for me at all. How's that sound? Does that work for you?"

In the four and a half years that Laura and I had been together this was the angriest I had ever seen her. My mind was spinning out ways to try to defuse the impact of my very late arrival (and the eavesdropping), but I wasn't coming up with much. Laura had every right to be furious. But in my Manhattan-drenched brain, I was pissed off too, for a multitude of reasons that of course had nothing to do with her.

First things first: I had to get us out of that purple light. I touched her elbow, which she immediately shook off, and moved us out of the alcove into a swatch of sky blue. "I'm just saying," I said, "I know what this guy's up to."

"I don't need to listen to your career advice right now."

She held my look, gave me the head bob, and tried to move past me.

"Yeah," I said, angling in front of her, "and I don't need to walk in on a conversation between some douchebag director who thinks he's God trying to talk my girlfriend into flying to Vancouver so he can try to fuck her for two months."

I turned slightly to follow Laura's eyes over my shoulder. Ingrid Claire, the actress who had played Laura's hot mother on the show, was standing behind us, hanging on every word. She gave me a look like I was a six-foot tumor and fell sobbing into Laura's arms.

After thirty seconds Ingrid broke the clinch and held Laura by the elbows.

"That's so exciting about Carlin Browne's movie," Ingrid said, spoken like someone who had spent thirty years playing the same character. Did everyone at this party know about Laura and the movie?

"Thank you," Laura said, teary-eyed herself. "It's only a reading."

"I have a very good feeling about it," Ingrid cooed, and then added emphatically, "And I *am* your mother."

With that last statement they both started to hug each other and cry again.

"I'm gonna get a drink," I said.

"Wait," Laura said, reaching for the back of my coat.

Ingrid dabbed at her eyes with a crumpled cocktail napkin. She said to Laura, "We'll talk later," and headed back into the thick of the party.

There was a mini-roar from the dance floor as the first chords of "Rockin' Around the Christmas Tree" came over the sound system.

"Why can't you just be happy for me?" Laura asked, this time without a note of anger in her voice.

Looking back on that moment, all I needed to do was reach down into the pit of my *inutile pezzo di merda* heart and deliver the most passionate "I am so happy for you" ever spoken in the history of relationships. And who deserved that affirmation more than Laura—supremely talented actress, terrific mother, loyal friend, and genuinely beautiful human being? Instead, I opened my mouth and waited for those six words to come out.

Laura looked at me, heartbroken. Then she stepped past me to join Julie on the edge of the dance floor.

I stood with my back up against the riveted metal bar and waited for the group of people next to me to finish ordering their half dozen shots of tequila with Corona chasers. It was funny how festive tequila shots became when people weren't paying for them. With my eyes closed the cathode tube lights ran over my eyelids like a bleeding watercolor, oranges and yellows and reds and greens spilling into each other before fading into a perfect shit brown. When I turned back to the counter the bartender, dressed like a billboard for a Nordic myth, had the faint outline of a smirk around the corners of his mouth.

"Let me have a double Remy," I said. "And a shot of tequila while I wait."

"I need to see some proof of age."

"That's a joke, right?"

"Sorry, pal," Thor said, glancing over at the front entrance. "Club rules."

My old friend the doorman was standing twenty feet away, fondling the cross in his nostril and giving me the middle finger at the same time. I waved and turned back to the bartender.

"Excuse me," I said, as politely as was humanly possible under these trying circumstances. "You do any acting?"

This caught him off-guard.

"Yeah," he said, the vanity meter ticking. "Why?"

"Why don't you act like you're not an asshole and get me a drink?"

And then I added, just because something finally felt good, "You giant cocksucking piece of shit."

CHAPTER EIGHTEEN

"Light My Fire"

JACKIE STOOD ON A MILK CRATE, swabbing my face, which I hadn't worked up the nerve to look at yet in the mirror behind the bar. It was four a.m., the Onion was closed, and I was sitting on a barstool with my head tilted back over the counter, trying to bring the wine glasses that were hanging from the ceiling rack into focus.

"Fuck."

"Relax, Muhammed." He held his handkerchief just below my left eye socket and dabbed delicately. Just breathing in felt like it was a little too much to ask of my tattooed nostrils.

"What is that?"

"Witch hazel."

The pungent smell came back to me—skinned knees, heat rashes, acne.

"I haven't smelled that in twenty years."

Jackie held the dark brown plastic bottle up to the overhead bar lights and checked the date.

"That's about right," he said, then poured some more into the handkerchief and returned it to my face.

"Don't get it in my eye."

"If you'd stay still, I won't."

"Fuck," I reiterated. My partner was killing me. "Where's Brendan again?"

"What's the matter?" Jackie said, pretending to be insulted. "You think a gay guy would be more gentle?"

"Of course."

"Too bad. He went home to see his kids for a couple of days. He'll be back tomorrow."

I tried to remember whether this was news to me or not, then decided it was.

"Brendan has kids?"

"Now you're scaring me," Jackie said. "You know he has kids."

"How many?"

"Three?" Jackie dabbed around my eyebrow. "They live in Cherry Hill with his ex-wife?" He looked at me like, how did I not remember this, like I was acquainted with these kids, like I had taken them to a matinee and treated them to soda floats at some point in the not-too-distant past.

"He can't be that gay," I said, which made Jackie laugh.

I very carefully re-positioned myself on the bar stool and listened to the drum of blood in my temples. One of the last customers had played a string of selections on the refurbished Wurlitzer, near the top of the list of Jackie's prized possessions. My partner had discovered the rusted juke box in the corner of a diner in Coney Island and bought it on the spot for two hundred bucks. Jose Feliciano's soulful version of "Light My Fire" rattled out of the old machine, which Jackie had hooked up to the speakers over the bar.

"You have a pretty deep cut across the bridge of your nose," Jackie said, appraising my wounds like Ferdie Pacheco. "Someone must've caught you with a ring." He leaned in a little closer. Although my partner was working hard to keep his patented nonchalance on high beams, every so often I caught a glimpse of alarm slip into his eyes. It scared the shit out of me. "I have to tell you, in my esteemed opinion as a bar owner for thirty years, a few stitches in the emergency room wouldn't be the worst thing in the world."

I swiveled my neck to take a peek in the mirror. Even though the incident had taken place only a couple of hours before, it had already taken on the blurry outline of a bad dream, which was fine with me. I didn't want to remember specifics—all I remembered were boots and fists and cursing and screaming. In the mercifully dark glass the bridge of my nose was nothing compared to the Rorschach blot that covered most of my right cheekbone. I knew what I was seeing between a bottle of Wild Turkey and a fifth of Jack Daniels was not even close to the worst of it.

"I'll live," I said, and closed my eyes again.

"Hold this."

Jackie put down the handkerchief and pressed a bar towel wrapped around some ice cubes against my battered cheek. I slowly raised my hand to hold it in place. Not surprisingly, my hands were unscathed and my knuckles unbruised, never a good sign in a barfight. Dinino's watch still held centerstage on my wrist.

"Are any parts of my face broken?" I asked.

"I don't think so," Jackie lied. My nose felt like overcooked rigatoni.

"Take a sip."

He held up a pint glass of Remy to my lips, which was as good an indication as any of what atrocious shape I must have been in. He usually poured out his top-shelf liquors in five-ounce Rocks glasses with fake bottoms. Once I was properly fortified, he laid a strip of gauze over my left eyebrow, then held it in place with two small pieces of adhesive tape that he pulled out of nowhere.

"Where'd you get all this stuff?"

"One of our regulars was a trauma nurse at St. Vincent's. He used to stop in for a drink after his shift and bring me some supplies."

After listening to my heartfelt assurances that I would survive the night, Jackie finally stepped down from the milk crate, moved behind the bar and poured himself a drink, looking a little unsteady himself. Obviously, seeing your partner beaten to a pulp was not the way you wanted to end your night, but whatever sense of awareness I still had left told me there was something else happening. I (very carefully) slid down off the stool, which roused Jackie a little.

"Why are you moving?" he asked.

"Where's our friend?"

I held onto Jackie's shoulder for support, and we tiptoed into the office. The brass lamp threw a small circle of light around the desk. On the floor next to the radiator, Virgil had curled his large body around a sleeping bag, his face pressed into one of Jackie's old jogging suits, his left arm cocked around the navy-blue Gap bag. His red sneakers were lined up neatly in front of the file cabinet. He once again seemed to be in the throes of a deep, untroubled sleep. The only time I had seen him conscious was when he was shoveling Chinese food into his mouth and lying to us about playing with DeAngelo. Either this poor bastard was exhausted from a life of homelessness, or he was passed out drunk again. Probably both. A blue-and-brown quilted comforter was spread across Jackie's desk chair. A bottle of Macallan and an empty glass were on the desk blotter next to it.

Jackie and I had used the room as an office since we first hooked up two years before. We had met at the blackjack tables in Sally's club.

Jackie had been working the phones forever, under Sally's umbrella, but was having a hard time juggling all his commitments, especially after Courtney arrived on the scene. After sharing a few laughs and a couple of long breakfasts, Jackie asked me if I'd be interested in a piece of the action. The specifics of our partnership were nothing to stop the presses—a fifty-fifty split on any new business, and twenty-five percent of his existing book. He said all he needed was someone he could trust to help him take some bets while he juggled his bar and his new girl-friend, whom he had met at a cocktail party fund raiser on the *USS Intrepid* and was trying his best to impress. My reasons for agreeing to this were a little more complicated.

The room was tight, and in trying to steady myself I knocked over the coat rack, sending it and a few jackets crashing into the wall next to the cabinet. Our guest stirred, then rolled over onto his back, his head resting flush against the metal of a New York Rangers Stanley Cup commemorative wastepaper basket. (There was a large dent in Messier's forehead, courtesy of Jackie and a field goal made by Dallas with no time left on the clock.) Even though the office was cold, it didn't stop the room from smelling like the E train in August. I started to feel nauseous, which I remembered was one sign of a concussion, and a little wobbly, which I knew was another. For the second time that night the floor seemed to rise up quickly, and I was seconds away from passing out. Jackie noticed I was fading, grabbed my waist and led me out of the office to a table where he handed me a glass of seltzer from the bar and another half pint of Remy.

I leaned my head against the wood paneling on the wall, closed my eyes, and tried not to think about the mess I'd made. The liquor burned as I took another long swallow; I felt it snake its way through my chest. I revved up my body to attempt another deep breath. I couldn't decide if I was having genuine trouble breathing, or the adrenaline that had flooded my nervous system was making my heart and lungs work triple-time.

As unbelievable as this might sound, I couldn't remember the last time I had inspired anyone to physical violence. Aside from the occasional flying elbow I took playing basketball in the cage on West 4th Street in my NYU days, nobody had laid a hand on me in almost twenty years. My nature tended to provoke more groans of indulgence and behind-my-back muttering than anything else. Even as a bookmaker, Jackie gleefully assumed the "bad cop" role, leaving me free to have a drink with our customers when it was time to collect. (Of course, Butchie was the notable exception, but that was more about Connie than what had transpired between me and him.) It was almost hard to believe that I had gone out of my way to turn Laura's special night into a prison riot. Like most catastrophes, the enormity of what had occurred between Laura and me hadn't fully sunk into my swollen brain yet.

Jackie must have assumed I had dozed off and took a moment to zero out the register. With my eyes closed, all I kept picturing was the sad, quilted comforter on Jackie's desk chair.

"When was the last time you were home?"

He looked up from the receipts as if he had forgotten I was there. Then, after putting some thought into the question, he said, "Friday afternoon." Sliding the cash from the register into a burlap bag, Jackie picked up his drink and sat down at the table.

"How did you finagle this with Courtney?"

At the mention of his wife's name, his face froze. He took a sip of his scotch and, despite his best efforts to remain stone-faced, I could see the glass tremble slightly in his hand. "I didn't have to," he said quietly.

It was a voice that had lost its "Don't Worry 'Bout a Thing" edge and was closing fast on "I Wish It Would Rain."

Then, to my absolute astonishment, tears threatened to spill out of his very heavy eyelids, which he again did his best to squeeze back.

"What happened?" I asked

"I don't know," he managed to say. "I haven't heard from her."

"Since when?"

"Two days ago," he said. "She's not calling me back, even though I've left forty messages on the answering machine, and her bitch of a sister is acting like she doesn't know anything."

"Did her sister sound concerned?"

"Not at all."

Since I was in no condition for deep thinking, my mind immediately went to the usual scenarios—quick getaway with a friend, sudden illness, torrid affair, home invasion. None of them sounded promising.

"Maybe she's visiting someone. She got any relatives around?"

"Yeah," he said, with a sigh. "Her sister."

"When was the last time you actually spoke with her?"

"Friday afternoon. She was still shaky about the car, so I stayed home for a couple of hours and took her out to lunch in Summit. We ate, we came home, checked out the new garage door. We even went upstairs for a little while. Then I drove back here for the Knick game. That was the last I heard from her. Saturday nothing. Today nothing. Tonight nothing."

Jesus Christ. Since we met, in keeping with Jackie's hit-or-miss nature, he and I had had a tradition of not sharing too many personal details. Even during times when our significant relationships seemed to be going well, when we could've shared something good, our friendship was focused primarily on our partnership. Besides setting our betting lines and moaning about our customers, there weren't a lot of heart-to-hearts. Our conversations were about one thing—money. While there were a couple of dinner foursomes and a Rangers game or two, we tried to lead our lives separate from the book. But in the last months, culminating with the derelict on the office floor, our personal screwups were hard to separate from the meltdown of our business.

"Could she have found out about the car?"

"Who the fuck knows?" he said. In the silver blue glow from the jukebox, the slow trickle of tears down his face looked like two strands of tinsel.

Granted that, at the moment, my senses were not particularly trustworthy, but the truth was, this was a Jackie I had never seen before. Sometimes, when I had an afternoon to kill, I'd sit in the bar with Brendan and listen to the old-timers talk about the neighborhood in the '60s and Jackie and how he made the Onion a "haven" (their word) in the time right after Stonewall, when "gay" and "welcome" were not two words that went together easily. He was in his late twenties (?) then, had maybe owned the bar for a couple of years. "Hero" was a tough tag to hang on anybody, especially someone who owned a bar in the city, but according to those old survivors, that was part of the rep Jackie had long before either Brendan or I had come into the picture.

Desperate events make us all into different people sometimes, but the change in my partner couldn't have just happened because of Courtney's car. I don't know if it was the booze he'd been slipping into his coffee, or the hours we kept, or Courtney herself, maybe all of the above and/or maybe something else I had absolutely no idea about, but I'd never seen him so wiped out.

What would Jackie have done if he were in my shoes? The Jackie of two years ago, flush with the idea of Courtney in his life, would've chased me out of the bar, would have said something along the lines of, "Do me a favor—go home and fuck your girlfriend. We'll all feel better," would have paid for a yellow cab to Staten Island or Connecticut, or wherever.

I leaned forward and looked out through the iron window bars onto Hudson Street. While it was very late and very cold and, most crucially, post-last call, the occasional party of revelers—remnants from a Christmas party, arms around each other, singing Oasis songs, or single strugglers looking for one last drink or at the very least an open deli—traipsed along the sidewalk chasing their frozen dreams.

"Go home," I said to my partner. "See if she left a note or something."

"I can't," he said, rubbing the corner of his eyes with the same handkerchief he had used to touch up my face.

"Why not?"

"What am I going to do with our friend in there?" Jackie nodded toward the office. "Tell him to stay in the car? We've tried that."

"I'll keep an eye on him."

He laughed. "You can't see."

I looked across the bar at the register, saw three of them, tried to focus, saw two of them, and realized Jackie was right. "We'll be fine for a few hours."

"I can't," Jackie said. "You're too fucked up. It's too much."

"You have to," I said. "Go home. Go to your sister-in-law's. Find out where Courtney is, and talk to her."

Jackie took a long look around his empire—the pocked, heavily varnished wooden tables, the bar, the plank wood floor, the faded posters of some of the legendary Off-Off-Off Broadway productions over the past forty years, the rows of liquor bottles lined up like soldiers on the front lines, the salvaged juke box. Then he turned his eyes back to me. I could see his mind had been made up three minutes before.

"All the guy does is sleep. Just let him stay in the office, maybe order a pizza or something. Brendan should be in by eleven. I'll be back by three o'clock."

"Whatever."

"I hired a lawyer," Jackie said, in a voice a little closer to the self-assured wheeler-dealer I was familiar with. "Some schmo that handled a few traffic tickets for Courtney. He's going to meet us in court on Tuesday. Open and shut case."

It dawned on me at that moment how many people it took to keep Jackie running—Brendan for this, me for that, Courtney until a few days ago. Some of his customers. God knows who else. Even Sally and Butchie played their parts. And now he'd told me out of the blue that he hired a lawyer. Despite some of his other failings, my partner still had a great instinct for self-preservation. He knew the absolute last thing we needed was a postponement, and a public defender would probably push the case back at least a week.

"As long as we get the money to Sally by Tuesday night," he said, pushing himself up from the table. "After that, we'll see what happens."

I WAS IN A HOSPITAL ROOM, A DINGY, DIMLY LIT hospital room, with very menacing-looking jungle animals painted on the walls. Even the giraffes looked vicious. I was hooked up to an array of machines and monitors, with a bunch of sad fluid bags hanging over my head. Dinino was seated in a chair by the bed, wrapped in his parka, felt hat pulled down low, absorbed in a porno magazine. It took a while for him to notice that I was conscious.

"*Pucchiacha*," he said. "About time you woke up." He held up the centerfold in front of me. "She's been asking for you."

Talk about a sight for (literally) sore eye sockets. But I was still having trouble focusing, even with a poster of some of my favorite body parts held up for me like an eye chart. Not getting the rise from me that he had hoped, Dinino rolled the magazine up.

"You look like Boris Karloff. *Cos' e successo qua?*"

"Bad decisions," I said weakly. My eyes moved down to my right wrist, which was connected to an IV and was minus the Bulgari. My heart froze.

"What's the matter?"

I shook my head and looked away.

"*Aspeto.*"

When he saw he had my attention, Dinino reached into his parka and from one of his many deep pockets pulled out the watch. Then he held it up to his ear.

"Still ticks like a motherfuck," he said and laughed. "*Fai attenzione.*"

He motioned for me to hold up my hand. He slipped the watch around my fingers just up to the IV and gave them a squeeze.

"Now that's the way you wear a watch."

I looked down at my hand. Even with the bandage and the IV tube the Bulgari was perfect.

"Why don't you hold it for me?"

"Keep it. Before I die down here and by the time they find me some skell from the Albanian pizza place is wearing it on deliveries."

The statement sounded vaguely familiar. When Dinino saw my confusion, he put a finger to his gray lips.

"*Pucchiacha,*" he continued, "now that you've rejoined the living, I'm going to close my eyes for a minute. *Capisce?*"

He flipped the magazine on my lap and slumped his body deeper into the chair.

"Capisce," I said.

BY THE TIME I OPENED MY EYES, gray light was falling through the iron window bars, and the smell of a fresh pot of coffee filled the air. I raised my chin off the folded comforter someone had slid under my face and very slowly tilted my head. Brendan was behind the counter, moving with the grace of a Dominican shortstop as he polished the speed racks and generally put the bar back in order. The good news was that my vision seemed to be a lot less multi-dimensional. The not-so-good news was that my body still felt like it had been thrown off a cliff.

Virgil, wearing a black and purple Golden Onion t-shirt and the NYU hat that I had bought Jackie, was wiping down the chrome and glass of the jukebox in the corner. Kneeling in front of the machine as if he was at an altar, he used a crumpled piece of newspaper and some Fantastic to remove last night's drunken finger smudges from the glass.

And even though the Bulgari was still on my wrist, there was no hospital room, no jungle animal, no porno mag, and no Dinino. My friend had been so fully himself in the hospital that it was hard to believe he wasn't still sitting next to me. It was only when I realized that there was also no Jackie that I remembered he was on the other side of the Hudson, hopefully reuniting with his wife, or at least figuring out where the hell she was.

I looked at the Bulgari again, then slowly put my head back down on the table.

CHAPTER NINETEEN

"Dedicated to the One I Love"

FROM THE MINUTE LAURA AND I MET (in the club with the soon-to-be divorced Ralphie, my high school friend with the unfaithful wife and the bottle of Southern Comfort), I knew that what was going to happen between us, if it was going to happen between us, was going to add up to a lot more than a one-shot deal. And despite the almighty physical attraction on my part, the heart-stopping first glimpse of her profile at the bar wearing the neck brace, a one-shot deal was the last thing on my mind.

Not that I was ever close to making that happen. Laura was a little wary after the ski bum made a mess of their brief marriage and put her back on the beginner slope, relationship-wise, with a very young son to raise and protect. She was not thrilled with the state of dating in 1993, to say the least. When I asked her for her phone number that first night, Laura gave me the name of her dentist's office in Connecticut. She said she had been going to Dr. Weiner since she was a little girl, that she trusted him and the people who worked in his office. If Doris, his receptionist, liked the sound of my voice, she would get in touch with her and Laura would call me back.

Which she did, two weeks later.

From the little I was able to piece together (since Laura never spoke badly about anybody), one of the issues Laura had had with her ex-husband was a lack of mutual interests. Captain of the University of Vermont ski team and big man on campus, Sean Loughlin was focused on three things: the side of an icy mountain, a crack at the Nationals, and banging every other female skier he passed on the slopes. Obviously, these interests didn't coincide with Laura's, which were simple enough: trying to finish her senior year with a six-month-old baby. And even though Laura did ski, it didn't sound like there was a lot of common ground between them even before Chris came along. They divorced the year after she graduated. Laura moved with Chris and Julie to the city and landed the shampoo commercials almost immediately.

But once Doris gave me the thumbs up, it was obvious that there was a lot of chemistry, physical and otherwise, between us. We could talk about everything. I never had to try to dream up a line to keep the conversation humming, and we didn't have to pop two bottles of Bordeaux to have a great time on a date. Laura had been a drama major in college, so we had acting, plus our budding careers, plus Chris, plus everything else. We both loved Manhattan and quickly acclimated our relationship to the rhythms of the city—one night the tasting menu at Po, the next day a picnic lunch for three at the Central Park zoo so Chris could say hello to the polar bears. It dawned on both of us very quickly that we were in love, and we started spending most of our free time together. Having a beautiful son, a sweet nature, and an already low tolerance for bullshit thanks to the father of her child, Laura wanted to limit the drama to our professional endeavors. She made it very clear that she didn't cherish the chills and thrills of an up-and-down romance.

After Aniko, neither did I.

But then a peculiar thing happened. Not that I was any less in love with her, but after a couple of years of bliss, I found myself getting a little distracted. The commercials were starting to bug me, and the plum acting roles weren't falling into my lap. I started to have too much time on my hands. As you can imagine, I was not the type of person who should have too much time on his hands. I was spending way too much money, which happens when you have nothing to do—drinks here, lunch there, a new pair of Cuccinelli loafers in the shop window on West Broadway.

An actor friend who was working in a café on Seventh Avenue told me about Sally's club. He was chasing an actress who was doing double-duty as a hostess (not Connie) in the casino, and he suggested that we stop in for a drink. One night, after he finished his shift, we put on suits and took a cab over to the brownstone. I knew it wasn't going to be five momos playing blackjack in Uncle Carmine's basement in Dyker Heights, but from the first night I was very impressed. The Toast operation was top shelf all the way, glitzy and very welcoming, if you spoke the language—style, money, connections. I played some blackjack, won a few dollars, had a few laughs, got checked out by the *gumadas*, and went back a couple of nights later, without my actor friend, when Laura took Chris home to visit her parents in Connecticut. Enter Jackie and the Onion.

"Sit down," I told Virgil Shepherd as I locked the door behind us and slipped on the chain. I hadn't been back to the apartment in almost twenty-four hours—the clothes that I had stepped out of before changing for last night's disaster were still on the floor, along with the 45s that'd been breaking Chris's heart before the Knick game. After sleeping on the floor in the office, Virgil's eyes lit on my white leather sofa like it was a giant pile of warm marshmallows.

"Bellissimo."

He lumbered across the room, stepping carefully over the records, and sank his body into the cushions, clearing a place for himself between the piles of dry cleaning. He propped the Gap bag in his lap.

"I'm going into the kitchen," I said. "I'll be right back. I'll put the television on." I found myself talking louder and slower, like I was trying to communicate with a deaf Rottweiler.

"Grazie."

The red lights on the cable box glowed 1:28. What does a homeless guy watch on cable? I put on the Cartoon Network, glanced back at my guest, and headed into the kitchen to check my messages.

I figured I'd take a quick and very hot shower, then order something for us to eat. Once he made a thorough inspection of my face (courtesy of the flashlight he kept behind the bar), Brendan had insisted that I leave Virgil at the Onion. But I had told Jackie I'd take him, and I figured Brendan could use a little space after his trip home. The greatest bartender in the world put up a brave front, but he was definitely not himself. Talk about a heartbreaker—leaving three kids for the holidays? Tough one. If I could have Virgil back to the Onion by six o'clock, hopefully Jackie could take him off my hands. That would give me some time to figure out my next move with Laura. This all made perfect sense to me, but I probably had a concussion, so of course it did. Very, very reluctantly Brendan had let the two of us walk out of the bar.

I filled a glass with ice cubes, pressed it between my nose and left eye, and listened for any sounds of movement in the living room. The old wooden floors in the building creaked when an ant took a leak, so I'd know if he was moving around. The only thing I heard were the voices of Scooby and Shaggy and the rest of the gang. I went into the bedroom to find a fresh towel.

The answering machine was on the stand next to my bed. There were eight messages when I sat down to play them back. There were four from my mother, two from my sister Pamela, and of course, two from my brother Michael. Every one of them said the same thing—please get home as fast as you can.

I MOVED INTO THE COCOON of Elsie's kitchen, staring at the wooden spice rack on the wall, running words like rosemary and oregano and thyme through my mind like a rosary to keep myself from thinking. A few years before, the cabinets had been replaced and the shape of the table had changed, but it was basically the same kitchen that I had sat in as a kid dreaming up any excuse not to finish my homework. The same philodendrons were still on the windowsill over the sink, spilling out of their ceramic flowerpots, and my mother's radio remained tucked in the corner behind the telephone, a lite-FM station playing softly just about around the clock.

My mother, sitting at the table, looked up at me.

"He's on the loveseat," I said. "He's eating cookies. He seems to like the Stella Doros."

She got up, moved to the refrigerator, and took out a bottle of Tropicana.

"I'm going to offer our guest some juice."

"No," I said, too quickly, prompting a flash of her eyes. "He's good for now."

If he stole something, the Romanos had too much of everything to begin with. If he wandered out of the front door, a seven-foor stranger walking quickly in this neighborhood would get noticed fast. But there was no way I was leaving Elsie alone with him, even for a second.

"How do you know this person?"

"He's a friend of Brendan's. From the bar. We have to take care of some business tomorrow morning."

Elsie nodded and sat back down next to me. Looking at her, it was hard to believe my mother was already in her early fifties, especially considering all the nonsense she had to put up with in this house. Her face still glowed with the smoothest of complexions, her Hungarian skin almost translucent, as if someone was holding a flashlight on a pearl. Her eyes shifted colors when she spoke, moving from the most brilliant green to a soft bluish yellow when she got upset or disappointed. My mother had the lightly frosted blonde hair of a 1960s movie star and the perfect nose of a Christian Dior model, courtesy of a sled and a parked car on some hill in the Bronx when she was twelve. Her only concession to age was to paint her blonde hair with Lady Clairol every summer to make the most of the Staten Island sun.

Mrs. Romano (born Elsie Juhasz) was Gabor-sisters-beautiful, maybe a little more Eva than Zsa Zsa or Magda, which was quite a compliment if you ever happened to catch any of the old *Green Acres* reruns. Her family had actually known the Gabor family back in the old country. There was also some weird connection to Bela Lugosi, another famous Hungarian, but they didn't like him too much.

In contrast to my father Jack, who was an only child, my mother had grown up in a large family of crazy Hungarians. She was the third youngest of seven sisters and one baby brother. When Elsie was nineteen and still living on Morris Avenue, two blocks from the old Yankee Stadium, she took a job as a receptionist for an employment office in Times Square. One night after work, she took a trip downtown with her friend Yvonne. They met a bunch of very well-dressed Italians at a social club on Mulberry Street, stayed for a hi-ball (my mother still referred to her mixed drinks that way) and just as The Crystals sang, here we were, thirty years later, nestled in the lap of luxury in the shadow of the mighty Verrazano.

Da do ron ron.

"Can I get you anything?" she asked softly. She looked at my black eyes and my swollen cheekbone and poured herself another cup of tea, the color of her own eyes betraying how concerned she was.

"I'm good," I answered.

She was treading very lightly. Unlike some of my other family members, Elsie was always happy to see me, but I could see I was wearing her down, too.

"You want to tell me what happened to you?"

"Not really," I said.

"You do realize," she said kindly, "as a mother it is within my rights to demand a little information."

"You're too good to embarrass your oldest son like that."

Elsie took a hearty sip of the steaming tea and said, "I know you don't want to hear this—"

I shook my head. "Please, don't even say it."

"Why can't you let your father help you?" she said, frustration slipping into her voice. "If whatever's going on involves Jackie and the bar. . . ."

"It'll all work out."

"Michael thinks you're in some kind of trouble."

Christ, was there anybody Michael wasn't talking to about me?

"For a smart guy, Michael needs to learn what brothers talk about should stay on ice at the fish market." I took a still-painful deep breath and ran more spice words through my head: coriander, paprika, cumin, sage, marjoram. What the hell was my mother cooking these days? "I know he's concerned," I said, more softly, "but he's got enough to think about."

"It's Michael's nature to worry. Just like it's Joseph's nature not to worry."

"What's my nature, Mom?"

Elsie gave me one of her cryptic Hungarian smiles. I listened for any footsteps in the living room, then looked up at the "Elsie's Kitchen" clock on the wall over the sink: 4:50. I wanted to make sure I got to the funeral parlor before anybody else.

"Who found him?"

"A couple of kids. They ran into the laundromat and the owner called 9-1-1."

"When was this?"

"Yesterday morning."

"Any word on how it happened?"

"According to what I heard in the superette, it was a massive heart attack. If that's true, at least he didn't suffer."

That's what I wanted to believe. That's what everybody wanted to believe. My mother was trying to spare me the ugly facts, but how would anybody know this fast anyway? Third-hand information got distorted very quickly in this neighborhood, especially when somebody died.

"I just saw him Tuesday night," I said, choosing not to mention my dream. "He looked like he always did." I thought back to the night of my birthday. Why didn't I notice anything? I wondered. Aside from Zenon pulling a diva act and blowing up, everything was the same. For the twenty-five years that I knew him, Dinino had never looked well. How could he? He ate crap, he drank blackberry brandy by the drum, he was never in sunlight. He always just looked like Dinino. He would've cursed me out for weeks if I had suggested a "well" check-up or even a Bayer aspirin for the hell of it. And he wouldn't've told me if anything was wrong anyway.

But of course, he had told me. It was on my wrist.

Elsie opened her mouth, hesitated, then looked away, but I caught the color of her eyes. I knew what was coming.

"Does Laura know?" she said softly.

Elsie had grown very close to Laura over the past five years. It would have been impossible for her not to, given who they both were, and especially with the amount of time Laura and Chris had spent at the Romano house for birthdays, holidays, and Sunday dinners. I wanted to explain that Laura'd had no part in what had happened, that it was all me, that I was the fuck-up. But that was unnecessary.

"Are you going to take Brendan's friend to the wake?" my mom asked very delicately.

"I don't have much of a choice," I answered.

LOCATED ON A CORNER HALFWAY BETWEEN my house and the arcade, Auriemma's Funeral Parlor was a throwback to the days when people spent their whole lives in the same place. It was one piece of the Staten Island puzzle that hadn't disappeared yet. Three generations of Auriemmas had served the dead of our neighborhood well since the family first opened the parlor fifty years before.

I pushed open the front door, Virgil following a few steps behind me. He had wolfed down an entire package of the breakfast treats and a quart of juice that Elsie had insisted on bringing him. Although the fact that he had said very little to anybody since Jackie split for Jersey made things easier, I still hadn't figured out a way to explain who he was and what he was doing there, aside from being Brendan's "friend."

Black eyes and all, my brothers and sister wouldn't interrogate me about how their oldest sibling had turned into the type of person who still got beat up. And despite a few second looks, none of my old neighbors would find the right way to ask, at least to my face, why Jack Romano's son was walking the streets with an enormous Black man. In a hurry to catch the Staten Island ferry, I had managed to squeeze Virgil into an extra-large Calvin Klein V-neck, my one pair of navy sweatpants, and an old camel overcoat from the back of my closet that I had worn at NYU when I was going through my Brando in *Last Tango* phase. Along with a liberal amount of cologne, it wasn't exactly *GQ*, but it was an improvement.

"Wait here," I said.

The entire funeral home was painted a soothing light blue, with dark gray carpet and light gray upholstery on the furniture. There was a laminated map of Italia framed next to the door marked *Office*.

Joseph Auriemma was straightening a vase of chrysanthemums when he saw us in the lobby. The grandson of the original funereal mastermind, and heir to the business, Joseph and I had spent eight unremarkable years in Holy Rosary playing soda can hockey with our classmates in the parking lot during recess. He was the first one back in his seat when the bell rang, and the only one the nuns didn't have to remind to tuck in his shirttails. Joseph was never a laugh a minute, but he was always a stand-up guy with only good intentions. Respectful to teachers and parents, helpful to the nuns, loyal to his friends, kind to the janitors, he was the classmate who put the work in and did the homework that many of us copied.

Now, standing somberly in front of me in his well-tailored black suit and tie, Joseph looked the picture of the professional undertaker, someone you could trust to bury you quickly and keep a lid on the costs. Sensible and steady. He probably went directly home when the last mourner slipped out into the night. He was the first in the household up in the morning to make breakfast for his family. Was Joseph getting fired from his agency? Was he causing a beat-down at his girlfriend's party? Was he dragging a homeless guy around with him to his friend's wake? Was he stiffing mobsters for thirty grand? Joseph was still just a good guy in a dark suit who wanted to do the right thing. Except he couldn't stop himself from looking at the bruises on my face, which were filling in nicely with different shades of navy blue and purple, tinged with a puky yellow and patches of red. A Caribbean sunset from the lips up.

We shook hands warmly. "We all loved him," he said solemnly. "He was a spesh-cial man."

I had forgotten about the lisp.

"I am scho schorry."

It was the same terrible lisp that we all hoped would go away when the braces came off, or maybe when he got laid for the first time. I could still remember, when he answered questions about the parts of a flower in third grade, we would all hold our breaths: "schtamen—deep breath—pish-til." It was as much a part of his character as the Southern drawl of Blanche Dubois, or Billy Bibbit's stutter in *Cuckoo's Nest*.

It took me a few seconds to refocus. In the silence, Joseph placed his hand on my shoulder.

"He was a neighborhood legend."

"You gave him something nice, right?"

"He had everything pre-paid. He was very spesh-cific. He requested a mahogany cash-ket with extra padding. Top of the line."

Wood—old school till the end. Dinino always said there was nothing worse than the drum of rain on a metal casket. Like being buried in a roasting pan.

"We just added some floral arrangements, just to make the room look full," he added modestly, still letting me copy his homework.

"I didn't think about the flowers," I admitted.

"No problem. Your mom schent a beautiful arrangement from the family," Joseph continued. "And Father Igna-schius schent schomething as well. Also schome of the neighborhood families and bus—"

"Anything from his nieces and nephews?" I asked, cutting him off, sparing both of us—a question that had slipped out and would have been at the top of Nanny's list.

Joseph shook his head.

"Nothing that I remember schetting up."

Disgraziati.

"Which room?"

"Parlor schee. One viewing was all he wanted."

"Joseph, thank you for everything," I said. Parlor C was the most spacious of the three viewing rooms. I smiled. "He should have nothing to complain about."

"We did our bescht," Joseph said sadly.

THE TELEPHONE WAS DOWNSTAIRS next to the restrooms. It was a quarter to six, and there was still no answer in the Onion. Why wasn't anything making sense? I wasn't shocked that Jackie hadn't surfaced yet, but I couldn't understand why Brendan wasn't picking up the telephone in the bar. Even with missing his kids, Brendan was the most reliable human being I had ever met, maybe even more so than Laura. Every day his regulars filled the stools for cocktail hour before heading home from work. I hoped Brendan was too busy pouring to get to the phone on the twentieth ring, but I doubted it. Just for the hell of it, I dialed Jackie's house in Jersey, with the same result.

The guestbook was open on the pedestal set up just inside the doorway to Parlor C, alongside a stack of cards:

> *In Loving Memory of Rudolpho Dinino*
> *December 20, 1997*
> *You sleep in God's beautiful garden,*
> *in the sunshine of perfect peace.*

I slipped a couple of laminated prayer cards in my pants pocket.

"Why don't you sit down in the back?" I said to Virgil. "I need a few minutes."

I watched him lumber over to the sofa against the light blue wall and ease himself into the cushions, which I figured should keep him busy for an hour. Then, without any excuses or emergencies that I could invent, I turned toward the casket.

CHAPTER TWENTY

"Along Comes Mary"

DININO WAS DRESSED IN A BLACK SUIT that I had never seen him wear before. His chapped hands were folded over a set of black Rosary beads, and the two lanterns on either side of the coffin cast a soft light on the silver crucifix resting under his thumb. I'm sure the Auriemma clan had their reasons for not decking him out in his parka and felt hat, but the body arranged in the casket in front of me was not close to the way Dinino had looked exactly one week before, when I brought him the cannolis on the night of my birthday. It was my last memory of him, other than the hospital dream. Rosy-cheeked, wispy hair parted on the side, looking robust enough to stretch out his humped shoulders and split the walls of his white satin-lined coffin in half, this was not a Dinino I could picture sitting up and saying, "Pucchiacha, what the fuck?" The idea that my friend had been betrayed by his own heart, within the walls of his own arcade, discovered by half-baked kids, was tying my stomach in knots. I lowered my chin and rested my forehead on the back of my hand.

When I opened my eyes, I was in a different room.

It was a lot smaller. There were no other visitors. The scent of white gardenias filled the air. And of course, the song was playing so softly in the background.

Her favorite—Grace Jones' version of "La Vie En Rose."

Gardenias and roses—Aniko always loved contrast.

I couldn't bring myself to look directly into the casket. I had seen her this way too many times in my dreams. But I felt I owed her at least that much. When I tried to raise my head, the room started to spin and I was falling over.

I felt a pair of very sturdy hands on my shoulders.

"You all right?"

It took me a couple of seconds to understand that I was back in Auriemma's. Jojo eased my body down on the cushioned bench and continued to stand behind me, his hands still firm on my shoulders. Through his fingers I could feel the same taut energy that had pulsed through my brother's wiry frame ever since he was a little kid. Then, once he knew I wasn't going to slide to the rug, he knelt beside me and bowed his head in prayer. His lips moved silently to the rhythm of the holy words in his head. I could tell it took every ounce of Jojo's self-control to keep his knees from bouncing up and down on the cushion.

When he finished, he put his arm around my shoulder and appraised my condition.

"*Madone*," he said loudly, then caught himself and said it again much more softly. "You look worse than he does."

I lifted my head and looked at Dinino. "It doesn't look like him."

Jojo moved his eyes from my face to the casket.

"Why's his hair so flat?" Jojo asked.

I made a move to get up. Jojo put his arm under my elbow and helped me to my feet. I glanced over my shoulder at Virgil, still sitting like a rock on the sofa. A few of the early mourners had taken seats, and the hum of funeral parlor chatter had started to build. My sister Pamela, dressed in a black pants suit, sat with one of her girlfriends in the third row, next to Michael. Nobody was sitting in the first two rows. I took a step toward the entrance.

Jojo nodded at the empty chairs.

"Why don't you sit down for a minute?"

"Your wife's got the kids?"

"She's got all the kids. She's going to switch off with Kristina at eight o'clock."

A few people gave me the solemn head nod. Pamela was waving me over.

"You see that man on the couch?" I said, directing Jojo's attention to the back of the room.

"The Black guy?"

"Yeah," I said. "Could you do me a big favor? Keep your eye on him. He's with me. If he tries to leave, get me."

Jojo took another look at Virgil.

"The Black guy back there?"

"Exactly."

"Where're *you* going?"

"I'm going to try to find Dinino's hat."

Jojo looked confused.

"That Black guy's with *you?*"

People started to head up to the casket, old-timers from the neighborhood who would want to hug me and express their condolences for a half an hour. I had to make a break. "He's with me."

Jojo shrugged and headed dutifully to the back of the room.

I SPLASHED MY FACE WITH COLD WATER and pressed a wet paper towel to my left temple. Auriemma's office was locked, as were all the rooms in the basement, so I figured I'd regroup in the men's room. Honestly, as much as I wanted to reunite Dinino with his beloved hat, I was relieved that the downstairs rooms were closed off. There were certain topics that the less I knew about the better, and mortuary science was one of them. And the episode in front of the casket had made me realize that I was too numb and too fucked up to tempt fate and pull open some locked doors.

I knew that I wouldn't be able to properly mourn my friend in that moment. Dinino's passing deserved my undivided attention, something that I had often given him when I was younger and that I gave less and less as I spent more time in the city with my friends, then my career, then Laura and Chris, then Jackie and Sally. My eyes in the bathroom mirror looked like two potholes on the BQE. I couldn't feel how much I would miss him, not yet. As terrible as it was to admit, to sit in the front row and, empty-eyed, welcome whoever came to pay their respects, would be close to acting.

Then I remembered something that I hadn't thought about in a long time, the cumulative effect of eight years of Catholic school. The nonsense that we were force-fed between social studies and math had a way of embedding itself into the brain and appearing in moments of extreme stress and exhaustion, which probably was the point anyway.

Where was Dinino's soul?

In Catholic school the soul was non-negotiable, a given. And for the handful of us who found the idea a little slippery, the teachers carted out that experiment, back in nineteen-something, where the doctor weighed people as they died and came up with a 21-gram difference. Okay class, there it was—21 grams equals weight of soul. Write it in your notebooks. Write it twenty-one times for homework. Test on Friday. But was that proof, or was it just some nut with a bad scale? Mrs. Hailey, our fourth-grade teacher, drilled the episode into us as if it were just as much a fact of science as Galileo and gravity, but she was a senile old bat who could never remember our names. Was *she* someone who could be trusted with the truth about the soul? She was still calling me "Mark" in April.

I threw some more water on my face.

My mind was racing.

Thinking about the way Dinino looked in his casket, there had to be something more. There was no way he was leaving us like that. Maybe Mrs. Hailey, so close to the threshold herself, had a little inside info. Wasn't that the deal with faith? In times of crisis. . .I knew that, somewhere in the basement, behind those locked doors there were basins for fluids and organs, but what provisions, if any, were made for the soul? Where did it go? Was it just lumped in with everything else? Did the Auriemma family open the window and turn their backs? Was that a trick of the trade they learned in mortuary school? Was Dinino's soul even here? Ever here? Was it back at the arcade? When the spark of his life was extinguished, did Dinino's soul float above the neighborhood, above the kids (and adults) that he had kept on eye on all these years, and hover in the mist over the bay?

Or was it all just bullshit?

I was making myself nuts, but that wasn't a terrible image and maybe even a good one—Dinino as a glow in the horizon, visible in the night once the sun went down and the neighborhood shut off its lights.

I suddenly became aware of a commotion just outside the bathroom door.

"I'm coming in."

Nanny's voice cut through the sanctuary of the men's room like a blow torch.

"Not now," I yelled.

"Here I come."

All I could think was, God, if there's such a thing as the soul, please have mercy on mine and make her go away. But so much for long shots. When I looked in the mirror again, Nanny was standing behind me. Enveloped in her funeral wear—a full-length mink coat and matching mink hat (courtesy of a very generous employee discount at L&T)-she looked like a Hun come to avenge the death of Attila. She was not happy.

"Who did this to your face?"

"I got mugged."

"Bullshit."

"How do you know I didn't get mugged?"

"Because I know," she said, and quickly added, "And who's the colored guy you have sitting next to your poor brother?"

"Nobody you need to worry about."

"Jojo's basically sitting in his lap."

"I gotta get back," I said, clutching the balled-up wet paper towel in my fist.

"Not until you tell me what's going on."

She gave me the look that had withered a couple thousand shoplifters as she decided their fates in the holding room on the fifth floor.

"Nothing's going on," I said, keeping my distance by the sink.

"I know your fat partner has something to do with this."

Among her many other unfathomable instincts, Nanny was inherently suspicious of anyone who was overweight. One of her favorite expressions was "People ain't fat for nothing." She seemed to take it personally.

"This is ridiculous," I said. "I'm not talking about this now."

"Where's Laura?"

"She'll be here later."

"Bullshit."

Both my head and my stomach were pounding.

"Is it too much to ask to go to my friend's wake in peace? Or take a pee for that matter?"

"Don't get smart with me."

"I'm not getting smart."

"Obviously," she said, nodding at my sorry reflection in the mirror. "I want to know why you look like that."

"I slipped in the shower."

Nanny nodded, then pulled a roll of peppermint Certs from the depths of her Louis bag. She carefully peeled back the foil, removed two mints from the roll and slipped both of them in her mouth.

"Bullshit," she said, but much more calmly. "Your grandfather said you're the talk of the Goddamn neighborhood."

"I'll explain everything after the wake."

"What you're forgetting," she responded, lowering her voice, "is that I deal with liars for a living. I spend a great deal of time with these people. I know how they think."

"I can't believe you're calling your grandson a liar."

I actually saw a split-second of stars (for the second time in two days) when Mrs. Mary the Blonde Romano buried her high heel in the soft part of my Ferragamo right below the tassel.

"I want you to cut this shit out."

"That *hurt*!" I yelled, grabbing my foot in my hand and leaning my thigh against the sink for support. Someone I didn't know was halfway through the men's room door. Nanny turned and glared at him until he backed out.

"Lower your voice," she said. "This is a funeral home. Have some respect for the dead. They don't want to hear that."

"They can't hear *anything*," I yelled, then very tentatively put my foot back down on the floor, turned to the sink, closed my eyes and splashed more water on my face. I was praying that, when I looked in the mirror again, she'd be gone, that my traumatized brain was hallucinating. But I wasn't that lucky.

"You and I have two very different definitions of what it means to be dead."

"That's a big part of your problem," she answered cryptically.

"I'm going upstairs," I said, and moved away from the sink.

Nanny reached for my elbow. "What's that on your wrist?"

She was staring at the Bulgari.

"Dinino's watch. He gave it to me Tuesday night for my birthday."

Nanny nodded, as if she were acknowledging something that only she knew. "That's the thing with you—people love you. You don't get that."

"You're right," I said, tired of arguing.

"I know I'm right. I'm too old to still be worrying about you. I want you to stop all this nonsense and get married already and let me live the rest of my life in peace."

"That's why you tracked me down? To tell me to get married?"

"I tracked you down because your sister said you looked like a racoon and you have your brother bodyguarding Leon Spinks. You need to wise up, marry this girl, and move on with your life. We're all going to follow Rudolpho into the ground if you don't stop being so God-damn selfish."

Rudolpho? What? I had never heard anyone call Dinino "Rudolpho."

"He deserves better than that."

I looked at Mary the Blonde, all five feet one inch of her minked-out self in front of the urinal, holding me in her unflinching gaze, the look in her eyes tinged with—what? Something I had never seen before and that was gone before I had a chance to figure it out.

"She'll take care of you," she continued, with a lot more tenderness than she had three minutes before when she impaled my big toe.

"Does anybody ever consider the possibility that I like the way that I live?"

"Please," she said. *"Chi va piano va sano e lontano."*

I knew I was on the ropes when Nanny broke into Italian, a language she reserved for curse words and grand pronouncements.

"Suppose she doesn't want to marry me?"

What I really wanted to ask was, What makes you think I deserve her?

"Of course she wants to marry you," Nanny said. "She's a good girl. She's a good mother. She's respectful. She's not Italian, and I don't care. Doesn't that tell you something?"

"Things are different these days."

"No, they're not," she said. "I've been watching people for seventy-two years. I know when people are in love." Again she looked at me intently, the fur on her mink rising and falling slightly. "The heart don't act."

"I'm not sure if that's true."

I flinched when she brought her hand close to my face, expecting a right jab, but she just reached for my chin. "How many times do I have to tell you? You don't see with your eyes. You see with this." She moved her hand from my chin and placed it gently over my heart.

It was impossible not to love this woman for what she was, even though what she was made it impossible not to want to strangle her from time to time. Did she speak the truth? Possibly. Did she have my best interests at heart? Definitely. Did she love me with the ferocity of a lioness facing down poachers in the savannah?

That was the worst part of it.

Having decided that she had said what I needed to hear, she removed her palm from my chest and turned toward the mirror. With the steadiest of hands Nanny pinched a Chanel classic red out of her bag and spread it perfectly over her lips. Once she was satisfied, she dropped the lipstick back in her bag and moved past me to the men's room door.

"By the way," she said, paused in the doorway, "I'm very sorry about Dinino."

"Thank you," I responded, and watched her leave the room.

When I finally made it back upstairs, Parlor C was packed. There was a line snaking from the back entrance of the funeral home past Parlors A and B and up to Dinino's casket. That was the thing about Staten Island. Even though the people were often nuts and there were way too many of them, they knew when to show up. "Respect" was a big commodity on the rock, and it was a legitimate deal-breaker when people didn't follow through. When a kid was born, everyone went to the hospital. Birthdays, anniversaries, christenings, confirmations, tonsillectomies—people came out, and when they couldn't, they sent something. Hallmark did a booming business on SI, as did the florists. And when someone died, the neighbors came to Auriemma's early and often, which evidently had happened while I was downstairs.

A lot of the old-timers had already staked out their territory and made a play for the chairs. The line itself was mostly teenagers, both girls and boys, their hoods pulled over their heads, their eyes a little red, the whiff of pot cutting periodically through the smell of carnations. It looked like a reform school reunion until you saw their faces, their genuinely sad faces, paying their final respects. Their presence made me feel very proud and also a little protective of my relationship with Dinino. The two kids who were there the night Zenon exploded stood next to each other, holding hands, silently sharing a bag of cheese doodles. No boombox.

I made my way through the crowd and up to the pedestal, where I surveyed the room. There was no one standing stage-right of the casket, greeting the mourners and accepting condolences. People moved up to the casket, stopped, said their prayers and looped around the chairs against the far wall, as if they were on a conveyor belt. The first row remained depressingly empty. Elsie, Pamela, and Michael had disappeared from the third row. Nanny was already holding court with some of the Holy Rosary bingo sharpies on a couch in the far corner.

Fighting off the smell of the flowers, I tasted the blackberry brandy on my lips and tried to make eye contact with Jojo. From the position of their bodies it looked like neither one of them had moved a muscle in an hour. Jojo sat with the tips of his feet planted on the carpet, staring straight out into space, not talking to anyone. Virgil's head rested against the light blue wallpaper on the back wall. I made a mental note that, if I survived the next two days, I'd buy my brother something extra nice for Christmas.

People had already formed their cliques, sitting half-turned in chairs or huddled in groups of three and four, chatting away. That was one of the many things that was ironic about wakes. One minute everybody's kissing each other on the cheek and hugging up a storm, and the next morning the same people were throwing themselves on the coffin. But again, who was I to say anything? While those people were at the grave site tomorrow morning I'd be in a shit court in New Jersey trying to save my ass. So who was the hypocrite?

I cut the line, knelt down in front of the coffin, and took in the sudden change of scenery inside the casket. In my absence Dinino's faithful had deposited tokens of their appreciation and remembrance on the white lining surrounding my friend—dozens and dozens of quarters, spirals of the cardboard tickets that came out of the ski-ball machines, a few small stuffed animals, and a couple of old Polaroids of a younger Dinino, hat firmly in place, sweeping the sidewalk in front of the arcade. Someone had even stuck what looked like a wrapped calzone in there. I had to admit, I was a bit overwhelmed. I bowed my head and put my hand on the glass bottle deep inside my coat.

Somewhere on the cab ride from the ferry I'd had the brilliant inspiration to slip a pint of blackberry brandy into the coffin. I thought maybe the brandy would help Dinino absolve me for not being at his funeral mass the following morning. And if forgiveness was too much to ask, how could it hurt to have a pint of his favorite booze along for the ride, even though by now there was less than half of it left? My plan had been to do it before anybody else showed up, but I'd been so thrown when I saw him that I forgot the bottle was in my pocket. Now with the room packed and what I sensed were all eyes on me, the window of opportunity had slammed shut once again.

I stood next to the kneeling bench and bent over the casket, my head close to Dinino's chest. From that angle I could work the pint with my right hand from my coat pocket into the coffin.

I was suddenly aware that the room had grown extremely quiet. After about thirty seconds I heard a voice in my ear. "Johnny, it's okay, son. Pull yourself together. He's with God now."

When I turned my head I saw that it was Father Ignatius.

"I just need a minute, Father," I said.

When he bent over to put his arm on my left shoulder to comfort me (and pry me off), he saw the top of the bottle sticking out of my pocket.

"What're you doing?" he whispered.

The thing with this guy was, even though he had his hands in more pockets than Butchie, he meant well, especially for a priest. And Dinino trusted him. Fuck it. With a little tug I slid the bottle out of my coat and nestled it into the soft white satin lining.

As solemn as an extra from *The Exorcist*, Father Ignatius eyed the pint of brandy and nodded.

"God bless you."

I looked up at him. "Is that a joke?"

He looked down at me with his pale lips, his black robe, and his crucifix dangling over my shoulder and said, "I never meant it more in my life." Then he helped me up, turned to face the mourners and lifted his Bible.

"Let us pray."

I WAS HEADED OUT OF THE PARLOR to call the Onion again when I felt a tap on my shoulder. It took me a couple of seconds to realize that my old friend Ralphie was standing next to me, shadowed by a distinguished looking gentleman in his mid-forties. Even in our carefree youth, when we were doing the plays together in high school, when we were hitting the bars on MacDougal, when he was playing "Maybe This Time" in the Empire Diner, Ralphie was a tormented soul. That was his look—collar up past his ears, dark circles under his eyes, too drunk, muttering. And then he would wonder why the phone number the girls gave him was always to a nail salon. But if Ralphie was still tormented, at least he looked terrific. He was wearing an expensive navy trench coat and his hair had that flippy center-part that was a big deal at Astor Place. I had to admit, he finally looked like the successful writer he had become.

I was a little adrenalized from my episode in the casket but happy to see Ralphie looking well. I had to give him credit—to show up to this wake with that haircut and with who I assumed was his boyfriend took courage. Ralphie, for his part, looked slightly unnerved when he got a closer look at the condition of my face.

After we shook hands and exchanged condolences, he introduced me to his friend.

"Paul, I told you about Johnny. He was like a son to Dinino."

The tears welled in my eyes so fast that I looked down at Paul's very tasteful black loafers until I could blink most of them back.

"I'm so sorry for your loss," Paul said respectfully, doing the tight-chin funeral parlor head nod. "I've also heard that you've been a very good friend to Raphael," he continued, looking at Ralphie. "He always tells me how you saved his life."

Here we go. "He makes it sound like an Elton John song," I said to Paul, who from the bright look in his eyes got the reference. "I just got him drunk. He's always been dramatic."

"Hey, I was in bad shape that night," Ralphie said, getting dramatic. "You hung with me, you took me to the club. You put me to bed. You let me stay in your apartment for a week. If you didn't pick up the phone, I had some weird thoughts in my head."

Truthfully, I *was* worried about Ralphie that night. Not worried enough not to lose sight of him for a few minutes in the club while I was trying to ingratiate myself to Laura. But definitely worried enough to bring him back to Sullivan Street and stash the bottle of extra-strength Tylenol and my one steak knife in the back of the oven once he had finally passed out. Also worried enough to miss my audition the next morning, so I wouldn't have to leave him alone. And it was closer to two weeks that he spent on my sofa, not one. But all that was between Ralphie and me. Paul didn't need to know this early in the game how crazy Ralphie was.

I glanced at the corner of the room, about twenty feet away. Jojo was still one hundred percent in Zen guardian mode. He had shifted his position on the couch and was studying Virgil like he was the Buddha. What would Virgil think when he opened his eyes and saw the way Jojo was staring at him? I had to get Virgil out of there.

"I gotta go," I said. "Very nice meeting you."

Ralphie grabbed my hand and looked at Paul. Out of the corner of my eye I saw Auriemma and Auriemma, Sr., carrying in a giant flower arrangement of carnations in the shape of a pinball machine.

"And If it wasn't for my crazy ex-wife Johnny would have never met Laura."

"What a lovely woman," Paul said. "Very sweet."

"How do you know her?"

"We just had the pleasure of talking with her."

"The four of us should go out to dinner one night," Ralphie chimed in.

I stepped back from my old friend and his new friend and caught my breath. Laura was seated on the far side of the folding chairs between Pamela and Elsie, who was passing out tissues. Pamela, as usual, was talking non-stop. Laura's blue sunglasses were fixed on the casket.

CHAPTER TWENTY-ONE

"Tell It Like It Is"

WHENEVER MY FAMILY DISCUSSED Laura behind her back, my grandfather would end up saying, more than anything just to shut everybody up, "She loves him, Goddammit. Would you spend four Christmases with us if you didn't have to?" After all the time we'd been together, those words had never really sunk in until I saw Laura sitting in that funeral parlor, paying respects to my oldest friend.

I moved past the pedestal and stood stage-left of the coffin. The parlor was starting to thin out a little. The pinball wizards had come and gone, as had most of the local business people. The old-timers were sitting tough, but this was their thing. They were superstitious about not putting in enough time, but, at this stage of the game, who could blame them? I tried my best to catch Laura's attention, but she was masterful at not making eye contact.

"Everybody's asking me about your friend," Jojo said, suddenly materializing next to me.

"What time is it?"

Jojo pushed up the sleeve of his suit jacket and squinted at the Gucci watch I had given him three birthdays ago.

"It's a quarter after nine."

I watched Laura stand up and embrace Elsie and Pam, an "I'm not going to see you for a while" hug if I ever saw one. Then she collected herself and began to thread her way past a couple of empty chairs to the aisle. I put my arm around Jojo.

"I need a few more minutes."

We both looked back at the sofa. Virgil was staring down at his knees, scribbling feverishly on one of the napkins he must've pulled from his coat pocket.

"What do you think he's writing?"

Laura stopped at the foot of the aisle to hug Jojo's wife.

"I have no idea," I said.

"Looks important," Jojo said.

She walked up the far side of the room toward the casket.

"At least tell me his name, in case he wants to leave."

I watched Laura kneel in front of the coffin, place her hands in prayer, and bow her head.

"His name is Virgil," I said, and for the first time since this disaster began, I remembered where I'd heard that name before. But the thought was gone, as quickly as it came, as I watched Laura rest her hand on Dinino's arm.

THE SITUATIONAL IRONY OF MAKING a desperate stab at saving our relationship in the middle of a funeral home was not lost on me. But the office was the only place I could think of to speak with Laura in relative privacy, and Auriemma, Jr., somewhat reluctantly I must say, gave me the key. I closed the door behind us and sat on the highly polished edge of my friend the undertaker's desk.

It was hard to get a read on Laura with her sunglasses still in place. She was wearing a black pants suit and had her hair pulled back behind her ears and falling on her shoulders, like Catherine Deneuve in *The Umbrellas of Cherbourg*. She stood with her back to me looking at the framed certificates on the wall.

So much for champagne bubbles—my heart was beating like the Fania All-Stars. But I was strangely buoyed by Nanny's words in the men's room, which kept repeating in my head.

"Thank you for coming tonight," I said.

"Your mother called me," she said, slipping her sunglasses into her coat but still keeping her distance. I very quickly realized that my optimism may have been misguided.

"I didn't know you were here until Ralphie's friend told me how lovely you are."

Laura shook her head to dismiss the compliment. "I am so sorry about Dinino. He was great," she said quietly. "He was the only one of your friends I ever believed."

"Believed?"

"I believed he had your best interests at heart." She considered what she'd just said, then added with a half-smile, "Ralphie, too."

She could've added, *Unlike every other creep you've surrounded yourself with*, but she didn't. I took a step toward her and watched as she moved away, closer to the bookcase, filled with huge textbooks detailing the ins and outs of embalming.

"I just want you to understand that I'm here for Dinino. This is not about what happened between you and me. Michael's taking me back at nine-thirty."

"I'll take you home."

"That's not a good idea."

"Where's Chris?"

"He's with my parents," she said, then added, "We're spending the holidays with them."

I thought back to Poppy's words about the four Christmases.

"I am so sorry about what happened at the party," I said, catching a glimpse of my reflection in the glass of one of Joseph's framed mortuary school diplomas. "I can't believe I did what I did."

She moved closer to me and examined my face. I tried to remain perfectly still to take in her presence—her perfume, her softness, her breath, which always reminded me of the icing on a vanilla cake.

"I can't believe *this*," she said, visibly upset.

"I know," I said. "I know how stupid I was. I had just had an argument with Evan. He fired me from the agency."

"I'm very sorry to hear that," she said.

"It was a matter of time."

I regretted what I said as soon as it came out of my mouth. She took a step back.

"But why?" she asked. "Why do you say that? Why has everything become a matter of time with you?"

I could see from the tension in her cheekbones that Laura was debating whether to have this conversation now or cut her losses and walk out of the office.

"It's like you insist on making things hard." Her words were not angry. "I thought I was going to have a happy marriage. Why not? My parents have a happy marriage. I know what a happy marriage looks like. I was in love. Why shouldn't I have expected a happy marriage? And look what happened." Laura pulled a tissue out of the sky-blue dispenser on Joseph's desk and held it at her side. "But we didn't make it miserable on purpose. When it fell apart, the only thing we both knew was that we didn't want to make Chris miserable."

"The last thing I would ever do," I said, "is make you and Chris unhappy."

"But you have. That's what you don't see. You're different—you don't enjoy *us* anymore."

"That's not true," I said.

"You didn't notice that things haven't been the same with us?"

"Look," I said. "I know it's been crazy. And I know the things I've done are terrible, starting with the night of my birthday. But I haven't told you everything that's going on."

"You haven't told me *anything* that's going on. *Before* the night of your birthday. For a long time now. I don't know what you do anymore. I don't know where you *are*. I don't even know who you're with."

"I'm not with anybody," I said.

"You're not with *me*," she corrected. "But you're with Jackie. You're with Sally Toast," she said. Then, after a pause, she added, "You're with a blonde woman who's hanging all over you."

And there it was. The waitress who tried her best to ignore us at the diner came into sharp focus—Carla. She did shampoo commercials with Laura. How did I not recognize her?

"That was just a breakfast."

"My friend told me it was obvious that the woman you were with was looking for a lot more than breakfast."

"Connie?" I said, too fast, and immediately saw in Laura's eyes the mistake I had made calling her by her name. "She's one of the bartenders in Sally's club. You know, scary Butchie? The bodyguard?" I asked. "She's Butchie's girlfriend. We went out for breakfast to talk about. . ." the word "fucking" popped into my pulsing brain, but mercifully I held it back.

"About what?"

"About nothing," I responded, feeling that the tide was very sadly turning back to a very ugly sea. "Stupid bullshit bookie stuff."

"Which I know nothing about."

I thought back on the conversation with Connie, how I was so quick to tell her about keeping Laura in the dark.

"And honestly," Laura continued, "I wouldn't know anymore if you were telling me the truth or not."

"I have never lied to you," I said, quick to add something to my miserable defense. "Things have been complicated. Not relationship-wise, I swear. I *swear*. Money-wise. Business-wise. Jackie-wise."

"I told you the night we met that the last thing I wanted in my life was complicated. It's complicated enough raising Chris by myself."

"By yourself?" I said, feeling a jolt of adrenaline. "How could you say, 'by yourself'?"

"Because you're not around us anymore. Think about all the things we used to do, the three of us. I saw you through the window, how hung over you were when you took Chris to the game. I actually thought about not leaving him with you."

"And we had a great time."

"Taking him to the fish market in the middle of the night five days before Christmas?"

"He was great. We were all watching him. He had a ball. How do you say no to a kid a week before Christmas?"

"You can't say no to anybody."

Who *had* I said no to in the last seven days? Jackie? Sally? Connie? I thought of standing in a New Jersey police precinct at two in the morning for Jackie. Of promising Sally thirty thousand dollars by Christmas Eve. Of drinking Bloody Marys with Connie at six in the morning. Of taking an eight-year-old to the fish market at eleven o'clock at night when it was twenty degrees out.

Who had I said no to, except Laura?

"You're right," I said.

She looked away, down at the quartz clock on Joseph's desk, the face set in cherry wood. The two hands ticking away told us it was ten minutes to ten. The clear sound of the ticking also told me that Laura wasn't crying. She was trying very hard to stay in control. Like Evan's speech, what I was about to hear had been in the works for a while.

"I think you like 'complicated'," she said softly. "I think 'complicated' has become a great excuse for you to avoid spending time with us and your family and your career and everything else that has a chance of making you happy."

Talk about opening with a knockout punch—she was a lot better at it than Evan. I took a deep breath, noticed that the edges of my vision had gone black, and that Laura looked like she was standing at the end of a tunnel.

Tick, tick, tick.

"Now can I tell you what I think?"

She nodded her chin slightly, then closed her eyes, as if she were hoping I'd disappear before she would have to listen to me again. When she opened her eyes and I was still there, she said, "Okay," as if she'd just agreed to identify a body in the morgue.

Her eyes were locked on mine. Now they were full of tears.

There was a soft knock at the office door. Joseph looked in the room, the expression on his face suggesting that he'd rather be in a cancer ward than standing in that doorway.

"I'm scho schorry to interrupt," he said, his nervousness kicking his lisp into overdrive. "No ru-sch. I just thought you might like to schee him again before we close up the parlor. I know you schaid you couldn't be here for the funeral tomorrow."

Motherfucker.

"Thanks. I'll be right there," I said, and watched Joseph vanish from the doorway.

Her chest heaving, her lower lip trembling, tears sliding down her cheeks, Laura tilted her head and looked almost sideways at me.

"Go ahead," she said, her voice shaky. "I have to get back."

She leaned into me and kissed me very tenderly on the cheek. "Please take care of yourself."

She reached into her coat, put her blue sunglasses back on, and tucked her hair behind her ears. Then she turned and moved through the half-open office door.

Nanny was right again.

The heart don't act.

CHAPTER TWENTY-TWO

"1-2-3"

FROM THE SCENT OF YESTERDAY'S COLOGNE on the pillowcase to the folds of the satin comforter on my chest, I figured the odds were pretty good that I was lying face down in my bedroom on Sullivan Street. I had the smell of Staten Island ferry beer in my nostrils and the sour taste of fermented blackberries at the back of my throat. I could make out the not-too-distant thread of trucks and car horns from Sixth Avenue, which was one block over. There was also a very good chance that I was naked, since I had one painful hard-on burrowing into my mattress. The hard-on was a pretty regular occurrence, with or without Laura. The lack of warmth in the apartment (tough to get the heat to the third floor in those old buildings), and the liberal consumption of alcohol, gave my kidneys a run for their money.

The snapshots that insisted on playing around the edges of my memory were in black-and-white—the look on Laura's face when she kissed me goodbye, Laura getting into Michael's car in the parking lot, some crazy argument with my brother, Dinino and me alone in the parlor, sitting on a bench at the ferry, cans in brown bags, the torch of the

Statue of Liberty passing in the window.

And Zenon, in Dinino's arcade, shooting sparks out of her head and laughing, the crew of smirking devils smirking at me now.

Not one of those was a scene that I needed to revisit in greater detail. I figured my best option, if I *was* in my bedroom, was to just stay there, face-down in the pillow, for as long as I could. My attempt at saving what was left of Laura and me had been a dismal failure. What could be a better answer at this moment than to do nothing?

The one thing I couldn't ignore was the music playing in the living room.

The sound, which had begun as the low grunt of bass and snare drum, started to come together, a trumpet line, the shake of a tambourine, some saxophone. And then a voice: "1-2-3, oh that's how elementary. . . ."

I pried my eyelids apart, pushed myself off the mattress, and swung my legs on the floor. For a change, I was right on three fronts—I *was* in my bedroom, I *was* naked, and I *did* have one raging boner. Outside the window, the sky over the west side of Manhattan was still dark.

The music was blasting.

Takin' candy...

Who the fuck was playing my 45s?

I threw on my bathrobe and opened my bedroom door. When I reached the kitchen, the digits on the microwave clock read 5:12. Fortunately, my landlords were all in their early eighties and slept like frozen vegetables, so there was no clamor from below. But the voice, also registering at an impressive volume, came from the bathroom, accompanied by the swoosh of running water.

It was the kind of voice that blended in so tunefully with the record that if hadn't been for an extra "baaa-by" I would never have heard it at all, especially at that decibel level. I grabbed a fork out of the sink and dropped it into my bathrobe pocket. Then I tiptoed over to the bathroom doorway.

Virgil was standing over the sink, stripped to the waist, my favorite Elvis commemorative postage stamp towel wrapped around his ass. He was singing his heart out, with a baritone that was a cross between Ben E. King and the white-haired guy from the Doobie Brothers. An empty bottle of Stoli stood next to the soap dish.

With each choppy hack of the razor—my razor! —patches of greyish black grizzle fell into the sink basin and were swept down the drain by the torrent of water pouring out of the faucets. Steam from the hot water had fogged up the room. His eyes were glued to the patches in the mirror he had cleared by making circles with his fist, and he was concentrating like a six-year-old trying to ride a bike with one training wheel. Between the singing, the shaving, the steam, and the vodka, he didn't notice me until I was almost past him.

The thing that really killed me? Not one trace of an Italian accent.

"Excuse me," I said, the urgent need to alleviate myself propelling me past my houseguest to the toilet, where I mercifully cut loose.

At least he showed some decorum and kept his eyes in the cloudy mirror. I belted up my bathrobe when I was done, then turned to the sink.

"What the fuck are you doing?"

He put the razor down on the sink counter and looked over at me as if I'd asked him a trick question. The scar, which I had first glimpsed at the precinct, was much more unnerving in the close quarters of my bathroom. It began just below his ear, zig-zagged down the side of his neck, and extended all the way to the middle of his chest, where it ended in a semi-circle just below his ribs. I tried to picture what size knife, or what size person for that matter, could have done so much damage.

What I hadn't noticed before were the bruises. Black-and-blue marks covered his lower body from the edge of the towel to just above his rib cage. They were not unlike the ones around my eyes and nose but much more thorough. They looked suspiciously like kick marks from a boot.

When he saw me looking at his back, he took Elvis off his ass and draped him over his shoulders. Len Barry finished the song solo, without the benefit of Virgil's almost note-for-note accompaniment.

"Mi stavo preparando."

"What?"

"Come si dice. . . .I get ready?"

"At five o'clock in the morning?"

Ssshhh–scratch, *ssshhh*–scratch. The record had come to an end.

"Scusa. I didn't want to get in your way."

A little late for that now, motherfucker.

"You put the record on?" I asked, attempting to maintain my last ounce of composure. After all the miserableness of the last few days, I knew that if Virgil Shepherd had in any way fucked with my 45 collection, I could not be held accountable for my actions.

Sss-hhh–scratch, *ssshhh*–scratch.

He shook his head, like he was embarrassed about something.

"Then how did the music get on?"

After some shifting and blinking, Virgil said, "You put it on. . . *quando siamo tornati."*

Ssshhh–scratch, *ssshhh*–scratch.

Occasionally, when I've had too much, I have been known to toss on a stack of 45s and pass out to the sound of them. And "1-2-3" *was* one of my late-night go-to records of choice and often served as the last song in the line-up. Of course, I had no recollection of doing this, but I also didn't remember entering the apartment, taking off my clothes, and falling face down on my mattress.

"You're saying that I put it on?"

"*Si.*"

Ssshhh–scratch, *ssshhh*–scratch.

"Why are you *si*-ing me now, when two minutes ago you were sing-ing like you were born in the Bronx?"

He shrugged again. A bone-chilling thought lightning bolted into my brain.

"How'd I get into bed?"

"*Tu camminavi. . .*you walked."

"By myself?" I said, more telling than asking.

"*Si.* Yes."

He nodded vigorously.

"You swear?"

Ssshhh–scratch, *ssshhh*–scratch.

"*Sulla Vergine Maria.*"

"How long's the music been playing?"

Ssshhh–scratch, *ssshhh*–scratch.

"*Non cosi a lungo*," he said. "Three hours maybe."

And with that, the bass and drums kicked in, the horns laid down on top, and the song started playing again.

"Leave some hot water for me," I said, and went into the kitchen to put on some coffee.

WE SAT IN THE BACK SEAT OF A YELLOW MEDALLION, moving steadily through the grimy confines of the Holland Tunnel and out past the toll booths. Traffic was already backed up coming into Manhattan on the last Tuesday morning before the Christmas holiday, the king of all grid-lock-alert days, but the trip to beautiful downtown Jersey City and bey-ond was relatively painless. I looked out the back window at the ever-present shades of gray in the morning sky, actually the title of one of the Monkees' more introspective songs. (I know they didn't write it, but they played all the instruments on it, so fuck you Monkee-haters.) I couldn't remember the last time the sun had graced the sky, but maybe I was too preoccupied to notice. Either way, the weather wasn't inspiring great confidence in the proceedings to come.

My guest vocalist sat beside me, looking out his own window, stretching the limits of whatever I had pulled out of my closet that I thought might fit him—a black Armani pull-over sweater that had been handwashed to an extra-large, a pair of tan loose-fit Ralph Lauren chinos, my old Gucci wing-tips. There were no songs coming out of his mouth, but there was a definite improvement in his appearance, and he didn't look too upset when we dropped his old outfit into a dumpster on 7th Avenue before we got into the cab.

I looked at him in the rearview mirror. It was crazy to think how some decent clothes and hot running water could make such a difference, but there he was, looking in my camel overcoat like a cross between Wilson Pickett and Wilt Chamberlain. As a matter of fact, despite my double-breasted wool navy pinstripe suit and pressed yellow tie, I was the one, with my black-and-blue eyes and purple cheekbone, who looked like he had spent the night in a particularly spirited lock-up.

I figured the more presentable he appeared, maybe the faster the thing would be over, either way. As ridiculous as this sounded, I still held out a faint hope of getting over to the cemetery to see the closed casket before I headed to Sally's club to settle up our debt. I felt terrible that I wouldn't be at the grave-side service, but it didn't seem too much to ask that I could get back to the site for a late afternoon moment of solitude.

Truthfully, I was having a hard time getting the business about Dinino's soul out of my mind. I didn't know what I was expecting, but I did know I had to get to the cemetery before the diggers put away their shovels and the burial was over.

Before we left the apartment, I tried both the bar and Jackie's home one more time, with no success. It wouldn't have been so distressing that Brendan wasn't picking up at the Onion at eight-thirty in the morning, if it hadn't been for Brendan not picking up at the Onion at 8:30 the night before. And Brendan, being Brendan, occasionally *did* open the bar at the crack of dawn to make sure everything was in order, especially before a big Holiday drinking weekend. I asked the cabdriver to pull over on our way to the tunnel— the metal gates were up, but there were no signs of life.

The best bookmakers on the planet wouldn't have been able to come up with a spread for what was going on in Jackie's life. For all I knew, my MIA partner was sitting on a beach in Aruba, Courtney cozying up next to him, his sandy hand under her ass, a ceremony to renew their wedding vows scheduled for later in the lush tropical evening. This was well within the sphere of possibility, if not reason. Although considering the unpredictability of Jackie's nature, I couldn't rule out him showing up in court either, dressed in a Santa suit, passing out ten-dollar bills to all the kids sitting in the pews waiting for their fathers to be sentenced. Kindness and generosity were also somewhere deep in the heart of his track suit.

It had always been a crap shoot with Jackie Parker, a fact that was finally starting to sink into my brain. Jackie's best moves were whims dressed up as instincts, even as far as inviting me into his operation. He was optimistic enough to trust his gut, but also savvy enough to know what pieces to pick up and which ones to kick to the side.

Too much had already happened to get my hopes up about court and getting most of our money back. I wanted the thing to be over with, with or without Jackie and/or his mystery lawyer. I wanted to turn Virgil Shepherd loose when we got back to the city and then say goodbye to my friend in an empty cemetery. Was that too much to ask?

After a few wrong turns and a stop in a gas station off 3 West, we tracked down the Dorwood Municipal Courthouse. The building was a stately Greek revival affair with two columns in front and a line of what I pictured were attractive trees when they weren't frozen solid stretching out on either side. Two blue Department of Corrections busses were parked on the left side of the building. The courthouse had the same efficient look as an elementary school in the suburbs and, from its size, seemed to be serving some of the other towns in the area, too. Our very patient cabdriver left us on the marble steps of the front entrance, and after I gave him a generous tip from the last of the cash I had stashed in the apartment, we headed into the hallowed halls of New Jersey justice.

The lobby was busy with court officers and lawyers and the families of the arrested, although it was nowhere near the spectacle we had witnessed at the precinct in the East Village when we were reunited with Virgil four nights before. I was bracing myself to see Chopsticks, '70s porno cop, and his cherry-faced partner from last Tuesday night parading past with neck braces and walkers, but they were nowhere to be seen.

We emptied our pockets for the metal detector. Virgil carefully laid his ratty blue plastic bag into the gray bin as if it was filled with precious jewels and anxiously awaited its reemergence on the other side of the X-ray tunnel. We passed with flying colors, but as we approached the large, curved stairway leading up to the second-floor courtroom, my vision blurred and the room started to spin a little. Virgil noticed as I reached out for the railing.

"*Cosa c'è che non va?*"

"Nothing," I said, my hand gripping the wooden bannister. Jesus Christ, we had come this far. There was no way I was going to collapse now.

I could see that he was sizing up my condition.

"*Io penso e discern,*" he said, "*che tu mi segue e io saro tua guifa.*"

"In English."

"You first," he said. "I walk behind."

The courtroom was packed, but we were able to find two seats in the back, which improved my situation immensely. I discreetly fingered the bail receipt in the pocket of my coat and checked out the room.

"You see anybody that looks like a lawyer Jackie would hire?"

Without making a big deal of it, I tried to imagine how the hell I was going to find Jackie's attorney. Everyone I squinted at was wearing a Men's Wearhouse three-piece and looked exactly like the type of boot-leg shyster my partner would hire. Virgil surveyed the men standing along the wall stage-left of the bench, then laid my folded coat neatly across his lap and put his Gap bag between his feet.

"You ever done this before?" I asked.

"No."

"You never been arrested for anything?"

He shook his head.

I knew that Officer Nikki told us that Virgil didn't have a criminal record, but I had been too disoriented at the time to believe it. Now, noticing the way his eyes took in the courtroom, I had to admit it was possible that this was a guy who had never stood in front of a judge before. While there were still a lot of gaping holes in his story, from the episode in the projects to the Archie DeAngelo fairy tale, for the first time I considered that maybe Virgil Shepherd was just a delusional alcoholic who had managed to teach himself Italian and who had figured out a way to stay off the cops' radar.

Until he met us, of course.

"Look at this crew," I said, nodding at the less than stellar collection of Jerseyites sitting around us. "When the D.A. asks you what happened, what're you going to say?"

Virgil gave me the same look he did squinting at me in the foggy mirror when I asked him about playing my 45s.

"*Non lo so.*"

I had to admit, some of the phrases that I had learned from Dinino (and Nanny) were coming back to me fast and furious.

"Alright, let's think about this," I said, lowering my voice, trying to keep the conversation between the two of us. "What did you think you were doing last Tuesday?"

"*Guida.*" He made a motion like he had his two hands on a steering wheel.

"That's it?"

"*Un favore.*"

"That's all Jackie told you?" I continued, eyeing a pair of deadbeats who were sitting in the aisle across from us, hanging on every word.

"*Si.*"

"Nothing else?"

"No," he said, shaking his head.

Interesting—the words "stealing", "stolen," "wife's car," "insurance money," "bankrupt," "fucking Mazda," didn't seem to enter into the picture.

"He told you which car to pick up?"

Virgil nodded.

"*Il giaguro,*" he said, then added, "*Nel garage.*"

"Excuse me!" I snapped, and the two deadbeats fixed their bug eyes front and center on the judge's still-empty bench.

"So if you were supposed to be doing Jackie a favor, why'd you drink so much?"

He looked at me and shrugged his large Armani-clad shoulders.

"All right," I said, my voice just above a whisper, "ready? Here's your story. You were drunk and you went to the wrong house," I said. "You found the keys in the car. When you heard the sirens, you panicked and put the car in Reverse instead of Park. You never meant to smash anything, you never meant to hurt anybody. You got confused." I tried to think of the word Dinino used when one of the kids in the arcade lost it. *"Sfasato?"*

Virgil nodded.

"The beauty of this state is that they don't really give a shit about what happened. They're looking for a payout. We take care of the fines, and we go back to the city. All of this is really about money."

Virgil nodded. When he spoke again his voice was just above a whisper. *"Grazie,"* he said.

I checked the Bulgari: 9:59. There was still no sign of Jackie, or our lawyer for that matter. From the way the bailiff was adjusting his belt and pulling up his pants, it looked like he was just about ready to kick things off.

There was only one thing wrong thing with the silver-lining scenario I had just painted for Virgil—it wasn't true. On a good day, the cops we dealt with on the night of my birthday were vengeful pricks. Now that they'd had a week to think about their smashed cars and their bruised egos, I'm sure they were looking forward to keeping Virgil around for a rematch.

I watched the judge enter the chamber and head straight to the bench, all three hundred plus pounds of him, the black robes definitely not making him look any slimmer. When he finally sat and peered over his courtroom, it was obvious from the look of impatience on his face that he was thinking about one thing—a long lunch.

"All rise," the bailiff said. "The Court is now in session, the Honorable Judge Philip Lockhart presiding."

"That's him," I said to Virgil. I had heard Chopsticks slip and call the judge by his name on the phone. "That's our judge."

But Virgil noticed the lack of enthusiasm in my voice as we sat down again.

"*Stai bene?*"

"Terrific," I lied.

Thirty seconds later, I saw the two cops (minus Chopsticks) slip into the courtroom from a side door. The motherfuckers *did* have neck braces on. The court personnel scrambled out of their way as though the cops were war heroes, and the two of them settled into seats in the first row.

I turned sideways and looked at Virgil in my Armani sweater. All I could picture were the bruises on his back that he was trying to hide under my Elvis towel. Then I stood up again.

"Take a walk with me," I said to Virgil.

He looked confused.

"*Non capisco.*"

After two dozen "Excuse me's," dirty looks, and psycho stares, I slid into the seat next to Porno cop.

"Remember us?"

He turned his neck brace and grinned when he saw my face. His partner laughed when he noticed my black eyes. But the expressions changed when they saw me pointing at the scuffed tips of their boots.

"We need to talk," I said. Then I pointed up at the judge. "Him, too."

CHAPTER TWENTY-THREE

"Ruby Tuesday"

BY THE TIME I GOT BACK TO MANHATTAN, it was after five o'clock. None of the upstanding cab drivers in the town of Dorwood would agree to drive me back into New York City, so I ended up taking fucking mass transit: two buses to get to a place called Harrison, where I was finally able to track down the PATH to take me to the World Trade Center.

The buzz on the street, the good will, and the general giddiness of Christmas week in downtown Manhattan were light years from what I was feeling as I stepped out of the train station and headed west. Walking up Varick Street towards the Onion, past the two-deep bars, the restaurants advertising Christmas Eve *prix fixe* specials, the liquor stores with their red-and-green window displays of Holiday booze guaranteeing a Holly Jolly bender, well-bundled people carrying shopping bags of silver- and gold-wrapped boxes, I was in the most miserable mood of my life.

The cops back in Dorwood had pretty much reacted the way I thought they would. They tried to put us both in handcuffs, until I convinced Virgil to stand on the bench and pull up the Armani sweater. The deep toe-prints on his back had morphed into a blue-black Van Gogh sky that caused quite a stir in the front of the courtroom. When the Honorable Judge Lockhurst noticed the commotion, he called a ten-minute recess, and the five of us found ourselves in his chambers.

That's when I played the Ralphie card.

I told them that a highly respected newspaper (I didn't tell them it was the *Village Voice*) would have pictures of Virgil's bruises in living color on the front page of tomorrow's edition, along with snapshots of their boots and a candid statement by yours truly about the bribes, if we couldn't come to some immediate understanding. The cops went nuts, but the wise Judge Lockhurst was a little more empathetic. In less than twenty minutes, the charges disappeared, and Virgil Shepherd, the vehicular terror of Dorwood, NJ, was a free man.

I let them keep the bribes for their time, asked them to give our best to Chopsticks, and walked out of the courthouse with the twenty grand in bail money.

But whatever optimism I had managed to drum up after getting the money back was very short-lived, along with any thought of making last call at the cemetery before the gates were locked. I wanted to finally part with Virgil Shepherd, get the money to Sally and return to the frame of mind I had been in right after Laura walked out of the funeral office. I was extraordinarily intent on getting drunk, and then getting really drunk.

As soon as we turned the corner onto Hudson, I saw Nadia the bagel girl standing in front of Ivar's store. She was crying.

"Brendan got shit beat into him."

"What?"

"They took him in ambulance."

"When was this?"

"Yesterday night."

"How?"

"Talk to Ivar. He said bad guys were looking for you and Jackie."

Fuck.

Nadia looked to the Onion and then back to me, using the sleeves from her black hoodie to blot the tears on her cheeks. I hugged her, kissed her on the top of her head, and told her (very convincingly, although how could I believe a word of it?) that Brendan would be all right. Then I ran over to St. Vincent's in three minutes, Virgil keeping pace with me the whole way.

St. Vincent's Hospital was on Seventh Avenue and 12th street. It had been there forever, one of the oldest hospitals in the city. To call it "run-down" would be a compliment, but it always seemed to rise to the occasion, especially over the last decade and a half when AIDS did its terrible number on the neighborhood. Each one of its pale green corridors, once you got past the disinfectant, smelled like the history of New York for the last hundred years: births, deaths, riots, celebrations, parties, fires, triumphs, and catastrophes. The patched-up cushions on the gurneys lining the emergency room screamed, *Don't let me die here*, but the staff was amazingly good at keeping people alive. Some of the old-timers from Sullivan Street had passed at St. Vincent's, but we had plenty of Romano births here, too, including my father fifty-four years before. Due to bureaucratic bullshit and funding issues, there were always dire rumors in the papers and in the neighborhood that the demise of the hospital was imminent, but then how would we live without the last-call ambulance sirens at four the morning?

We bolted through the Emergency Room doors.

"Excuse me, I need some help," I said to a nurse in the first cubicle I saw.

A middle-aged Latina in red scrubs, she glanced at my face for a split second and then handed over a clipboard and a pen. She was wearing a pair of heavy-duty purple surgical gloves that would've given Jojo's mittens a run for their money.

"Sir, just fill this out and take a seat. Triage will call you in a few minutes."

"No, I need to *see* someone."

"I understand, sir," she said patiently. "I promise, someone will see you in a few minutes. Just please fill out the form on the clipboard."

Why couldn't anyone understand me anymore?

"I need to *visit* someone."

"Oh," she said, still eyeing my bruises. She nodded and took her clipboard back.

By the time we tracked Brendan down he had been settled into a private room on the fourth floor. According to the nurses at the desk, he was more banged up than anything else, although the outside possibility of internal bleeding was something the doctors wanted to keep an eye on for at least another forty-eight hours. The three cracked ribs and a bruised sternum would heal themselves in a couple of months.

The hospital room looked exactly like the one in my Dinino dream, minus the mural of ferocious animals. I pulled the curtain back slowly and pushed a chair alongside the bed. Virgil walked around the other side and stood next to the crucifix on the wall. Brendan was hooked up to four different monitors, and his left side was bandaged over. His lower lip looked like a box spring.

"Hey."

His eyes got brighter when he realized it was us, though it was obvious from the size of his pupils that he was on some top-flight sedation.

"Remember the time," he said, speaking in a measured, opiate-laden rhythm, "when you told the drunk fireman to keep his hands off me?"

"Yeah, I do."

"We're even."

When he tried to put his lips together to form a smile his right hand reached for his side.

"The nurse at the desk told us about your ribs," I said, and leaned over the bedside bars to raise the blanket a little. "She said give them a few weeks, and you'll be back behind the stick like this never happened."

"Can't wait," he whispered, looking like the only stick Brendan had on his mind was a morphine lollipop. I peeked at the label on his I.V. bag.

"They got you on the good stuff," I said. (Just what I suspected, but with a codeine chaser.) "Beats Jackie's watered-down Remy Martin."

There was a large bouquet of flowers on the table next to the window, along with a plastic water pitcher and a sad little unopened tub of applesauce. The blinds were drawn, shutting out the lights from Seventh Avenue and throwing the far corner of the room, where Virgil was still standing, into shadow.

"Nice flowers," I said.

"My kids were here before. Cheryl drove them up to see their poor battered father."

Cheryl. That's right. I did know that. Maybe the fog was starting to lift.

"How'd you find out?"

"Nadia. I never saw her so emotional," I said, and then decided to stop being glib. "Actually, she was crying hysterically."

Brendan was visibly moved by this info and closed his eyes for a half a minute to regroup. When he started to speak again, there was anger in his voice.

"The police came by. They think it's a bias crime. I told them a couple of guys I never saw before got carried away."

"You should have told them the truth."

He seemed to consider this.

"The fat boy did call me nigger."

Anthony.

"Butchie was there, too?"

Brendan closed his eyes, took a deep breath through his nostrils.

"I wasn't a nigger when I was pouring him free drinks and listening to his bullshit for ten years when he came in for his envelopes."

"That's the way they are," I said. I was especially thinking about their boss. For all his sheen of refinement and tuxedo-clad cool, Sally was the one who had sent them to the bar to make a statement. His henchmen would never have made that move without the consent of the boss.

"Stupid me, I thought it was business as usual," he laughed bitterly. "Like church, a second collection before the Holidays, until Butchie's sidekick pulled out the bat."

Most likely the same bat Butchie used every ounce of self-control he had in his body not to bring down on Anthony's fat head. Talk about irony. I could see Brendan was getting more agitated.

"Squeeze the pain pump."

Brendan pushed on it a couple of times and then looked over at Virgil.

"How are you, Virgil?"

Virgil moved a little closer to the bed rail. "*Bene*," he said. But the expression on his face when he looked down at Brendan was anything but *bene*.

"Your friend handled himself real well this morning."

"What's today?"

"Tuesday," I said, and very gently slid the pump out of his hand and laid it on the blanket next to him.

"That's great," Brendan said, letting the words out slowly. His eyelids fluttered for a second and then drifted close.

An announcement about the end of visiting hours came over the speaker. As if on cue, a nurse stuck her "He's mine now" face in front of the curtain to see how many of us she would have to kick out. I smiled and held up my index finger for one more minute. She narrowed her eyes with a mock look of *Don't fuck with me*, said, "I'll be back in *two* minutes," and left the room.

I looked over at Virgil and stood up. "*I'll* be back tomorrow," I said. "You need anything?"

"I do," he said very softly.

"What do you need?"

Brendan shook his head slightly. "Promise me you're not going to be an asshole about this."

Me? An asshole? That promise had been out of my hands for a while now.

"Absolutely," I said, and put my hand very carefully on his shoulder. "The two of us took enough beatings for one week."

He looked up at me—the pupils of his eyes were spinning like pinballs. "That wasn't a promise."

"I promise."

"Thank you," he said. He closed his eyes and floated off like a dope fiend.

TAKING THE CREAKY ELEVATOR BACK DOWN to the lobby, I thought about what I had just promised Brendan, and realized it was the truth. I'd been a complete asshole in the Cathode Club with the bouncers, but that didn't mean I was going to stop at Astor Place for a quick Mohawk and then pull a Travis Bickle, charging into Sally's club with guns blazing. I may have become a lot of things in the past two years, but a shooter wasn't one of them. I had never fired a gun in my life and wanted to keep it that way. I knew my father kept a pistol somewhere in the house, but I'd never felt compelled to track it down and blast a few tin cans off the back deck. Michael actually had a permit to carry, but that was about the large wads of cash he often trekked from the market to his Cherokee Chief parked in the lot sixty feet away under the shadow of the FDR Drive. I wasn't about to go out and exact my revenge in a hail of bullets. And I wasn't crazy, either. People had guns in the club. That was part of the territory. I wasn't going to be a jackass, at least not in that way.

So the problem was, how could I get even with these pieces of shit without turning it into a bloodbath? I could opt not to pay, but that would only create more excuses for them to do terrible things to the people around us. I could pretend that everything was good, pay off what I could, then wait for an opportunity to get back at them—but there was no way I had that much self-control after I saw what they had done to Brendan. Seeing my friend banged up like that because of my own selfishness and stupidity broke my heart—again.

And if I was finally going to be honest with myself for a change, it was more than Brendan. It was Evan. It was Dinino. It was Laura. What had set this insane chain of events into place? Was it Laura and the show, or Zenon sending a bolt of electricity into my body? Was it Courtney's car? Was it Carlin Browne showing up on the set, or Virgil materializing at the precinct? Was it Jackie disappearing? Was it me sending my career down the drain? Was it too many drinks, too many six a.m. breakfasts, too much time spent with people who would fuck you in a second if it meant putting an extra twenty in their pockets? In the end it was all of those things, but it was really only one. And it had been in the works for a long time.

As I stepped out of the hospital onto West 12th Street, I also realized something else. I didn't want a drink anymore. Actually, the last thing I wanted was a drink. A part of my brain must have sensed that I was going to need a clear head. When the time came, I would trust my instincts and improvise, then figure out where that would take me.

But first I had to get on with the business of making whatever I was going to do a one-man show.

CHAPTER TWENTY-FOUR

"Could This Be Magic"

T HE ACTION DIDN'T BEGIN IN THE CLUB until after eleven, which gave me a couple of hours to kill. There had been a moment on our way out of the courthouse when I thought about putting some money in Virgil's hand and leaving him at the Staten Island ferry. But by the time we got back to Manhattan it was after four o'clock. There was no way I was going to make it over to the cemetery before the gray sky turned black and the gates were closed for the night. And when we found out about Brendan, I felt a little bad about cutting Virgil loose, especially when I saw the look on his face in the hospital room.

I could swear he started to shake when he first saw Brendan connected to all the tubes and monitors, although maybe it was alcohol withdrawal. Unless he had an airport bottle with him on our trip into Jersey, he probably hadn't had a taste since we supposedly downed a bottle of vodka at our record bash the night before. Now, walking alongside me as we headed down Seventh Avenue, Virgil looked "mushy," as Nanny liked to say. It was a word she used whenever any

of her grandchildren got a little overwhelmed in her presence and didn't
rise to the level of intensity she brought to her daily encounters.

After seeing what they had done to Brendan, I was in no mood for
conversation myself. So I settled for a last supper at a pizza place I
knew on Bleecker. The food was good, the place was primarily take-
out, and the owner, once he hugged everybody hello, couldn't stay still
long enough for a lengthy Q and A.

Bobby was one of those big-hearted Neopolitans who was always
in motion. His bushy black mustache covered a third of his face, and
the wild waves of his thick black hair were rarely heading to the same
shore. A big basketball fan (and a decent bettor), Bobby had on his
blue and orange New York Knicks sweatshirt under his tomato sauce-
splattered apron, in anticipation of the big rematch with the Heat in
twenty-four hours. If you caught him out of the corner of your eye, he
looked a lot like a Jackson Pollock painting, minus the frame.

After he bear-hugged me hello and heartily shook Virgil's hand, we
sat down at one of the two tables in the back and soaked up the orange
heat from the pizza oven. Garcia the cook, dressed like his boss but
half as tall, immediately brought us two large glasses of house red. (I
know—but for someone raised with Italian grandparents, that didn't
qualify as drinking.)

I took a sip. Virgil drank his wine down in one gulp.

"Brendan's going to be all right," I said, more to rally his spirits
than to convince myself. "Those nurses are sharp, and he's such a great
guy, they'll want to take extra good care of him. If the next few days
are stable, he'll be out by the weekend." (Christmas in a hospital bed
won't be a lot of fun, I thought, but at least I'd be up there to keep him
company.)

Virgil stayed quiet, his deep brown eyes wandering around the pizzeria, which, between the strings of Christmas lights looped over the

wall paneling and the cheaply framed posters of Italian soccer teams, wasn't all that riveting.

He hadn't taken my coat off yet, even though we were five feet from the oven, and he kept the collar up. What struck me, without the distraction of the scar, was how smooth the rest of the skin on his face was, especially now that he had shaved. This didn't look like a man who had spent his days and nights on the street.

Nobody has skin like the Hungarians, and obviously he was forty shades darker, but Virgil's face had the same glow that Elsie and Pamela had been blessed with. How crazy was that? When I first saw him in the cell in Jersey, I'd figured he was close to fifty. But now, sitting face to face across a small table, I realized that my math was way off.

He was staring at the flames in the pizza oven but turned back to me when he realized I was studying him.

"The flames, they are hot," he said.

"Bobby's old school. Only wood," I said, and then added, "Very crispy."

"*Proprio come le anime dei dannati.*"

I had no idea what he had just said, but he seemed to get a kick out of it. He reached into his pocket, took out Jackie's pen and started writing something down.

"Could I take a look?"

When he was finished, he pushed the napkin toward me. I read the words out loud, stumbling through the pronunciation, as Bobby slid a steaming pizza and a basket of garlic knots on the table in front of us.

"*Minchia*, whose souls are damned?" he asked, laughing.

"What?"

"You just said, like the souls of the damned."

I looked at Virgil.

"I was just reading what he wrote."

"You speak Italian?" Bobby asked Virgil.

"*Si.*"

"*Come conosci Johnny?*"

"Sono stato mandato per salvare la sua anima."

"*Minchia*," Bobby laughed. "Garcia, we're gonna need some more wine at this table."

Then Bobby turned to me, still smiling.

"Johnny, where'd you find this guy?"

"Jackie's bar."

"*Minchia*," Bobby said, again eyeing my wounds, then sizing up Virgil. "Wouldn't be a bad bodyguard." He laughed and headed back to the counter, where a couple of customers were waiting for pick up.

Virgil put a slice of pizza on his plate and took a bite as Garcia refilled our wine glasses.

"*Grazie.*"

"What was that business with Bobby about souls?"

Virgil took the napkin from the table and very carefully tucked it into his pocket.

"I don't understand what you wrote," I said. "Are you talking about Dinino?"

But how could he have known what I was thinking back in the funeral parlor?

He shook his head.

"*Devi fidarti di me*," he said. "You must trust me."

"Trust you with what? Why do I have to trust you?"

He reached for another napkin and started writing down words in Italian like his life depended on it

"*A te convien tenere altro viaggio se vuo' campare d'esto loco selvaggio.*"

I pulled the receipt out of the pocket of my coat and put it on the table.

"Why'd you leave this in the car?"

"For you," he said quietly. "To know."

I looked over the words that Philomena had told me to write down. Then I took a second sip of wine, this one much heartier than the first. Virgil's glass was empty again.

Even though the fiftyish Bobby had been born a true pizza maker from Naples, he grew up in the Bronx, not too far from the legendary Arthur Avenue and another famous Italian-American singer. His love for doo-wop and all things Dion translated into a soundtrack for the pizzeria that favored street-corner records from the late-fifties and early-sixties. I was so focused on trying to figure out what Virgil was not saying that I hadn't picked up on the music. But filling the space between Virgil and me were the beautiful voices of The Dubs singing "Could This Be Magic."

Virgil stopped writing and looked up.

"You know The Dubs?"

"*Magnifico.*"

I was waiting for him to break out in song, but this time he just listened. I closed my eyes and let the harmonies coming out of the speaker on the back wall fill my ears. For a hole-in-the-wall pizza place, I had to give Bobby credit. He had a terrific sound system. Listening to the Dubs sing, I thought about how soft Laura's lips were when she kissed me goodbye.

When I opened my eyes, Bobby was hovering over the table. He was looking at us suspiciously.

"What's wrong?" he said.

He was staring down at our plates.

"You're not eatin'."

Virgil spoke up.

"The pizza. . .deliziosa. L'appetito. . .non e cosi buona."

Bobby looked at Virgil with the most serious look I had ever seen above his mustache. Then he said: "Let me wrap it up."

"Grazie."

"Fellas," Bobby said, picking up our pizza tray and pointing to a table by the front window, "I'll be right back. Help yourselves."

A small folding table draped with a plastic red tablecloth had been set up across from the counter. The scrawny Christmas tree was dwarfed by an impressive array of Holiday favorites—a bottle of Baileys, anisette (nice old school touch), Frangelico, a bottle of whiskey, and a platter of *pignoli* cookies and *struffoli*. There was a sleeve of two-ounce plastic cups on the table and a stack of green napkins.

Virgil's eyes moved past the cookies and the honey balls but caught fire when he zeroed in on the bottle of Jameson.

"Go 'head," I said.

I pushed the sleeve of my leather coat up and looked at the Bulgari—the clock was ticking. Virgil stood up, walked over and filled his wine glass to the brim with whiskey, then brought the glass and the bottle back to our table.

THE TEMPERATURE MUST HAVE DROPPED another five degrees as we made our way over to the corner of Bleecker and Sixth. Two enterprising hustlers had set up a makeshift Christmas tree operation on the corner. They were doing a pretty brisk business, moving what was left of the forest into the apartments over the storefronts on Sixth and Seventh and into the luxury buildings opposite the park two blocks away on lower Fifth. All the people who had been too busy making money over the past few weeks must have suddenly realized that they were down a tree.

They were dragging the last specimens past us over the cold sidewalks up and down Sixth. I took a deep, painful breath and let the smell of half-dead spruce fill my nostrils.

Just under the deal-making and the sound of the buzz saw I could make out an instrumental version of "O Holy Night."

"You got the food?" I asked.

Virgil held up the white paper bag, which, thanks to good-hearted Bobby, had a few extra delicacies packed in with our uneaten pizza.

"You got the whiskey?"

Virgil pulled the neck of the bottle of Jameson, another gift, from the side pocket in my Brando coat.

"You got your Gap bag?"

Virgil held up the blue bag with his other hand.

"You got some place you could go tonight?"

Virgil nodded his head unconvincingly.

"You want to stop back at my apartment and get another coat?"

He looked down at my ex-coat.

"*Perfecto.*"

Virgil was already swaying a little in the frigid wind that was running cross-town. I tried to imagine where this night would take him, but I was having a hard enough time figuring out where it would take *me*. I told myself, if he hadn't gotten blitzed in the first place, he could've just driven Courtney's car away and maybe none of this would've happened. But the time for that fantasy had come and gone. So what if he sang in tune (and in English) when he was drunk? So what if he was upset about Brendan? So what if he said I had to trust him? Did that mean I had to feel bad about wrapping this up and figuring out my next move?

I looked at the man standing in front of me. Just his size—and that scar—would send most people running. Who knew why he was homeless, what crazy things he had seen, where he stayed? What the hell he was writing down on those napkins he kept stuffing in his pocket? I had managed to avoid thinking about his side of the story for as long as I could. Now was not the time to start, especially since I'd be walking into Sally's club without any hint of a plan in less than an hour.

He had a bag of food and a bottle of whiskey. He was wearing better clothes, and he wasn't spending a single night in prison, or New Jersey, for that matter. So why did I feel like shit when I held out my hand to shake goodbye?

I reached into my coat and pulled out a hundred-dollar bill.

"I want you to take this."

Virgil took a step back and shook his head. "No."

"Just put it in your pocket."

"You've done enough for me already."

There wasn't a trace of irony in his voice.

"That's exactly why I want you to have it."

"*Non lo voglio,*" he said, waving the money away.

"I got news for you," I said and smiled. "Neither do I."

CHAPTER TWENTY-FIVE

"Jingle Bell Rock"

S INCE SALLY HAD ENOUGH ROMAN CATHOLIC in him to close the club on Christmas Eve, the night before was wall-to-wall, three-deep at the bar, every seat at the tables taken. The roulette table seemed to be an especially big hit with the gumadas. Decked out in shiny low-cut dresses, black bras, lace-up heels and very expensive hair, they had formed a double semi-circle around the wheel, trying to parlay their Christmas clubs into plane tickets to Aruba. I had to give them credit—the gumadas knew exactly what they wanted for Christmas.

I was hoping to share some choice season's greetings with Anthony in the lobby, but another fat youth stood guard by the door, not a chair in sight. I'm sure Anthony II had been told to expect me—at the mention of my name, some dim form of awareness flickered in his dull eye sockets, and he walked me, already winded, over to the elevator.

I scanned the casino for familiar faces, thinking that maybe Jackie would turn up, but aside from JW, the ex-body building bouncer who greeted the elevator on the third floor, Sally's regular dealers and Connie, there was no one there I knew. I caught bits of half-assed conversations about money and sex and midnight mass at St. Patrick's. I thought about heading straight to the office for my audience of one with Mr. Tosterelli, but my ex-breakfast partner and favorite mob temptress would have been highly insulted if I didn't stop at the bar. At this stage of the game, the last thing I needed was more drama.

Connie, dressed in a strapless red jumpsuit, looked like she could have been the Christmas edition of one of Zenon's perverse helpers. She saw me (always alert) while she was pouring out glasses of Maker's at the far end of the bar and immediately made her way over.

"Oh. . .my. . .God!"

She was looking at me like someone had taken a paintball gun to the ceiling of the Sistine chapel. I took a step back.

"What happened to your face?"

"Stupidity."

"Oh, my God."

"You said that already."

Connie waved me closer, leaned across the bar, and very softly licked the bruise above my left eye. Then she whispered in my ear, "You still have your dimples?"

"They're there somewhere," I said.

This seemed to reassure her a little, and she leaned back.

"What're you drinking?"

"Club soda."

Connie rolled her eyes under a line of green eyeshadow, another nice Holiday touch. Just past the crap table, I saw the sea of tuxes and evening dresses part, and Butchie, like an Orca mowing through a pod of penguins, barreled up to me, a vicious smirk appearing on his face.

"Hey, I see you're a popular guy," he said, nodding at my bruises. "They did a nice job." He laughed approvingly. "I guess I should feel lucky that I got to your fag bartender in time."

Breathe, I thought. Deal with Sally first. Work the diaphragm. Keep your cool. Maybe even act a little.

"You proud of that?"

"Just a friendly reminder," Butchie said. "Just in case you and Jackie forgot about tonight. Believe me, Anthony was enjoying himself. It's a good thing I like Brandon."

You just put my friend in the hospital, you giant piece of shit. The least you could do is get his name right.

"I heard," I said casually.

I could see the comment hit home.

"What's that mean?"

Exhale.

"Nothing," I said, taking a sip of my soda. Breathe in through one nostril, out the other.

But he wouldn't let it go, which I knew would happen, especially in front of Connie.

"You heard *what*?"

I flashed Connie a smile, hopefully with some dimples.

"Hey, Connie," I said, "when a guy enjoys going to a bar, spending some quality time with the bartender, there's nothing peculiar about that, right?"

Connie, being the shrewd study of human dynamics that she was, nodded her assent. "I've never thought so," she said. "As long as they leave a big tip."

And just for good measure, I winked at Butchie and took a healthy look down Connie's halter.

I saw Connie's eyes shift from my face to a place over my right shoulder. Fat Anthony the First had lumbered over to my side. A black suit had replaced the jogging outfit—maybe he'd gotten a promotion for a job well done on Brendan's rib cage. He also smirked when he saw my face.

"Sally's ready for you."

MR. TOSTERELLI WAS SEATED BEHIND HIS DESK when Anthony ushered me into his office, his eyes moving from the closed-circuit monitor to my face. A single china coffee cup sat on the glass surface next to the phone. He waved me over to the chair and nodded for me to sit down.

"Where's your partner?" Sally asked.

"I don't know," I answered truthfully.

"Not surprising," Sally said. "He'll surface."

I didn't know if Sally had some knowledge that I wasn't aware of, but he didn't look or sound too concerned that my partner wasn't occupying the chair next to me. More resigned than anything. His voice was measured, calm, as if he was on the phone with a travel agent.

"Jackie Parker's like a buoy in a hurricane—everything else is swept away and he pops up two weeks later," he said. "He's been pulling this disappearing act for years. Let me guess—his latest wife's fucked him over." Sally shook his head. "It's always the same story. He could never get past a pair of big tits."

"I'm sure I'll see him soon."

"Yeah, me, too," Sally said, and then laughed. "You know he's nuts, right? Every four, five years he goes off the rails. Ends up in the bin. I think he's got—what do they call that, a Napoleonic complex?" Sally laughed. "I mean, he's got other things, too. Poor fuck."

Sally glanced back at the closed-circuit TV, studied the screen for a couple of seconds, then looked back at me. "I heard his father was the same way. Lost his mind over a go-go dancer," Sally said. "Poor fuck senior."

I didn't know what to say to any of this, so I kept my mouth shut. Sure, Jackie had always been up and down, at times a little erratic, with delusions of grandeur, but that was every other actor I knew. Why was he giving me the psychiatric history of the Parker family?

Sally was measuring me across his desk, watching for my reaction. He was so low-key, so unlike the way Butchie was seething in the casino, that I had to admit I was a little thrown off. There was just a hint of pink in his cheeks, but I also knew that could change quickly.

"You know how many times I've owned that bar over the years? I take it when he goes away. I make some money, then I give him the keys back when he straightens his head out and he can pay the vig again." Sally took a sip of expresso from the cup on his desk. "The Black guy he's got there does a great job keeping it running," Sally added, "whether he's working for him or for us."

I couldn't be sure whether Sally was telling me the truth or trying to make me feel like an even bigger asshole. Either way, it was time for me to get some color into his face.

"So if you like Brendan so much, why did you send Butchie and Anthony down to the bar?"

"Every now and then they get something in their head, you got to let them do these things. Gets the blood up."

"You let them put Brendan in the hospital with three cracked ribs to get their blood up?"

"That's the way they think," Sally said matter-of-factly. "What're you going to do? They weren't going to kill him. And if either of you had the brains to pay your debts when you were supposed to, it would've never come to that." He pushed the cup away from him and straightened up in his chair. "Now what do you got for me?"

I pulled the envelope out of my coat and placed it next to the empty cup. He pushed back in his chair, his face still not betraying any color, as if this were just one more test to which he already had all the answers.

"You know something?" he said, raising his voice slightly but still trying to keep the tone neutral, "I don't know what happened to you. You used to walk in here with your nice clothes, have a drink, tell us a funny story, share a little inside entertainment bullshit. To be honest, I never thought of you as an earner. But of all the wannabees hanging around here, at least you looked the part. I didn't mind you hanging around."

Of course, these were thoughts that I had considered myself over the past week, but Sally expressed them perfectly. It was impressive how good people were getting at summing up my life, or at least the last few years of it.

When he reached for the money, he knew exactly how light the envelope was and what he had to do about it.

He nodded at my wrist.

"Take off the watch."

A flush of rose in his cheeks, not much more than that. I slipped the Bulgari off my wrist and handed it to him.

"Beautiful piece of jewelry," he said. He looked at it approvingly. "I'd say about ten grand?" When I didn't respond, he added, "We're even."

He placed the watch back on his desk, where the glass surface made it glow.

"Now get out of here. Your book is closed. If you ever try to take a bet in this city or set foot near this club, that would be a bad decision. Stay away from the Onion, too. That's between me and your ex-partner. Any money you have out on the street, Butchie and Anthony will collect. Nobody's going to pay you anyway."

He saw me look down at Dinino's watch.

"Am I clear?"

I stood up.

"We're done," he said.

I took three steps toward the office door, then turned around. "You remember that conversation we had about *Othello*? When you said you and Butchie were Iago?"

This last bit did actually seem to throw him off a little. "Yeah. And?"

"You do realize that, after the play ends, they torture the shit out of that miserable fuck."

Sally sat up in his chair and smiled, but his face was the color of open-heart surgery. "Should I consider that a threat?"

I smiled back. "Don't let it get your blood up."

I SHOULDERED MY BODY THROUGH THE CROWD and pushed myself into a space at the bar. Connie reached for the bottle of Absolut and filled a soda glass, dropping two ice cubes and a wedge of lemon in for good measure.

"I think we should skip the club soda," she said.

I wasn't sure how much Connie knew about the details of our meltdown, but the expression on her face was equal parts concern (like she wanted to hug me), lust (like she wanted to fuck me), and self-satisfaction (like this is what you get for not fucking me when you had the chance). It was not something I wanted to think about any more.

"As a matter of fact, skip the drink," I said. "I'm done."

She curled her long fingernails, decorated with Christmas trees, over the veins in my wrist and leaned over the counter.

"What can I do?"

When no response came out of my mouth fast enough, she pulled back and smiled. "Think about it," she said, "while I bring another drink to your friend."

I thought Connie was being sarcastic until I watched her pour out a glass of Cutty Sark and look down the length of the bar. That's when I saw the Camel coat. Virgil was at the other end, glass in hand. He leaned forward and waved.

I was standing next to him in a second and a half. "How'd you get in here?" I said, trying to curb the rising panic in my voice. He looked just as he had when I left him on Sixth Avenue, only much drunker. The blue Gap bag was between his legs.

"I give the hundred dollars to the man downstairs."

Virgil smiled and held up his empty glass of scotch, jiggling the ice cubes like it was the most natural thing in the world.

"We got to go."

"*E per nulla offensione che mi sia fatta,*" he said, "*non temer tu, ch'i' ho le cose conte, per ch'altra volta fui a tal baratta.*"

He delivered the words with great calm, but it was obvious from the burning intensity in his eyes that, whatever he had just said, he believed from the bottom of his soul.

"Johnny, introduce me to your friend."

Connie had appeared in front of us, delivering a refill for Virgil and my quadruple Absolut.

To this day I still don't know why I didn't grab him by my overcoat and drag him out of the casino. Elsie claimed it was my flair for the dramatic. Nanny claimed I wasn't being alert. Anybody else I've told the story to said it was probably my desire to commit suicide in the most spectacular manner possible.

Whatever the reason was, I finished my drink in two gulps and pointed to the empty glass for a refill.

"*Very* pleased to meet any friend of Johnny Romano's." Connie dangled her right hand out over the counter like God in Michelangelo's fresco.

I had never seen a Black man blush before, but Virgil's face got shinier. He didn't say a word, but from his expression it was obvious that he appreciated Connie's Santa suit.

After a moment of hesitation, he reached his huge hand over our glasses and shook her fingers delicately, much to Connie's amusement. When I turned, Butchie was standing next to us.

"I should've figured he belonged to you," Butchie said. "Fags, moulies. You got any other garbage you want us to take out?"

With no witty comeback springing immediately to mind, I nailed Butchie with a sharp right to the side of his nose. His body wobbled backwards into a clique of startled customers, knocking them all to the floor like dominoes. Then I looked down at my hand. Three of my knuckles were bloody, a major improvement from my episode at the Cathode Club.

It was funny, but after I hit him I felt cemented to the spot, like a dream where my feet were too heavy for my body. In the pandemonium that followed the only thing I heard was Bobby Helm's voice singing "Jingle Bell Rock" out of the speaker in the ceiling.

By the time I realized that Anthony had wrapped his giant hands around my throat, it was too late to do anything but gasp for air.

After thirty years of breathing freely, not getting any oxygen into my windpipe sent my body into shock. As Anthony pressed his fingers deeper into my neck, I watched what happened next with a peculiar combination of resignation and fascination. Dragging me backwards towards Sally's office, Anthony the First gave me a bird's eye view of Butchie as he climbed to his feet, blood pouring from his nose into his hands, which he wiped on the suit of the guy standing next to him. Then he moved toward the two of us, holding the neck of an Absolut bottle in his right hand. As he raised the glass bottle over my head Virgil took him down with a perfectly placed elbow to his throat. For the second time in sixty seconds Butchie went flying, this time into the crap table ten feet away.

People ran for the elevator, tables were thrown over, and chips flew in a hundred different directions. Anthony let go of me and lunged at Virgil as I slumped to the floor, desperate for air. All I saw was a parade of Italian loafers and gumada pumps moving past my face and emptying out of the casino. Even the loyal dealers had split. It was essential personnel only.

When I caught sight of Virgil again, Anthony and the bouncer JW had his head pinned to the counter of the bar.

Butchie was sitting on the floor in front of the crap table, his hands wrapped around his own neck for a change, gasping and coughing, his nose still bleeding. His gun was lying on the carpet about five feet away from me. I picked up the Absolut bottle and threw it against the wall, just to get everybody's attention. Then I picked up the revolver.

"You're fuckin' dead," Anthony croaked, breathing heavily.

I aimed the gun directly at Anthony's fat head.

"Get away from him," I said.

Anthony and JW each took a couple of steps back. Virgil looked surprised as hell when he lifted his head and saw that I was the one who was holding the gun.

I steadied my voice and said, "Walk over to me."

Anthony took a step forward. I looked at him and shook my head. "Not you, asshole." I pointed at Virgil. "Him."

Straightening up slowly, Virgil took four steps in my direction, then teetered forward and fell to his knees about halfway down the length of the bar.

At some point Sally must have stepped out of his office. He surveyed the damage to the club, looked down at Virgil, then spoke very softly to me. I noticed that he had already slipped the Bulgari on his wrist. "You want to be a player?" he asked from across the room. When I didn't say anything, he added, "You want to be one of us? Wasn't that the point of all of this? Then put the gun down."

I have to admit, I wasn't surprised that Sally was the calmest person in the room. How do you not have a certain level of poise when you run a Mob casino in the heart of Manhattan? But what he said next went way beyond composure. "Better yet," Sally said, and looked at Virgil again. "Shoot him."

Virgil was still on his knees, but he had put his hands down on the rug to hold his chest up. His head was bowed to the floor.

"Listen to me," Sally continued. "You really fucked us here. This is serious business. This is not something you walk away from. You want to make it right? Shoot him."

All I could hear was the sound of Zenon's voice in my ears: "What's wrong with you?" "That's the best you got?" "Give it to him."

But who was she talking about?

"It's just us. Nobody else here," Sally said quietly. "Just clip him, if you don't have the balls. We'll finish him off."

And, in Zenon's throaty tease, "Shoot again."

I fired one shot at the mirrored panel five feet to the right of Anthony the First's head and paused for effect as chunks of silver glass collapsed to the floor. Nanny had always told us stories about her uncles in Italy, how they were all members of the *carabinieri*. Maybe it was in my blood, or maybe Butchie just had a really good gun. Or maybe I didn't give a fuck anymore. Whatever it was, the recoil wasn't half as bad as I had expected. I sent another shot into the mirror over the blackjack table to the left of them.

Holding the gun as steady as I could, I moved forward and crouched next to Virgil.

"Can you get up?"

He closed his eyes and nodded. "*Si.*"

Leaning his head and chest against me, Virgil managed to get to his feet but was still doubled over. I was starting to think along the lines of a broken spine when he grabbed onto my shoulders and pulled himself up. I took a few steps backward, the gun steady in my right hand. Virgil's hands were on my shoulders, as if we were doing some very fucked-up tango.

Butchie was still on the floor, his back against the side of the crap table, struggling to get some air into his windpipe, making choking, guttural noises. There was pure hatred in his eyes.

Sally stared at me but said nothing. Even though he didn't move a muscle, his face was purple. So much for poise. I felt Virgil slump his head over my shoulder. Terrific, I thought, here's where we both go down. But somehow I was able to hold him up as he struggled to get his balance.

There was one thing left to do. "Connie?"

A high-pitched squeak came from somewhere behind the bar.

"You all right?"

"Yeah."

She still hadn't shown her face.

"Go into Sally's office."

Connie slowly emerged from behind the bar. She looked at Sally, who nodded. Then she tiptoed carefully through the debris. When she reached the door that led to the office, she waved goodbye and blew me a kiss. I heard the door slam behind her.

"Ready?" I said to Virgil, keeping my eyes, and the gun, pointed straight ahead. Sally and Butchie shared a quick glance, trying to read each other's minds. I put one last bullet into the heart of the glass chandelier over the crap table, just to close out the festivities. We stood at the entrance for two seconds and watched as the antique crystals exploded and a kaleidoscope of silver and blue glass rained down to the floor.

Then Virgil and I took the back staircase out of the brownstone.

CHAPTER TWENTY-SIX

I SAT IN THE DARK, THE PICTURE FRAME IN MY LAP. The streetlight on Sullivan Street cast a dull glow on the photograph. The looks on our faces told the whole story.

Chris was sitting on Dinino's stool, which we had pulled up to Zenon. He was chipping away at a giant pistachio ice cream sundae that we had picked up before we headed to the arcade. From the look of intense concentration on his face, Chris could have been working the gold mines in South Africa. Each nugget he found through the layers of chocolate syrup and whipped cream was lined up in sized places on the gameboard. It was a brilliant move only a four-year-old kid (and maybe Jojo) could pull off—order pistachio, and then take out every nut.

Laura was on one side of Chris, and I was on the other. We were smiling at Dinino, who took the picture, after a few choice words and some minor grunting, on Laura's new digital camera.

At this point, maybe a couple of you might be thinking, Johnny Romano has written about all these songs, all these scratchy 45s, all these "momentous" records that held such meaning for him. What was

Laura's song? What was the melody that connected the two of them? What were the lyrics that brought back the smell of her hair and the scent of her perfume? What was the vocal that sent a smile to his lips and a light in his eyes, even when he fucked up his one-line opposite Gillian Anderson on the set of *The X-Files* or when Michigan upset Ohio State last year and everyone bet the underdog?

It was the song that was playing on Dinino's radio in the arcade the moment the picture was taken. Just to torture myself a little more, I pulled the 45 out of its sleeve and put Laura's record under the needle.

"My Cherie Amour."

I sat back in my chair, closed my eyes, and listened to Stevie Wonder's la-la-las, the flute, the beautiful string arrangement, allusions to summer days and cafes, distant clouds and beating hearts. I saw Laura's smile and Chris's pistachios and heard Dinino cursing the camera—and every other moment that had meant the world to me over the past four and a half years.

When I opened my eyes, Virgil was staring at me. He was on the sofa, wrapped in blankets and throws, his two bare feet resting on the rug.

He had hit the white couch as soon as we got back from Sally's, put his hands behind his head, and sacked out immediately, not moving a muscle in two hours. On our journey downtown, before we got back to the apartment, he had insisted that they never laid a hand on him, even though I swore I had seen Anthony the First drive Virgil's head into the corner of the bar a couple of times before I managed to get my hands on Butchie's gun. I have to tell you, I was relieved to see his eyes open.

I moved over to the stereo, picked up the tone arm, put the song on again, and stacked a few gems behind it. Then I settled back in my chair. Virgil pulled the red Christmas throw from around his shoulders, draped it over his legs, and sat up on the sofa, resting his folded hands in his lap. He didn't say anything, just continued to look at me.

It was hard to read his expression with just the streetlight in the room. He seemed there but not quite there, too calm, no movement. I was thinking skull fracture and an imminent return to St. Vincent's when he spoke up.

"*Chiedo scusa.*"

"What?"

"I am sorry. . .for the *confusione.*"

His voice was barely above a whisper. I leaned over, lit a candle on the coffee table, and studied Virgil's face in the flickering light. There were no cuts, no black-and-blues, not one bruise to suggest that he had taken on some of the meanest pricks in the city. The fact that he had just apologized made me assume he thought I was an even bigger asshole than I had suspected.

He leaned his head back and stared up at the cracks in the plaster ceiling. After a minute, I started to get a little nervous and tried to coax him back into the conversation. "The last thing you need to do is apologize," I said.

He tilted his chin forward and fixed me with that same too-calm stare. "*Molto brutto.*"

I thought about his episode in the Avenue D projects. "What do you do, make a career of being at the wrong place at the right time?"

He shrugged, then said, "*Essi volevano.* . .kill you."

I understood that much. Virgil took a deep breath, the heap of blankets slowly rising and falling. Then he shifted his body very slowly to the edge of the sofa and reached out his long arm.

"*Posso io. . . ?*"

I leaned forward and handed him the photo. He held the brass frame by the edges, like a Polaroid that was fresh out of the camera.

"*Bellissima.*"

"Happier times."

Talk about an understatement.

"*Sì.*"

Virgil smiled at the picture.

"Tell me about her."

"What do you want to know?"

"*Una cosa,*" he said, and held up one finger.

I thought about all the things I could say about Laura: how soft her hands were, the way she bent her knees when she played ski ball in the arcade, how she always shakes her head when it starts to rain, the way she hugged Dinino the first time she met him like he was a member of the family. . . .

Virgil was still holding up one finger.

"When Laura hears a song for the first time, she immediately knows all the words," I said. "I've never figured out how she does it. She sings along like she's heard it her whole life."

Virgil nodded.

"*Un regalo. . .*a gift. . .*ancora.*"

"Whenever we go to a restaurant, Laura orders the least expensive thing on the menu, and it tastes so much better than anything I get."

"*Saggia. . . .* Very wise. . . . *Ancora uno.*"

"She's the loveliest human being I've ever seen in my life." When Virgil didn't look away, I added, "If there was ever anybody on this earth who I wanted to make happy, it was Laura."

Virgil moved his eyes from my face to the picture, taking it in like he was seeing the stars for the first time. Then he reached across the room and very gently handed the frame back to me.

"*Grazie.*"

He held up the bottle of gin. "*Posso io. . . ?*" he asked and raised the bottle to his lips.

"Be my guest" I said.

With that, he slugged down what was left and put the bottle on the floor.

I had found a few other empty bottles stashed around the apartment besides the ones we had drunk together, stuff that I had when I first moved in—Cointreau, Domaine de Canton, something called Tia Maria, booze gifts that I had never opened. Virgil Shepherd was very undiscriminating in his tastes.

He was eyeing the cabinet next to the stereo. "Anything else?"

"Take a look in the kitchen by the toaster oven."

"*Grazie.*"

Virgil slid down to the rug, shook off some of the blankets, and lumbered into the hallway. He returned holding a bottle of Campari. It was decorated with dust and hardened streaks of red-brown liqueur.

He offered the bottle to me, but I waved it off and made a sound that could pass for a very sad laugh.

"Don't take this the wrong way," I said. "But what the *fuck* happened?" I held my hands out, indicating the living room, Virgil, the crusty red bottle in his hand, the blankets on the floor, the unlit Christmas tree. "How did I go from *this* (I nodded at the photo) to *this?*" I looked back at Laura and Chris's faces in the picture. "I'm sitting here in the dark, I don't have two nickels to my name, and I've lost the two people I love the most."

"*Un momento.*"

Virgil twisted the top open, then re-assumed his position on the couch and pulled the blankets back up over his knees.

"*Persone*, they fuck up," he said, matter-of-factly. "*Succede. . .*it happens. They try. They make excuses. They make promises. They try harder. *Poi. . .*they fuck up again. *Cosa sai faire?*"

I knew what Virgil was trying to do, and I appreciated the effort, but the last thing I needed to hear was a pep talk on human frailty. I'd been in enough Arthur Miller plays to know that the flesh was weak. I wasn't about to let myself off the hook that easily.

"Not everybody fucks up."

"You'd be surprised."

I ran through a list of people in my head, starting with Laura, through most of my family, Dinino, Brendan, Auriemma the undertaker, even Neapolitan Bobby. All of them had found a way to steer clear of the swamp and stay above water. I couldn't believe that it was doom-and-gloom for everybody. And the crazy part was, I didn't think Virgil believed it either.

He had obviously seen a lot of low points in his life, but there were moments over the past week when he didn't seem particularly grim, not even in court. Only when he saw Brendan, which had been a kick in the gut for both of us. If you saw the look on his face when he was singing "1-2-3." Or listening to the Dubs. Or drinking the whiskey from Bobby's hospitality table. Or the way his eyes lit up when he saw Archie DeAngelo on the television in Uncle Feng's. Even when he laid eyes on Connie's Christmas cleavage and turned maroon. This didn't seem like a man who believed we were all destined to fuck up, repeatedly, and die.

What was I missing here?

"Why did you follow me to the club?"

The way he held my look and then leaned back and closed his eyes made it clear that whatever he was about to tell me was something he had wanted me to know for a while.

"*Sono stato mandato per salvare la tua anima.*"

"I don't understand."

"I was sent here for you. To save your soul."

The soul again. I laughed.

"It's that bad?" I asked. When I saw that Virgil wasn't laughing, I added, "What do you think, you're some kind of angel or something?"

"I am a poet."

"A poet who wants to save my soul?"

"*Esattamente.*"

"You wait 'til now to tell me this?"

"I tell you *prima*," he said softly. "You were not listening."

"Why me? What about Jackie?"

Virgil shook his head solemnly.

"Jesus Christ. You're serious about this."

"*Sì.*"

"I didn't think poets were in the business of saving souls."

Virgil smiled. "We save them all the time."

My eyes moved from his face to the flame of the candle flickering on the coffee table. When I looked up again I felt like I was watching myself from another room, sitting there in the dark, wrapped in blankets, the bottle of Campari on the coffee table between me and my would-be poet savior.

My eyes moved to the empty corner where the Christmas tree had been. The freshly painted coils of the radiator were hissing heat into the room, and the stacks of my 45s were piled on the bare wooden floor. I was back in the apartment that I had first moved into nine years before.

When I looked at Virgil, he was pointing to the picture frame.

"*Che dire*. . .the other picture?"

"What other picture?"

Virgil got up off the couch and moved to the stereo.

"What're you doing?"

I felt the same tingling in my hands that I had at the arcade just before Zenon exploded.

Virgil reached under the turntable and pulled out the hidden picture frame. Without looking at it he walked over to the chair and handed me the photo. Then he sat back down on the couch and drank some more Campari.

The picture was of Aniko, in black-and-white. It had been taken at Rockefeller Center. She was leaning over the railing watching the ice skaters in the rink below. I had gone to buy two hot chocolates, and when I got back, a tourist was taking her picture with a Polaroid. She didn't care. As a matter of fact, I don't think she even noticed. People were always taking pictures of Aniko. She was wearing her long black coat, and she had a silk pasha around her head. The look on her face, even in profile, even with her sunglasses on, was full of life.

I gave the tourist twenty bucks and my hot chocolate for it.

And I took it from the apartment the day I left.

"How'd you know about the picture?"

"I tell you, I am a poet. *Quella foto e poesia.*"

"It's ancient history," I said, but he saw that my hands were trembling. For nine years I had tried my best to forget it was there.

Stretching his arm across the coffee table, Virgil offered me the Campari. But when I reached out to take it from him, he held on to the bottle and stared into my eyes.

"*Ascoltami*," he said. "You had nothing to do with it."

"I had everything to do with it."

"No," Virgil said. "*Quello non e vero.* . . .that is not the truth."

He let go of the bottle and pushed himself back on the sofa.

One night, after we had broken up, I had gotten drunk and stopped into Dumpling to see her. I don't know what I was thinking, or if I was thinking, but I figured it had been four months, how could this hurt? And I missed her. When I walked in there was another girl behind the music stand.

Aniko had died of a brain aneurysm two months earlier. One of the bartenders found her in the apartment when she hadn't shown up for work. She had been dead for two days and nobody knew.

I looked from the polaroid to Virgil. I felt the tears on my lips. I felt the blood rush out of my heart and into my throat. The words that finally came out of my mouth had been there for a long time.

"It wouldn't have happened if we were together."

"Yes," he said, very softly. "Yes. It was her. . . *destino*."

"If I was with her, I could've helped her," I said. "I would've been there. She wouldn't have died alone."

"*Lasciarlo andare*. Let it go," he said. "You are destroying yourself."

"Yeah, well," I said, and took a long slug from the bottle. "That's the least I can do."

"*E qualunque cosa* you can give to the people who love you, and who you love."

I looked at the bare floor, the candle burning down.

"A dark place can be very easy to find," he said. "*Lo so*. . .she doesn't want that."

She? Aniko? I stared at his face, trying to see something that I couldn't see.

"How do you know any of this?"

"I am—"

"Right, I forgot. You're an angel."

He shook his head. "A poet."

I pulled the blanket tighter around my shoulders.

"Can I see the *foto* again?" he asked. "The first one."

I put the polaroid of Aniko down on the table. Then I leaned over and handed him the picture of Laura and Chris. He held it up about twelve inches from his face, looked at it hard for a few minutes, then very gently put it back down on the coffee table next to the picture of Aniko.

"The people in the *fotos*. They love you."

"I can't believe that," I said. "Too much has happened."

Virgil looked at the window, staring into the streetlight as if he were trying to pull words out of the air. His face, in the silver light, was full of emotion. I saw pain, regret, suffering, hurt, loss, all pass over his features and settle into the deep brown of his eyes. In other words, I saw everything that I had felt, that I was still feeling, since I had betrayed Aniko and left her to die alone.

If he were an actor, if this had been a performance on a stage, it would have brought the house down. But it was definitely no performance. When he turned to me again, there were tears in his eyes, too.

"There is nothing sadder than looking back with a broken heart at a time of great joy."

He said it in perfect English. As if he was singing. My eyes fell on the two pictures. "She made me feel that I deserved what she gave me," I said to Virgil, "her faith in me, her love. The way she looked at me— I believed that's who I really was."

"But that is who you are," Virgil said quietly. "*La tua anima*. Your soul. Still."

He motioned for me to hand over the Campari. I reached the bottle out to him and felt the rug under my feet. I saw the Christmas presents under the giant tree.

"*Grazie*," he said.

CHAPTER TWENTY-SEVEN

"Jumpin' Jack Flash"

THE PHONE STARTED RINGING AT 6:00 A.M. Before I picked it up, I knew who it was. "I'm on the corner, in the phonebooth." I took a breath, waited.

"You awake?"

"You heard?"

"Meet me in Dante's. In the back."

"Not a good idea."

"Fifteen minutes," he said, and hung up the phone.

I walked into the living room. The two pictures were still side by side on the coffee table. Virgil's body was spread across the sofa, dead to the world, covered in a dozen comforters. The way he was lying there reminded me of the first time I saw him, under the canvas blanket on the cot in the jail cell. The good old days of one week ago, when Laura and I were still together, Dinino was still alive, and I hadn't shot up anybody's social club yet.

This time, however, instead of a dirty cement floor, his right hand was resting lovingly on the empty bottle of Campari.

WE SAT IN THE FAR CORNER OF THE CAFÉ. The two electric candela-
bras on either side of the entrance kept the room a notch above dusk,
which worked for me. Besides the two middle-aged men by the front
door, dressed in paint-speckled Carhartt jackets, talking in Spanish and
waiting for a take-out order, the place was empty, a quiet start to Wednesday, December 24th.

My father sipped his coffee cup-sized serving of expresso, then
gently wiped the blue tint of his eyeglass lenses with a napkin. His cologne more than held its own against the smell of fresh pastries a few
feet away from us in the kitchen. Our very tired waitress, who looked
a little stunned to be serving anyone that early on Christmas Eve,
moved over to our table and refilled my glass. Sitting across from Jack
Romano, talking about what had happened a few hours ago, the only
thing my stomach could handle was another half glass of lukewarm
water.

"What'd you think was going to happen?" he said. "I hear my son
shot up a fancy social club. I'm going to sit home and wait for the
'Price is Right'?"

"Will you get insulted if I tell you I wasn't sure?"

He ignored my remark. I don't know if Jack had any other plans
later in the day, but the way he was dressed suggested drinks and a
matinee. Or maybe he just got decked out for the old neighborhood.
There wasn't a single wrinkle in his navy blazer, and his light gray dress
shirt, monogrammed *J.R.* on the pocket, was open one button at the
collar. A fitted cashmere overcoat was draped neatly over the back of
the chair next to him, a stark contrast to my floppy camel Brando coat
that Virgil had been wearing. I had never seen a person respond to ca-
lamity with such elegance.

"Who reached out to you?" I asked.

"Not you," he said.

My turn to ignore a remark.

"Uncle Jimmy?" I asked. Uncle Jimmy was my godfather. He had taken my father under his wing when he first arrived on Staten Island. To repay him, Jack had bestowed upon him the honor of watching over me.

Very smart man—I hadn't seen the guy in twenty years.

"Jimmy got a phone call from his boss in Brooklyn, who got a phone call from our friend in the city." He paused when he saw my eyes widen. "Yeah. Him. You were a hot topic of conversation last night."

"I'm sorry this got back to you."

"A little late for that now."

He returned his cup to the saucer without making a sound, as if he had just docked a 20-foot cabin cruiser on a windless morning in May.

"You seem so calm."

"What am I gonna do? It happened. Now we have to figure it out."

After spending so much of my childhood thinking about what my father was thinking or not thinking about me, I wondered what was going through his mind now. How did he feel about his oldest son creating such a mess in his old playground? As far as I knew, Jack had never shot up a gambling club. But then, as far as I knew wasn't very far.

"You sure you don't want nothing to eat?"

Let's be honest—the real question he had to be asking himself was, *How do I feel about my oldest son, period?*

I shook my head and laughed to myself, thinking about how much my life had changed since I picked up the cannolis for Dinino in this very establishment on the afternoon of my birthday.

"I don't have much of an appetite."

"Me neither."

Another silence settled in the space between us, but we were the kings of silence, so it wasn't like I was tapping my foot under the table. Every now and then Jack would train his sunglasses on the bruises on my face, but he seemed most concerned with the state of my sweatshirt, a faded maroon relic from my high school lacrosse team that, despite the frigid cold, I had pulled off a chair and thrown over my tee-shirt without thinking to grab a coat.

"You look like a vagabond."

Interesting choice of words. Definitely Mary the Blonde's son.

I apologized for my fashion sense, explaining that I was a little too preoccupied to handwash my Burberry merino crew neck.

Jack took another sip of his coffee.

"You know," he said, "I've been waiting for this phone call for a while."

"Why would that be?"

"Because you treated this like a game."

"You always seemed to be enjoying yourself."

The muscles in his face tensed for the first time since we had sat down.

"You had no business getting involved in this," he said. "Your grandmother's right. You live with your head up your ass. And when you finally take it out, you think with your dick. And never more than five minutes ahead."

"Nanny said I think with my dick?"

"No," Jack admitted. "That's me. But she did say that you have your head up your ass." When he saw the look on my face, he added, "You also know what it took to keep Mary the Blonde out of the car this morning? She was ready to ring Genovese's doorbell. She doesn't care that he's been dead for thirty years."

"I know."

"I don't understand. All you ever did was moan about the way I treated you and your mother, how I was never around. Why would you want to live the same way I did? I don't get it."

"How come you never said anything to me?"

"Like what?"

"I don't know, something like, 'Why're you getting involved with this?' or 'This isn't for you.' Maybe 'Why don't you stick with acting?' Something that would've clued me in that you had my best interests—me—at heart."

"Now you're being ridiculous," Jack said. "I'm not gonna tell a grown man how to live his life."

"Even when he's your son?"

"Keep your voice down," he said without anger. "Maybe I didn't expect you to start listening to me."

I was temporarily out of smart-ass answers. I tugged at the sleeve of my sweatshirt and thought about how I had given up Dinino's watch. I pictured the look on Sally's face as I took it off my wrist, as if he knew how this was going to play out all along.

"Where's your partner?" my father asked, breaking what seemed like an hour of lost time.

"Not around."

I explained how I had encouraged Jackie to go home and make up with his wife. By now I was sure Jackie, with or without Courtney, was long departed for higher ground, whether that was a trip to Atlantic City or a one-way plane ticket to the Cayman Islands. Either way, as Nanny would say, "No good deed."

"What about Laura and Chris? Do they know?"

"No," I said, happy to deliver some good news. "Laura took Chris to Connecticut for Christmas."

My father registered this information without surprise. Maybe Elsie had told him what had happened at the wake, or maybe in his eyes Laura was just another piece of the puzzle that was bound to get kicked under the refrigerator. One day I wanted to ask Jack how he had managed to keep such a terrific woman interested long enough to put up with all his bullshit. But obviously this wasn't the time for that conversation. The question I did manage to ask, after he had slid a ten-dollar bill on the table in lieu of the check, was this: "What do you want me to do?"

"Look," he said, his voice barely above a whisper, "nobody got killed. That's something. But you did put your hands on them. We're going to have to pay for the damages to the club—Jimmy mentioned something about a lighting fixture—and the money that was on the tables that they lost, the days they have to close. . .maybe two hundred thousand. We'll get a figure. In the meantime, we're gonna walk out of here straight to my car, and I'm going to drive you to Newark Airport. You need to leave the city for a few days. Go to California. Put a few thousand miles between you and them. I got an envelope for you in my coat. Buy your ticket cash."

I wondered if he knew that, in addition to what happened last night, I didn't have two nickels in my pocket.

"I'll ask Jimmy who I have to reach out to. I have some ideas. I might even ask our friend to get involved. What the fuck, we were neighbors once, right? Then we'll set up a sit-down, and you come back for that maybe in a week and be very sorry for what you did."

He held my look until I nodded. Seeing Jack Romano sitting across the table from me at seven o'clock in the morning on Christmas Eve, a man of action, a man who was able to think things out, a man who was able to control a situation, a feeling not unlike respect started spreading deep across my chest.

The only thing I had left to say was, "Thank you."

Jack finished his coffee and turned the cup over in its saucer. "*Everything* about me isn't bad," he said, with just the right amount of irony in his inflection.

I took another sip of water while I considered how I was going to bring up the next part.

"There's one other thing," I said, and when he didn't ask, I added, "What about Virgil?"

"Who?" Jack asked, reaching for his coat.

"He was with me in the club," I said. "He was the one who took Tosterelli's guy out when he was about to smash a bottle of vodka on my face."

"You mean the guy who broke his jaw?" My father dismissed this idea with a wave of his hand. "Stay away from him."

"I can't."

"We're not talking about an easy thing here," he said. "Even with the people we know."

"I know," I said.

"No, you *don't* know," he said. "You *don't* know." He hesitated, and I could see he was debating whether or not to share what he was thinking. After a couple of seconds, he dropped his coat back on the chair and closed his eyes for a second.

I had never seen my father express much emotion in his life. Even anger seemed to require too much of an investment in the daily proceedings of the Romano household. We knew we had to tiptoe around the house when his bedroom door was shut, even if it was four o'clock in the afternoon, but we never saw the consequence if we didn't. When he finally emerged, after my mother had already fed us and before he got dressed and left the house for the night, it was always a challenge to figure out what was going on behind his prescription sunglasses, which made what he said next knock the hell out of me.

"Let me tell you something else you don't know. Do you think we moved to Staten Island because of the fresh air? We *had* to move. I had two detectives sleeping in front of our building on Sullivan Street for months. Every time your mother took you out in the stroller, she passed the same brown Buick. The cocksuckers wanted everyone to know they were there. They used to use the bathroom in the back of Gerardi's candy store on the corner. I never forgave that prick Gerardi's son for letting them do that. The old man would've never allowed that."

"Why were they there?"

"They were trying to pin a murder on me."

Jack saw me flinch.

"They were crooked. Some neighborhood deadbeat went missing. The loan sharks turned the bulls on to me. They figured they'd put pressure on from both sides." Once again, he delivered this revelation evenly, without the drama that usually accompanies the word *murder*. I guess I was sitting there staring at him with my mouth open for a little too long, so he felt compelled to break another silence. "I didn't do it," he said, "if that's what you're thinking."

Was *that* what I was thinking? Did I *believe* him?

"Then why you?" I managed to ask.

"I owed the loan sharks a lot of money," he said, a rare concession that almost caused him to smile. "And I was paying them, but not fast enough. One day one of the bulls, this detective named Stuckey, made a not-so-nice comment to your mother. I got in the backseat and told them I would blow up the car with them in it if they every spoke to your mother like that again. They disappeared like the cowards that they were, and the loan sharks went after your grandfather. They said they would kill me if they didn't have the money in a week. Your grandfather cashed out his pension from the Parks Department to pay them off. They took three-quarters of what I owed and the promise that I'd never show my face in their clubs again. They called off the crooked piece-of-shit cops, and we went to Staten Island two weeks later."

This wasn't the departure story I had always heard from Nanny and Poppy. That story was all about how drugs had flooded the neighborhood and it was too heartbreaking to watch the neighbors' kids OD on their own front stoops. That was a very sad scenario, but this story made a lot more sense.

"Mom knew about the murder?"

"You mean the *alleged* murder?" he said, making another point. "Of *course* she knew. She knew what I did when she married me. I never hid anything from her. That's how we met, as a matter of fact, how we got together. A lot different from all the Irish boys who chased after her in the Bronx."

In the most unpredictable stretches of my father's life, when we wouldn't see him for days at a time, I knew that my mother always believed that her husband loved us, even when I was sure the opposite had to be true. I never understood how a man could not want to be around a woman like Elsie as much as he could, and then expect so much from her during the few hours he was home.

And then something happened that I hadn't seen happen in a very long time: the set of Jack Romano's jaw relaxed, *his* dimples appeared, and my father laughed.

"Maybe we're more alike than either one of us wants to admit."

Then he reached for his coat again.

"Now let's go to the airport."

"I can't."

"Why not?"

"The guy from the club? Who broke Butchie's jaw? He's sleeping on the sofa in my apartment."

He stared at me across the table. And for the first time in my life I saw the look my father would've given us if he had ever actually opened the bedroom door at four o'clock in the afternoon.

CHAPTER TWENTY-EIGHT

"A Hazy Shade of Winter"

JACK PULLED UP THE BLINDS SIX INCHES and looked out the window on Sullivan Street. Then he turned back to me. "Anytime you're ready."

I had double-checked the bedroom, the closets, the shower, under the bed, behind the goddamn Christmas tree. I figured maybe he'd gotten nervous when he heard more than one set of footsteps moving up the stairs, but even that didn't make sense. If there was one thing I knew about Virgil Shepherd, it's that he wasn't easily unnerved. And he would have been way too hung over to make it down the fire escape.

Jack watched me stare at the empty sofa, then moved away from the window. He started to pace alongside the coffee table, like a tiger in the Bronx Zoo trying to figure out the best way back to the jungle. Dramatic revelations of the fuck-up gene aside, I still wasn't completely convinced that his presence in my apartment was all paternal concern and not embarrassment at having his namesake whacked. But it was a start.

I pushed the blankets aside and sat down.

"Why're you getting comfortable?" Jack was getting more frustrated by the second. "Come on, get up. Get your things."

I looked at the pictures on the coffee table, still side by side, looked at the expressions on our faces, and thought about what Virgil had said the night before.

My father looked at me, registering—what? What was the expression on my face at that second when I raised my eyes from the photos and realized a window had opened up, and I was seeing things that finally started to make sense? My headache, which had been with me on and off since Zenon, had levelled off to a low static. Whatever distortion Zenon's jolt had contributed to the disharmony playing in my head had disappeared. For better or worse, I seemed to have most of my mental faculties back.

"It was a set-up," I said, mostly to myself. "Butchie thought I had something with his girlfriend. He put Brendan in the hospital because he knew how I'd react. That's why Sally didn't care that Jackie was MIA."

My father looked at me as if I had just woken up from a coma.

"I would've never made it out of the club. Even if I had all the money. Even if I didn't hit Butchie." I looked at Jack. "He knew what was going to happen."

"Who knew?"

"Virgil."

Despite the urgency of my epiphany, Jack was unmoved.

"Let's go."

"He followed me to the club to save my life."

"That remains to be seen," my father said. "I mean, what were you thinking? You fuck around with a wise guy's girlfriend? I could've told you how this would turn out."

"I wasn't *fucking around* with her," I said. I felt my jaw tighten.

"I *never* cheated on Laura."

The unspoken "unlike you" hung in the air between us.

He held my look for a long time. "Well, good for you," he finally said.

I decided to sidestep that minefield for now and kept my mouth shut.

Jack sat down on the sofa on the other side of the blankets. From the expression on his face he looked like he felt the same way.

"I'm telling you," I said, lowering my voice. "That's why Virgil went to the club."

"Could be true," he responded. "But I'm telling *you*, Sally has to do something before word gets out that he didn't. So we don't have a lot of time to sit here and debate the obvious."

"There's nothing to debate," I said.

"Good. Whatever happened is done," he said. "It's history. You understand?" That was about as much of a concession as I was going to get out of him. When I nodded, he went on. "Your friend's smart enough to be scared," he said. "Now get your stuff."

He got up and stood by the door.

"He's not scared," I said. "He's trying to tell me something."

"Yeah, to disappear like he did. That's a good message. I wish you would've thought of it."

"I have to do this."

"Do what?"

"I have to find him."

"*Find* him? And *then* what?"

"I don't know," I said. "Maybe I could put him on a bus and send him somewhere."

"Why can't he put himself on a bus?"

"Because he won't," I said.

Jack moved away from the door and stood over me, his breathing heavy.

"Now you're getting me mad," he said. "Haven't you heard anything I've said?"

"I'm sorry," I said, and I was. "I have to do this."

"Think about yourself."

"You know something?" I got up off the sofa, moved to the closet, and pulled my new leather coat over my old sweatshirt. "I'm tired of thinking about myself."

EVEN THOUGH IT WAS CHRISTMAS EVE, there wasn't a lot of cheer in the neighborhood east of Little Italy and north of Canal Street. The Bowery looked like a war zone with a whole-sale sign—run down, busted-up, with cracked brick walls, broken windows, metal gates coated with urine, and charred mattresses on the curb. The cold had bleached the streets white, and the relentless gray that had shrouded the city over the past week came, not from the sky anymore, but rose like mist from the sidewalks. It was like walking in a graveyard after a thunderstorm.

Aside from the supply businesses, the music club CBGBs, and a handful of outposts (mainly noodle shops and a couple of thrift stores) that had begun to crop up, the effects of gentrification hadn't kicked in yet. Ten blocks from the boutiques and the art galleries in Soho there were garbage cans burning at eight o'clock in the morning to keep people like Virgil Shepherd from freezing to death.

The neighborhood seemed a lot sadder and more desperate than when I'd done a once-over here the previous Sunday. An army of volunteers was already combing the streets, getting those they could on their feet. They were handing out food and helping some people into vans, probably taking them to one of the missions. But there were still dozens of men and women on the sidewalks wrapped in tarps and cardboard boxes who were not going anywhere. I wondered what the plan was for them.

Jack had done his best to hijack me out of the city. First, he had argued with me to get in his car to go to the airport. Then he had insisted that he was driving me over to the Bowery to cruise the streets, which we both knew was a lie. As soon as we hit Canal Street the childproof locks would have gone down, and we would have been off through the Holland tunnel.

Some of it was about what he was going to tell my mother (and Nanny) when he got back to Staten Island without me. A lot of it was that a man like Jack Romano was used to getting his way. He kept telling me how dangerous these guys were. I kept repeating that I knew how badly I had fucked up, but this was something I had to do. My father finally accepted the fact that his son wasn't going to stop acting like an asshole and save his own life when I swore on Chris' head that I would call Jack the second that I was ready to get out of the city, whether I found Virgil or not.

We had talked more in the past two hours than we had in thirty years. Neither one of us was very good at it. And there had been a couple of moments when we were both ready to blow it up. But we didn't.

I could also tell that the situation had taken something out of him. Jack had not been quite as dapper when he got into the Eldorado to drive back to Staten Island, alone. And he definitely wasn't happy— good luck facing Mary the Blonde when he stepped through the front door. But when he grabbed and shook my hand on the corner of Sullivan and Spring, there was a look in his eyes that I hadn't seen in a long time. I was pretty sure that same look was in my eyes as well.

The morning drifted into the afternoon as I moved through the neighborhood, checking the hotels and bars and empty lots. So many bottles had broken on these streets that the glass looked like it had been pulverized into the pavement, creating patches of glitter that shone through the mist on the white sidewalks. When I asked if anybody had heard of Virgil Shepherd, most didn't answer, didn't even look up, as if names and words meant nothing. One poor soul took a swing at me. (What else is new?) A few people asked for money, but most of the time I felt like a ghost drifting past eyes that never saw me.

I thought about what Virgil had said about a dark place.

Up around Delancey Street I saw a yellow cab cut off a banged-up delivery van trying to pull over to the curb. The two drivers got out of their cars. The cabbie was a young Arabic kid in a red soccer jersey, and the man who was driving the van was dressed in jeans with stringy hair halfway down the back of his sweatshirt. Cursing and then pushing, they were ready to tear each other apart when a white Cadillac gunned the engine and jumped the sidewalk. The car stopped about a yard from the two men, forcing them to jump back, almost into each other's arms. The driver's window rolled down, and a man, maybe forty and wearing a red Santa hat and bushy white beard, stuck his head out.

With a wild grin on his face Santa yelled, "Merry Christmas, mother fuckers!" and flung a bottle of something at them, which smashed at their feet. Gleefully giving them his middle finger, he swerved the Cadillac past a fire hydrant and pulled back into traffic. The two men followed the car with their eyes. Then they turned back to each other and started laughing.

My last inspiration was a community center around East 10th Street, not too far from Aniko's friend Officer Gee and the 9th Precinct. I thought that, since the police had picked up Virgil in the projects a couple of blocks away, maybe he had some connection to the neighborhood.

The center tried hard to offer some Holiday spirit. Lit-up wreaths hung inside the grates on the front windows. A small Christmas tree, not unlike the one Neapolitan Bobby had on his hospitality table, was perched on a milk crate by the front door, its green skirt weighted down with bricks. A line of people had already formed in the alley on the side of the building, which was attended to very compassionately by two young women who looked like they could've been college students. They smiled and passed out hot beverages from a couple of urns on a folding table. It was hard to ignore the number of children who stood on the line with everyone else.

A *Welcome* sign was posted over the front door frame.

The inside was full of chairs and couches. There were lamps on tables throughout the room, the shades casting a soft yellow glow. Some of the people were sleeping, while others sat at the tables, playing cards or talking quietly. A few small kids wandered around the room or sat in front of the television console, which flickered cartoons in the corner. Another small Christmas tree sat on an end table in the corner.

"Can I help you?"

The woman who approached me from behind a small desk was also young, mid-twenties, a pretty face framed with brown hair and a Duke baseball cap. She had a pull-string ceramic Santa sled pinned to her red Holiday sweater.

"I was looking for someone," I said. "I thought he might've come here."

"What's his name?"

"Virgil Shepherd," I said, and when I didn't see any recognition in her eyes, I added, "Big guy. Big shoulders. Tall. Black. He was wearing a camel overcoat and brown Gucci loafers."

It was obvious that the description didn't register, but she made a show of peeking over my shoulder to survey the people around us.

"I think I would remember him," she said kindly. "We don't get too many people in here wearing Gucci."

"He's got a big scar on the side of his neck."

"Maybe he came in earlier. I just got here a couple of hours ago. Are you a relative?"

"Friend," I said.

"Would you know if he's been with us before? If he's already been here for services, we may have some information."

"To be honest, I don't really know much about where he goes or what he does," I said. I watched two kids chase each other around the room until a young man grabbed them by their hands and led them over to a sofa.

"I'll check anyway," she said.

"Thank you."

"Virgil Shepherd, right?" she asked, but she didn't move. She was looking at my face. I could feel myself shudder, and I hunched my shoulders.

"It's always cold in here," she said, and smiled apologetically. "It's an old building."

"Could I ask you one more question?"

"Sure."

"What's the deal with the line outside?"

"Do you smell that?" She took a deep breath and nodded her head proudly. "We're serving Christmas Eve dinner in the cafeteria in the back. We start at four," she said, then checked her watch. "Maybe your friend will come in."

"How come the line's not moving?"

"We're still setting up," she said. "We'll probably open for seating around 3:30. "Would you like me to check our files for Mr. Shepherd?"

"No, thank you," I said. I knew it in my heart. "He's not here."

I shook my head and took two steps toward the door. Then I turned back.

"I just have one more question," I said. "Why are some people standing out there and some people are in here already?"

"The people you see in here arrived very early."

"But it's so cold for those kids outside," I said. "They can't come in here?"

"It gets too crowded if we bring everybody in at once," she explained. "We would just bring the children in, but the parents don't like to separate from them. Even for a short time." She lowered her voice. "It can cause some issues."

"That doesn't seem fair."

Miraculously, I hadn't exhausted this very nice woman's patience yet.

"I'm sorry," she said, still very sweetly. "What was your name again?"

"Johnny Romano."

"Mr. Romano," she said with a very deep sigh. "Nothing about this is fair."

When I left building, the line had grown. The two Samaritans, looking a little frigid themselves, were still handing out hot chocolates, the steam from the cups blown sideways by the wind, which was picking up again. I noticed a young mother sitting on the sidewalk with her back against the building. She had a picture book in her lap and two children nestled against her, one under each arm, to keep them from the cold.

I approached them slowly, angling into the line and provoking a few angry stares.

"Maybe you could use this," I said.

I slipped out of my leather coat and held it in front of them. The woman on the ground nodded. I took the coat and wrapped it around the three of them, tucking their chins just under the collar.

She looked up at me and mouthed, "Thank you," and then, "Merry Christmas."

The old man on the line in front of them, wrapped in a dirty Con Ed windbreaker, looked over.

"You got anything for me, Santa?"

"You like the sweatshirt?" I asked, tugging at the front of the pullover. "Vintage."

He gave it a quick once-over, then said, "I'm good."

I had to laugh. One vagabond to another.

CHAPTER TWENTY-NINE

"Baby, Now that I've Found You"

I WALKED WEST ALONG ST. MARK'S PLACE, my hands in the front pouch of my unwanted pullover, my eyes crisscrossing the street, trying to pick out Virgil through the throng of last-minute shoppers. On the corner of St. Marks and Second Avenue, a boombox blasted a reggae version of "God Rest Ye Merry Gentleman," while a hip-looking teenaged kid pulled off some impressive dance moves and passed around a Yankee cap.

On the next corner a tired middle-aged couple, wearing red- and-green ponchos, were peddling a table full of hand-carved Santas and Christmas tree candles.

Two blocks down, I gave the Salvation Army lady whatever change I had left in my jeans and made a left on Fifth Avenue, heading toward Washington Square Park.

The late afternoon sky had turned dark as I moved past Evan's apartment building, bits of Christmas carols staying in my ears from the store speakers on 8th Street. I figured I would start at the arch and work my way south, but there was nobody to see. The park was empty. The bitter cold had taken care of business, sending the starving artists, musicians, and NYU kids home early for the Holidays. Even the drug dealers had packed it in. Aside from a few psycho joggers, bare legs sticking out of their shorts like candy canes, the only people left in the park were a couple of undercover cops. They were both dressed like a cross between Serpico and Kurt Cobain and looked even more miserable than I was.

They were worth a shot.

"Fellas, I'm looking for a friend," I said as I approached slowly, my hands out in front of me where they could see them.

Kurt looked my ragged-ass presence over and kept a straight face.

"We may have a little something you're interested in." Real slick.

"I mean a real friend," I said patiently, already realizing that this was a mistake. "Big guy, black. Nicely dressed. Camel coat."

"Nah, bud, he ain't working the park anymore. We're here now," Serpico said. "What can we do you for?"

Standing there sizing me up, trying to contain their glee, these boys already had my frozen wrists in cuffs—an easy bust that would make their shift merry and bright. It wouldn't matter that I didn't have enough money on me to buy a Claritin. I tried a different tactic.

"Let me ask you another question," I said. "Did either one of you see a black Range Rover circling the neighborhood over the last few hours?"

Kurt looked intrigued. Maybe a supplier.

"Why?"

"The driver wants to kill me," I said. "He's a big mob guy and he thinks I've been fucking his girlfriend." I turned up the wild eyes. "Can you help me? Please?"

With that they both laughed, dismissed me with a "Get lost, jerkoff," and headed east in the direction of Broadway.

I crossed the west-bound half of Houston Street, then walked along the traffic island toward St. Anthony's church. The closer I got to the apartment, the colder I felt, and the more my brain buzzed with unanswered questions and brutal scenarios. *Why did Virgil leave the apartment? Did Jack's phone call spook him? Did he look out the window and see Butchie and Anthony on the sidewalk? Did he make a quick exit through the courtyard in back? Was he just trying to save himself, as my father had reiterated a dozen times? Or was there some crazy point to all of this that I wasn't seeing yet?*

If Virgil had managed to disappear, God bless him. But what if Virgil had already been cornered by Sally's guys? How would I find out? And what would I do if it was too late? The scene in Sally's club kept playing itself over and over, always ending with Butchie's *"You're fuckin' dead"* ringing in my ears.

Whatever blackbelt degree of asshole I had become in the last few years, even I wouldn't be able to live with myself after this one.

Jack had made me promise him that I wouldn't do anything extreme. I told him that I'd just try to find Virgil and get out fast, but some dark thoughts had settled over my brain and I was not too far away from convincing myself that I had the guts to carry them through. Honestly—and at this stage of the game what was left not to be honest about?—I'd never been a person who thought about packing it in. I did have a couple of friends who'd come a little too close to the brink and, despite what I told Ralphie's boyfriend about being dramatic, they had scared the shit out of me. I would never lay that on my friends and family, and I would never do that to Laura and Chris. But walking down Sullivan Street on Christmas Eve, I told myself that, if I found out that they had hurt Virgil, I would find a way to get even, in whatever way I could, and not think too much about the consequences.

And what about Aniko? How could Virgil know about the picture?

What had he meant when he said, "She doesn't want that?"

Was I losing my mind? Had any of it really happened last night?

But then I looked down at the knuckles on my right hand—cut, bruised, bloodied—and the empty spot on my wrist where the Bulgari had been.

I had questions about Jackie, too. I kept waiting for him, first at the Onion, then at court, then at Sally's club. Even as I crossed Prince Street, still checking doorways for Virgil, I wouldn't have been surprised if Jackie had popped out instead, cursing, waving his arms, insisting that we bring Brendan a Christmas Eve dinner from Delmonico's. How could he just disappear on us? I didn't want to believe that Jackie knew what was in store for me at Sally's and didn't show.

But Virgil had shown. My mind kept going back to that. If Virgil had by some miracle managed to get out of the city, would he try to get a message to me? Or was that too much to ask from someone who had totally trashed this poor guy's life? The expression in his eyes when he turned to me the night before, after staring into the streetlight—he looked like he'd been to hell and back. And it was because of me.

BY THE TIME I MADE IT BACK TO MY APARTMENT, eight hours later, the living room looked as if it had been poured out of one of Joe D.'s giant cocktail shakers. Furniture, glass, clothes, dishes, were ankle-deep on the rug. It was almost impressive how the Anthonys had taken their time destroying the place, scattering a couple of layers of everything I owned evenly around the apartment. With every step I took I crunched something into the rug. Even the Christmas presents for Laura, Chris, Dinino, and the rest of the family had been compacted like garbage in a chute.

Giving credit where credit was due, whoever demolished my belongings had done an especially enthusiastic job on my 45 collection, which had been shoe-heeled into bite-sized pieces and stuffed into the toilet.

I reached into the bowl and picked up the record on top. The jagged plastic was sticking out from the label like a black iceberg: "Beyond the Sea."

At least somebody still had a sense of humor.

The kitchen was equally wrecked, with one exception: My answering machine, although hanging by its cord off the counter, was still plugged in and blinking away.

I took the phone off the hook and played back the messages.

Three were from my mother, requesting, first calmly and then not so calmly, that I call her. There were two from Michael and one from Jojo, telling me, whatever I needed, just let them know, they were both at the market waiting for my call. Nanny had left four, the first one telling me to *cut out the shit and get home*. But the last message was very different. Her voice on the tape had lost its street-smart, know-it-all edge. Mary the Blonde sounded like a grandmother whose own heart was on the verge of being broken.

My father had left his own *sotto voce* message, probably calling from the extension in the den, asking me to please tell him where and when to pick me up and that we had to move fast. Even though she knew something bad was going on, I was sure my mother hadn't been told the whole sordid story.

But the last message really put everything into perspective. It came from somebody called Dean Flicker, co-director of Patient Services at Maryhaven Hospital for Psychiatric Behaviors. In a very clear, professional manner, Mr. Flicker stated that patient Jonathan Parker had named me as his next-of-kin, and could I stop by the admissions office at my earliest convenience to complete the paperwork.

I left the phone off the receiver and walked back into the living room, shuffling through my ex-possessions and surveying the rubble. The thing was, I didn't give a shit about any of it. The only thing I needed to find were the photographs.

I had left them on the coffee table, but the coffee table was now four coffee tables, with each leg scattered in a different corner of the room. I cleared a spot in the middle of the floor where the table had been and started sifting through my belongings piece by piece: keys, scripts, old sunglasses, a slipper, my wallet, one of Chris's Mutant Turtle action figures (I couldn't remember which one), the tone arm of my turntable. All smashed. All not the photographs.

About half an hour later I found the frame from the Laura and Chris photo under the sofa, glass spider-webbed, but the picture had been removed. Fuck. Could Butchie have really been crazed enough to take the time to slide the picture out and destroy it?

The answer was on the credenza by the door, which I had walked past when I first stepped into the apartment. The antique, which had probably been in the apartment since World War I, had been cleared of everything in order to spotlight the photographs. They had been torn to shreds, stacked into a pile on the green marble top, and set on fire. In the ashes I saw pieces from the black-and-white polaroid and the once beautiful colors from the arcade photo melted together, all charred.

Now *that* was sadism. Connie, thank you very much.

Even though all the ornaments had been smashed, I plugged in the lights to my monster of a Christmas tree. Then I cleared some glass off the cushions and fell into my sofa, next to the blankets, which appeared to be the one thing in the room that hadn't been touched.

I was cold, I was tired, and what I most wanted to do was close my eyes and wait for the sequel. Now that they had figured out where I lived, I was sure it was only a matter of time before they'd be back.

Obviously, if there was one thing Sally's men were, it was thorough.

When I pulled a blanket off the stack to wrap around my chest, something fell to the rug. It was Virgil's blue pull-string Gap bag, which must have been stuck between the comforters. In all the chaos of the chandelier exploding and our dramatic exit, I didn't remember Virgil taking it out of the club.

I picked it up and laid it across my lap. I don't know what I expected to find in there—a pair of socks? A toothbrush? Another thing I hadn't given much thought to. I unknotted the strings and pulled the frayed plastic open. Inside the bag there was only one thing: a yearbook from a school called JHS 49 on 116th Street. The book was dated *1981* and was in very bad shape. The front cover had a faded photocopied drawing of what looked like a prospector with a pickaxe, chopping at a stack of books.

There was a lot of writing on the inside cover, but it was impossible to read. The different colored inks had run and blurred, creating a finger painting out of the well-wishes and "Remember when's" that had been recorded there sixteen years earlier. The first few pages fell out as soon as I opened it, but the back of the book was a little more intact. That's where I saw the picture, on page 34.

It was a black-and-white photo of the eighth-grade basketball team. There were seven skinny kids huddled together, maybe fourteen, fifteen years old, brown and black, with one white kid on the far end who had the biggest afro in the picture. They were all in dark gym shorts and light T-shirts that read *Dreyfus Miners*. Underneath the photo was a list of the players. And stuck between Juan Carlos Ramirez and Gerald Smith were two names that I recognized: Archibald DeAngelo and Virgil Shepherd Brown.

There they were, standing next to each other in the center of the group. And even though there was a "Brown" added to his name, it was definitely Virgil. He was the tallest one in the photo. The scar on his neck wasn't there yet, but his dark eyes already looked like they knew what the future would hold. De Angelo stared straight into the camera, the same "I don't give a shit" attitude that had defined his up and down NBA career already evident in his cocky smile. De Angelo had his right hand resting on the shoulder of his much larger teammate.

Two phone numbers were scrawled in pencil in big, loopy handwriting next to the picture. The first one was a local number. The second had an out-of-state area code.

I ran into the kitchen and dialed the 212 number. A woman answered on the second ring.

"Thank you for calling the Paramount Marquis. Stacey speaking. How may we help you?"

"The Paramount Marquis?" I repeated stupidly into the receiver.

"Yes, sir," Stacey replied pleasantly. "Thirty-second Street and Seventh Avenue. Would you like to speak with reservations?"

"No," I said. "I'd like to speak with Virgil Shepherd."

"Surely. Please hold."

An absolutely terrible new-age version of "Silent Night" came over the line while I struggled to contain a rising euphoria that I knew was too good to be true. My hand was shaking as I held the phone to my jaw.

Stacey came back on the line ten seconds later.

"I'm sorry," she said evenly. "A Mister Virgil Shepherd does not appear to be registered at our hotel. Perhaps he's checking in today."

"How about Virgil Brown? Could you check the register to see if he stayed there recently?"

"I'm sorry, sir. I don't see anything."

"This doesn't make sense."

"Sir?"

"Why would he have this number written in his junior high school yearbook?" I asked.

"I couldn't tell you, sir."

I hung up the phone and dialed the second number.

The phone rang for a while, but maybe on the eighth or ninth ring a woman picked up.

"De Angelo residence."

Holy shit.

"Hello?"

"Where am I calling?"

"Chu don't know where you're calling?"

I detected a Spanish lilt to the ridicule.

"I'm sorry. I'm not sure."

"Miami," she said, followed by a very low and maybe not meant to be heard "Chu idiot."

"I need to speak with Archie. It's an emergency."

"He's out of town."

"Where out of town?"

Some cursing in Spanish, followed by silence.

"How about V—"

Click.

I dialed the first number again.

"Stacey, it's me. From a minute ago."

"Okay?"

"Listen, Stacy, can I speak with Mr. De Angelo?"

"Surely. Please hold."

Another woman came on the line five seconds later, this one not nearly as pleasant as Stacey.

"How may we help you?"

"I need to speak with Archie De Angelo. It's an emergency."

"I'm sorry, sir. We are not allowed to put calls through to our guests on game day."

I looked at the red digits on the microwave clock. Then I ripped the page out of the yearbook and shoved it into my back pocket.

CHAPTER THIRTY

"Nowhere to Run"

THANKS TO A PAIR OF VERSACE CUFFLINKS, I was able to find a cabbie on Sixth Avenue who had very little respect for Holiday traffic. I was standing in front of the Paramount Marquis less than fifteen minutes later. In a town famous for its luxury hotels, this wasn't one of them, but it still had some Holiday charm. The lobby was decked out with a gold-and-silver Christmas tree set up to the left of the front desk. A very inviting six-stool bar buzzed with guests off to the right.

But its biggest selling point was the location. The hotel was diagonally across Seventh Avenue from Madison Square Garden, which made it very convenient for visiting teams. And even though I was out of the bookie business, I knew that the Miami Heat had an eight o'clock rematch with the Knicks. They had to be somewhere in the Goddamn hotel.

The lobby was busy: businessmen checking out, a line of tourists checking in, hotel personnel darting around. A professional-looking young woman (*Nina* on the name tag), in a tailored maroon blazer and white blouse, was standing behind the front desk, quickly losing patience with me. Stacey was nowhere to be found.

"Perhaps I wasn't clear—Mr. DeAngelo is not available."

"Look, Nina," I said calmly. "I know he's here. I just need to ask him one question."

Maybe I wasn't as calm and cool with Nina as I thought, because within thirty seconds Bruce and Julian, wearing their own much larger maroon blazers and sporting headsets, converged on either side of me.

"Sir," Julian, the slightly larger one, said, "may we help you with something?"

While I was explaining my predicament, I saw Julian glance over my shoulder as two more men in maroon assumed positions on either side of the front desk.

Bruce had an idea. "If it means so much to see Mr. DeAngelo, maybe you could purchase a ticket to the game?"

I thanked him for his brilliant suggestion, then told him I had another idea. "I don't need to see him dribble," I said. "I need to ask him one very important life-and-death motherfucking question."

"Sir," Bruce said, "may we escort you out of the lobby?"

Thirty seconds later, I shook free of Bruce's steel-fingered grip on my elbow as he and Julian "escorted" me through the hotel entrance onto Seventh Avenue. When I turned, caught in a whirlwind of guests and pedestrians, I glimpsed my reflection in the frosted glass panel of the front doors. Days without sleep, food, or a shave, and fueled with nothing except gin and Campari, had definitely taken their toll on the healing process. The mementos on my face had massed into the color of a ripe eggplant. Factor in my uncombed hair, and I looked like a long-lost relative dug out of the tundra in Ivar the baker's backyard in Belarus. I even detected a certain odor about myself that JP Gaultier himself wouldn't be able to fix. But the thing that impressed me the most about my frozen reflection in front of the Paramount Marquis was the astonishing fact that I didn't give a shit.

I just needed to keep Virgil alive.

I waved to Bruce and Julian, who stood just inside the front doors, arms crossed in front of their maroon blazers. Then I turned and fell face-first over a luggage rack in the middle of the sidewalk.

The kid who'd been pushing the cart knelt alongside my body, his own maroon blazer accessorized by a black scarf wrapped around his neck. He couldn't have been more than twenty years old. He was milk-white, with a shock of dark hair hanging in his eyes and cheekbones that had "New School Acting Seminar" written all over them.

I knew the look well.

"Mister, you alright?"

My fingers groped for traction on the pavement, which felt like the flipside of an ice cube tray— I had missed the maroon outdoor carpet by two feet. The kid looked me over for a second, then reached out a hand to help me up. I rolled over on my back and noticed that I was surrounded by suitcases and garment bags featuring the Miami Heat logo. That's when I also noticed the large luxury bus idling at the curb, the door to the luggage compartment swung open.

"What time is it?"

He pushed up his sleeve and checked his watch.

"Shit," he said, slightly panicked. "Look, I'm sorry, but I really need to get these bags on the bus."

I thanked him and moved about ten feet down Seventh, close to the building and out of view of Bruce and Julian, as the kid loaded the bags into the bus with a strong sense of urgency. The pedestrian traffic was thick on my side of the street but nowhere near what it was in front of the world's most famous arena. According to the clock on Chase Bank, it was still three hours before game-time, but it looked like New Year's

Eve. A vocal throng had already staked out the entrance to MSG, waiting for the rematch that could avenge the Knicks' ugly loss six days before and move the team into first place.

A line of large men, wrapped in very expensive outerwear, moved quickly from the hotel entrance through the front doors of the bus. At the end of the line, the last to leave the warmth of the hotel lobby, were the stars—Alonzo Mourning, Tim Hardaway and the man of the moment, Archie DeAngelo, followed closely by my friend Julian.

I had an inspiration.

"Who's got tickets?" I yelled, walking half backwards, half forwards, pretending that I was in need of a scalper, and moving closer to the front of the bus. "I need tickets. Who's got tickets?"

This caught the interest of a small army of shady men who materialized from ten different directions and quickly converged on me, which is exactly the cover I wanted.

Mourning was standing behind a player I didn't recognize. He was staring straight into the entrance to the bus, waiting his turn like a gentleman, already with his game face on. Hardaway was right behind him, saying something to DeAngelo, their eyes taking in the sights of Seventh Avenue on Christmas Eve. Then they both started to laugh.

Virgil's old teammate was larger than he looked on television, a pair of gold aviators wrapped around his shaved head, the fur collar to his brown suede coat up past his ears. Time had hardened his features, but that same cocky look from the yearbook photo was in his smile and in his eyes, which at that moment were checking out a woman's ass as she bent over to re-bundle her Jack Russel terrier.

I pulled away from one friendly ticket agent, who wanted to sell me a seat on the floor for twelve hundred dollars, and made my move.

"Archie!"

He looked up from the woman's ass.

"You gotta help me find Virgil."

"What?"

"Virgil Shepherd."

Our eyes met. I had his attention. "How you know about Virgil?"

"You have to tell me where he is."

He thought about it for a split second, then took a step toward the bus. I stepped in front of him.

"Look," I pleaded, and held the yearbook page in front of his face. When he saw the picture and the phone number, he looked as if he had just run into a pick set by Daryl Dawkins. The expression on his face changed from annoyance to anger. "Where'd you get this?"

"It was in your junior high school yearbook."

"Why's my number here?"

"I don't know."

"Man, you fucked up."

"They're going to hurt him."

DeAngelo eyed me like I was out of my mind. "Ain't *nobody* gonna hurt Virgil anymore." Then he turned back to the bus doors.

I glanced over at the entrance to the hotel. My old friend Julian, who had gone back inside the lobby, came rushing through the doors, waving his arms like a praying mantis. He did not look happy to see me again. I grabbed DeAngelo's elbow.

"What does that mean?"

DeAngelo moved his eyes from his elbow to my face. Then he lunged at me and snatched the page out of my hand, just as the nice kid with the great cheekbones rolled the empty luggage cart behind us. Both the kid and DeAngelo hit the maroon carpet at the same time. The luggage cart spun around and toppled over, creating about six feet of sidewalk between me and a half dozen men in maroon blazers.

Bruce took three of the men around one end of the cart. But Julian, crazed that I had made such of mess out of things, charged wildly right under the brass bar. Just as he was about to wrap his arms around my waist, DeAngelo, trying to get up himself, rolled over and stuck his leg out. Julian lost his balance and fell over the base of the cart into a second group of maroon blazers.

The page from the yearbook was on the curb in front of the bus. I ran over to grab it, but the wind picked it up and carried it into the middle of Seventh Avenue.

I charged into the street just as the traffic light changed.

Cars were passing me on both sides, horns blaring, drivers rolling down their windows offering me Holiday greetings:

"Get the fuck out of the *street*."

"What're you fucking *stupid*?"

"You're going to *kill* yourself."

"*Asshole*."

Weaving through the traffic, I managed to grab the page and make it to the taxi area on the Madison Square Garden side of the street. My lungs felt ready to explode, but it didn't matter. I leaned against the side of a yellow cab and looked down at Virgil's yearbook picture, which, aside from a few tire threads, was still in one piece.

And then I did something that I hadn't done in a long time: I broke into a smile.

The last thing I remembered was the mounted cop, on the largest horse I had ever seen in my life, bearing down on me in the cab lane, his night stick the size of a telephone pole.

CHAPTER THIRTY-ONE

"Joy to the World"

WHEN I OPENED MY EYES, I was staring into the dark corner of a holding cell. My feet, hands, and especially my chest felt as if they were weighted down to the metal cot with stones. The rest of my body was numb. I tilted my face toward a dim light in the corridor. I was still in last night's clothes—my high school pullover, sweatpants (minus the tie string, just in case I wanted to kill myself), and my very beat-up Ferragamo loafers. I could hear other people making some very peculiar noises in the cells around me, but mercifully whoever was in charge the previous night had given me a single.

A police officer was standing on the other side of the bars. I heard the heavy clang of metal, and the door to the cell slid open, then his footsteps on the concrete floor. He hit the door with something solid and took a step toward the cot.

"Come with me," he said flatly.

At the front desk, all was relatively calm. The clock on the wall next to the *Midtown South* sign claimed it was 7:20. I wasn't sure if that was a.m. or p.m. until a pair of cops came through the front doors to the precinct, throwing some daylight onto the gray concrete floor.

A couple, maybe in their late twenties, was sitting on a bench against the far-right wall, nodding off, their heads bobbing forward, then jerking back, and finally coming together like Siamese twins. Aside from a few uniforms circulating with their coffee cups, it was quiet enough to hear the Holiday songs the officer at the desk had playing out of the small radio behind him. The desk sergeant was probably in his late fifties, with Pillsbury doughboy cheeks and thinning brown hair. He nodded at a pen and told me to sign a couple of forms if I didn't mind.

When I handed the pen back to him, he levelled his curious eyes at me.

"You know Archie DeAngelo?"

"We have a mutual friend."

"Guy couldn't miss last night. Played like he was on fire."

"The Heat won?"

"Knicks beat 'em at the buzzer." The officer laughed. "Best game I ever saw in my life."

When I didn't say anything, he added, "DeAngelo came by late last night. Said he wanted to drop the charges, said he knew you and it was a misunderstanding." He leaned closer to me and thought he was lowering his voice, but instead spoke in a very loud whisper. "Tell you the truth, he didn't look overjoyed to be here, but the other guy pressed him, so good for you."

The other guy? Somewhere deep in my very tender, still frozen rib cage, my heart jumped. I tried to take a deep breath.

"What did the other guy look like?" I asked, my voice trembling.

"Short white guy, nice coat, well-spoken. Lawyer-type. I don't know, maybe his agent?"

I closed my eyes.

"You alright?" he asked.

"Did DeAngelo say anything else?"

The desk sergeant shook his head.

"All I know is you're a lucky guy. The charges weren't pretty."

I did a quick inventory in my head.

Then he said, "You're on television, right?"

It was much more of a statement than a question, and I wasn't about to argue. "Yes, Officer."

"We thought so," he said. "The cold syrup?"

"That's me."

"I gotta tell you," he said, pointing his finger at me with conviction, "that sneeze reminds me of the way my uncle Andy used to sneeze, God rest his soul. We'd see him snorting a little, and we'd all say, here it comes, here it comes." He laughed at the memory. "He used to clear the room."

When I didn't say anything he added, "Funny stuff."

"Thank you," I said, and I meant it.

"Between us," he said, "we get our share of celebs in here. A lot of them stay at the Plaza and whatnot." Once again, he got quieter and louder at the same time. "You'd be surprised at what trouble they could get into."

Not surprised at all, I thought, but I said, "Yeah, I can imagine."

And for the third time, his whisper drowned out the radio playing "Oh Little Town of Bethlehem" behind us.

"You know, we tried to keep you separate." When what he was saying didn't immediately register with me, he added, "You know, away from some of the rougher elements." He nodded at the bruises on my face. "Looks like you been through enough."

I nodded.

The sergeant looked over the paperwork, then handed me a plastic baggie with the tie string to my sweatpants. "You're good to go."

I checked the pockets to my sweatpants, which were empty.

"You missing something?" the officer asked.

I shook my head, then thanked him and turned to leave.

"Oh, yeah," he said, waving me back. "Someone left this for you."

He slid a sealed envelope toward me, as flat as if it was empty.

WHEN I STEPPED THROUGH THE HEAVY WOODEN DOORS onto West 35th Street it was Christmas morning in New York City. The cold air made everything look sharp and clean. I wanted to put some distance between me and last night's accommodations, so I tied the string around the outside of my sweatpants and headed east towards Eighth Avenue. Aside from a passing cab, the streets were so quiet I could hear my footsteps, slow as they were, on the sidewalk. I noticed an open Starbucks on the corner and thought about ducking in for something warm, but that was easier said than done. Not everybody was as generous as Nadia and Ivar.

A line of purple clouds, already tinged with gold, was fading fast into the dawn sky. The sun was rising over the East River and sat just north of the Empire State building. I couldn't remember the last time I had seen it. I reached for my sunglasses out of habit, but God knew where they were. I closed my eyes as I walked, letting the rays work their warm magic on my eyelids and my bruises. I heard church bells, probably coming from St. Francis of Assisi, a church on 32nd that Laura and her parents would hit when her parents stayed in the city.

They were announcing the eight o'clock services. I followed the sound of the bells and made a right down Seventh Avenue.

The Excelsior Marquis was across the street. Not much action on the maroon carpet—people were pretty much where they needed to be at that time of the morning on a holiday. I was sure Archie DeAngelo and the Miami Heat were long departed. I wondered what he was thinking when he stepped on the court last night? Was he thinking about his 8th grade friend? What did he mean when he said nobody could hurt Virgil anymore? And what was that look he had in his eyes when he watched me leave the curb and chase the picture into the middle of Seventh Avenue?

I held the metal railing as I climbed up and then sat down at the top of the steps in front of the entrance to Madison Square Garden.

There was no sign of the crazed fans who had packed the street a little more than twelve hours before. No sign either of all the garbage that was usually left in the wake of a big game. The city cleans up well when it has to—who wants to see a filthy city on Christmas Day? A couple of young cops, looking not particularly upset to be working a Holiday, stopped and eyeballed me for a second. Then they continued walking down Seventh.

I thought about everything that had happened in the last ten days. Laura and Chris. Dinino. Jackie and Brendan. Evan. Sally and Butchie. My father. DeAngelo. Aniko. Much of it didn't make sense and already seemed like one of my peculiar dreams. But then in some ways it was perfect.

Virgil the poet knew what he was writing all along.

In a couple of minutes, I would walk the thirty-five blocks to Sullivan Street. I'd knock on my landlords' door, wish them a Merry Christmas, and thank them for putting up with me for nine years. I'd also let them know that I'd be moving out for January 1. Then I'd go upstairs and make some phone calls. I'd call Laura's home in Connecticut. I'd call my father and mother. I'd call Nanny and tell her that she had been right about everything. I'd call St. Vincent's Hospital. I'd call Nadia at the bakery and let her know how Brendan was doing. I'd even call Maryhaven and wish Jackie a happy holiday.

I eased the envelope out of the front pocket of my pullover and laid it in my lap. Besides my name, there were no other marks on it. I used my fingernail to open the flap across the back.

Two nickels dropped out of the envelope into the palm of my hand.

And even though I was cold, and I had a lot to do, it felt good to sit on those steps in a small pocket of sunshine. From here I would watch the city open its eyes and come back to life. And I would never forget what I held in my hand, which for all the world felt like two silver stars.

About the Author

Michael DeConzo has had the good fortune to teach in the same schools that he attended as a student: IS 49, Curtis High School, and the College of Staten Island. Before that, he owned a candy store, a video store, drove a truck for a bar and restaurant supply, and kept uneven tempos in a few rock and roll bands. He has had an original screenplay optioned and a play produced on Staten Island. *Two Nickels* is his first novel.

CPSIA information can be obtained
at www.ICGtesting.com
Printed in the USA
LVHW091439040221
678105LV00019B/255

9 781946 989840